To Winona,

Cherish your great library as I did as a youth (many years ago).

The Funeral Home Murders

DISCARDED

Rob Hahn

vanity

North Star Press of St. Cloud, Inc.
St. Cloud, Minnesota

This is a work of fiction, while based on actual events,
all characters and dialogue are of the author's own creation
and are not meant to represent any person living or dead.

Author photo: Megan Hahn

ISBN-10: 0-87839-287-4
ISBN-13: 978-0-87839-287-2

First Edition: September 1, 2008

Printed in Canada at Friesens.

Published by
North Star Press of St. Cloud, Inc.
P.O. Box 451
St. Cloud, Minnesota 56302

northstarpress.com

info@northstarpress.com

For my mom and dad.

SIN

P hillip Grady knew death. He'd been around it nearly his entire life. Since boyhood, he'd worked at the funeral home that bore his family's name in the small town of Hudson, Wisconsin. He started with trash duty and filing. Later, he attended mortuary school at the University of Minnesota and eventually took over the family business when his dad died in 1991. He had seen so many different forms of death—the elderly dying long past their prime to young children succumbing to accident or disease way too soon. He didn't like death in any form but dealt with each instance in a stoic, professional manner, which many in the tiny Wisconsin town had come to appreciate. Phillip was sure he had seen every trick death could play on humans. As it turned out, he'd missed one very important one.

The killer walked purposefully up to the front door of the Grady Funeral Home just after twelve noon. His partner had spent the previous two weeks scoping out the home, watching for patterns, seeing how people came and went. They knew some of the employees took lunch away from the funeral home, and, as expected, Shirley Hennan, the funeral home's secretary, left precisely at noon. She had done the exact same thing the previous ten workdays, his partner had reported.

As soon as her car was gone from sight, the killer walked up the front walk to the funeral home. The front door, as the killer hoped, was unlocked, and he made certain to wipe his goulashes, just like his partner had told him, on the carpet in the entry way to avoid leaving muddy prints where cops could ID them.

From under his overcoat, the killer slid a rifle and began a stalk through the funeral home. He didn't relish what he had to do, but his partner had convinced him that it had to be done.

He knew where the offices were, and he headed in that direction. He listened outside Grady's office, then confirmed with a peek inside that it was vacant. He knew what that likely meant, turned and made his way down the long hallway that led to the basement stairs.

The killer eased open the door to the basement and began a silent tiptoe down. At the bottom, he checked his weapon and turned into the low-ceilinged prep-room. Phillip Grady, working over a cadaver with his intern, Charles Illsmere, froze and stared speechless at the intruder, his eyes quickly fixing on the rifle pointed at him.

"What are you doing here . . . with that?" Grady asked.

Though his partner made him swear not to engage Grady in conversation, the killer said, "You know too much. This is the way it has to be."

"He knows I'd never take things as far as I said I would," Grady said. The register of his voice had risen in fear.

"Like that changes anything," said the killer, through gritted teeth. He raised his rifle to Grady's chest, and Phillip understood one very important thing. He knew nothing of death. Before he could protest or move to protect himself, the killer squeezed off two deafening shots, which hit Grady in the chest and the head.

Illsmere, the intern, stared wide-eyed throughout the exchange. Nothing in mortuary school had prepared him to face death like this. He held up his right hand as if to stave off his murder. The killer swung his weapon and squeezed two more concussive blasts from the rifle, instantly killing the young intern. The second murder wasn't part of the original plan, but was the only way to ensure that there would be no witnesses.

In the silence following the rifle blasts, the killer surveyed the room and the damage he'd wrought. Two dead human beings. Three counting the cadaver on the gurney. Blood splattered everywhere, dripping from the counter and gurney and pooling on the terrazzo floor. He cast his eyes around the room and spotted what he was looking for. Careful not to step in any of the spattered blood, he made his way to a cabinet on the right side of the room. Quickly he cleared the bottles off one shelf, stuffing them into the pockets of his dark overcoat. Theft had not been part of his main objective when he'd arrived at the funeral home, but when would he ever have another opportunity like this?

Mission accomplished, the killer retraced his steps out of the funeral home. From start to finish, he had spent all of seven minutes inside the building. He was numb when he got into the car a little more than a block away. His partner was safe now.

The call came over the scanner shortly after one o'clock. A 187, a double murder, at the Grady Funeral Home in Hudson. Jerry Gray, one of the scanner monitors at Channel 6 in Minneapolis, was the first to hear it.

"Sounds like there are two dead bodies at a funeral home in Hudson," Gray said to the Assignment Desk and anyone else within earshot. Gray snickered.

"Just two? Business must be slow," quipped reporter Sean Kelly.

Gray rolled his eyes. "Are you interested in investigating this or do you just want to make bad jokes?"

"If there's a double murder, I'm there," Kelly proclaimed to the news room in general. "I'll get Benson. We'll update you once we're on the scene." He picked up his rain coat and headed for the door.

"Hey! Wait a minute," said Assignment Editor Julie Watson, stepping in front of him. "Did you forget that I decide who goes where?"

"Of course you do," crooned Kelly. "But maybe you've forgotten the most important part of the equation," Kelly added, presenting his chiseled profile for her admiration. "*I'm* the one with brains." His hand made an elegant flourish.

Watson didn't respond to either profile or flourish, but instead looked over the assignment schedule. Most of the reporters and photographers were already in the field working on stories for the evening newscasts.

"All right," she grumbled, "but be sure to keep me informed if we have a good story."

Kelly flashed his best grin and left to track down photographer Cindy Benson, and the two headed east to Hudson in one of the station's remote-broadcast vans.

Adam Fagley, Hudson's chief detective, surveyed the crime scene without saying a word. As he looked at the bodies of Grady and Illsmere, he acutely remembered why he had left St. Paul after fifteen years as a detective; it was precisely to get away from grisly scenes like this. He supposed he should be grateful that he'd gone three years in Hudson without seeing this kind of mess.

"What do we have so far?" Fagley asked Sam May, one of the two police lieutenants who had been first on the scene. May looked a bit pale and greenish around the gills, Fagley thought. Small-town cops, even seasoned ones, just didn't see crime scenes awash in blood.

The officer focused on him. "Shirley Hennan, the secretary, phoned it in shortly after one," May said. "She discovered the bodies when she got back from lunch. We've talked to her briefly, and she's currently upstairs in one of the rooms."

"What's your guess?" Fagley asked. "Any idea who might have done this?"

May swallowed and shook his head. "It could be a robbery gone bad. Look at this."

May pointed to a cabinet with an open door. One shelf was completely empty and every other shelf held at least a couple bottles.

"Do we know what was usually on that shelf?"

"No, not yet."

Fagley nodded and continued to survey the room.

"I just don't get it," May said. "Phillip Grady was a decent guy. Involved in civic matters. Active at church. This is ridiculous. I've never heard anyone utter one bad word about him. Or his family. Never. And the intern . . . was just a kid."

Fagley, taking pity on the cop, whose color was getting greener by the moment, motioned May to follow him up the stairs.

Kelly had covered enough murders in his reporting career to sense the acrid stench of death the minute he arrived at the funeral home. There was, of course, no particular odor, but he filed the phrase for use in his story, nonetheless. Actually, he could smell the bakery down the street. He knew scanner chatter couldn't be used as the main source for a story, but what Kelly saw immediately indicated something horrendous had taken place. The police had cordoned off the entire funeral home and its parking lots with yellow police tape.

As they passed the funeral home, looking for parking, two black SUVs, presumably there to take away the victims, waited in front of the main entrance, pulled up on the lawn to the steps just below the double doors. Law enforcement officials from the city, county, and state traipsed in and out of the funeral home, and a large Wisconsin Bureau of Criminal Apprehension crime-scene truck arrived. The Channel 6 van was forced to continue two blocks for parking, which was as close as they could get.

Kelly, already frustrated with having to walk to the scene, ordered Benson to get as much B-roll (video that covered a story's narration) as possible. He then ducked under the yellow police tape and began to walk around the premises.

A double murder, particularly one like this, intrigued Kelly. He told himself that he did "feel great sympathy for the victims and their families," but he also knew that a double murder in a small town like Hudson could get him the lead on the news, acing out the fifteen-odd other reporters also vying for the day's big story.

He placed a quick call to Watson's assignment desk.

"Just a quick update," Kelly said, in full reporter mode with on-screen voice. "It does appear, though nothing has been made official, that there were two murders at the Grady Funeral Home today. I suspect there will be a briefing later this afternoon. You should clear the lead segments on both the five and six for me."

Watson sighed. "Yeah, well, we'll discuss that when I see what you've really got."

"Give me a fucking break," Kelly snapped. "I've got a big story here, something a little more engrossing than that Pee Wee Herman-look alike weatherman waxing poetic about the possibility of flurries sometime next week. Oh, yeah, it gets cold in January, too. Big fucking breaking news."

"Kelly!" Watson barked. Then she paused. "I'll get back in touch with you in a little bit. Keep me informed."

Kelly smiled as he closed his cell phone. A murder, even a double murder, in a place like north Minneapolis or the Frogtown neighborhood of St. Paul would garner attention, but, unfortunately, killings in those areas were considered everyday occurrences. But an incident "in a small community impacted everyone in it in one way or another." Kelly knew this could be a big story. *If it bleeds, it leads*, especially when "blood sullied a community for the first time in years."

Hudson Police Chief Kevin Walsh arrived at the funeral home in his city-issued unmarked black Ford Crown Victoria. Kelly spotted him as he got out of his car, pegged him as the chief because he looked like a chief. At six-foot-four and 240 pounds, Walsh carried himself like a man in charge. His dark suit, crisp white shirt, and power tie weren't from a department store's discount rack. With the sloppy weather, he wore a camel-hair overcoat. When he entered the front doors of the funeral home, Kelly moved in a bit closer, but not so close as to force the officers to ask him to leave.

Once inside the funeral home, Chief Walsh's minions quickly guided him to the room where Fagley and others were gathered with Shirley Hennan. The chief conversed quietly with Fagley, then sat.

"Ms. Hennan, I'm Chief Walsh," he said. "I think we may have met previously."

Shirley sniffed and looked up. She nodded briefly.

"I'm truly sorry for what you're going through. Is there anything my staff or I can do for you?"

"Thanks, but I doubt it," she said, dabbing her bloodshot eyes with Kleenex.

"I know this is very difficult for you, but it's important," Walsh continued. "I'd like you to review for me when and how you found the bodies. I know you've already spoken with Detective Fagley, but it would help me if we could review a few details. Would that be okay?"

She nodded, looking exhausted but willing.

"You're the gatekeeper here."

Shirley smiled a little. "Receptionist, yes."

Chief Walsh pushed on. "I'm sure you've dealt with everyone the funeral home has done business with, one way or another. Can you think of anyone who might have had a reason to kill Phillip Grady?"

"No," she said.

"Did he have any arguments with anyone over the last couple months that you can recall?" the chief asked.

She started to shake her head, then paused. "Well, I overheard a few heated discussions on the phone during the last couple weeks, but I don't know what Mr. Grady was upset about or who he was talking to."

The two spent the next few minutes discussing Hennan's regular lunch routine, when she left and when she returned. Shirley told the chief how, when she returned from lunch, she saw that the front door was slightly open. This was odd, but it didn't concern her that much. She returned to her desk in the reception area and picked up where she'd left off on her work.

"The office was quiet, nearly silent," she explained, working to maintain control, "which wasn't all that strange, especially if the only other people in the building were working in the basement. We'd just got in Stanley Shaw's grandpa that morning. Then I got a phone call. It was for Mr. Grady. I paged him in his office out of habit, but I got no response, so I paged him downstairs, figuring I should have paged him there first. When I still got no reply, I took a message. Then I went downstairs." Shirley paused, trying to control her emotions. "I . . . I saw . . . *so* much blood." She dabbed her eyes. "Mr. Grady and Charles . . ." Again she wiped her eyes and paused to gather herself. She slowly shook her head a moment, then met the chief's eyes. "I got scared. I didn't know if the killer was still here, you know. I ran back upstairs and called 911. Then I ran outside to my car. I locked all the doors and waited for the police."

The chief thanked Hennan, then headed to an adjoining room. He gathered Fagley and others to discuss the case.

Lieutenant Sam May walked into the room where the chief and Detective Fagley were. He unbuttoned his winter coat but did not remove it. "What've you got?" the chief asked without preamble or small talk.

"I spent about fifteen minutes with Grady's wife at her house," May said. "As you might expect, she's in shock over this.

"At first Mrs. Grady couldn't think of anyone who might have done this or anything that might have prompted someone to kill her husband. But as we talked, she seemed to wander in and out of different thoughts. At one point she made reference to St. Timothy's Church, where the Gradys are members and where Phillip was very involved. She said there might have been a problem with something he was involved with at the church, but she wasn't more specific. I'm not sure if she didn't know or just wasn't willing to say. But she did indicate that something had happened here at the funeral home in the last couple weeks. She wasn't sure what it was because, as she said, Phillip wasn't one to bring home his work." He paused, thinking about what he said but decided not to consider it a joke as the chief's stone face had not cracked. "She said she'd noticed a major change in his personality over the last two weeks. He was morose at times and uptight and short-tempered at others, which, she said, was not at all like him. You guys got anything different or anything that fits along these lines?"

"Not a thing," Fagley admitted. "Our guys are still dusting for prints. The bodies have just been removed. We'll do an autopsy on them to find out what type of bullets were used. Whoever did this, I'm guessing, knew Hennan's lunchtime routine, which she told us rarely varied. But there's something else. Near the end of our conversation, she indicated something." He consulted his note pad. "I quote, 'I bet those druggies had something to do with this. Phillip was on to them. He knew something.'"

Chapter Two

Chief Walsh emerged from the funeral home at precisely four o'clock. He scanned the flock of reporters just outside the yellow tape. He had long since learned how to control the media, managing the info they received, making sure whenever possible they received it in time for deadlines but not with so much time to badger him with questions. And he occasionally used a little quid-pro-quo to help in police investigations.

"I'll make a short statement and then take a few questions," Walsh began as the TV lights turned on and cameras flashed in the darkening scene. "At approximately one o'clock this afternoon, a secretary from the Grady Family Funeral Home returned from her lunch to discover two bodies. She phoned police. When police arrived, they discovered two victims who died from apparent gunshot wounds. The victims have been identified as Daniel Grady, age forty-two, of Hudson, and Charles Illsmere, twenty-two, of Woodbury. Grady was co-owner of the funeral home, and Illsmere was a graduate student at the U of M, interning with Grady. There are no motives and no suspects at this time. Now I'll take a few questions."

"When did the killings occur?" yelled a Channel 8 reporter.

Walsh faced the woman. *How had she forgotten what he had said already?* "Most likely between noon and one."

"Were there any other employees at the funeral home during that time?" asked a male reporter from Channel 5.

"Not that we know of at this time."

"What type of weapon was used?"

Yeah, like we'd reveal that. "We won't be certain until the autopsies are performed, but we think it might have been a high-powered pistol, a hunting rifle, or a shotgun." *Yup, that about covers the possibilities.*

"Have family members been interviewed yet?"

"Yes, but we're not going to discuss that at this time." *Four questions. Good enough.* "That's it for now. I'll try to make an update around 8:30 if we have any new information. Thanks." He walked to his car amid more camera flashes, but, being a big man, none of that stopped him. Veteran reporters knew to get out of the way or be mowed down.

Kelly pondered the situation. Two dead, one of whom was the owner of the funeral home. No suspects, at least as far as police were saying. What was he missing? An inveterate reader of mysteries and spy thrillers, Kelly's mind raced through plots he had read. He often filled his mind with conspiracies, and that had sometimes worked to his advantage when reporting a story like this. Not too many years previous, he'd actually helped police solve a serial robbery case using a novel's plot as the basis for finding a motive and the eventual suspect. Turned out the thief had read the same novel.

After gathering his thoughts, Kelly pulled his cell phone out of his pocket, thumbed through the directory and called the newsroom.

"Assignment Desk, Watson."

"It's your favorite reporter," he purred arrogantly with a glance in the van's side mirror. "Do you have the lead slot cleared for the best?"

"No, I have it cleared for *you*. What do you have that's new?"

"Not much. Have Ms. Perky Anchor ask me whether the police have any suspects. She can ask about the time of the murders and maybe how the guys died. Oh, but if she asks dumb questions or mentions that it must be cold because you can see my breath, tell her I'll cut off her silicon-enhanced micro jugs when I get back to the station. Got it?"

"Tactful and charming as ever."

"And better looking every day." He wiped off the wing window with his handkerchief, then made sure his hair was in place.

Adam Fagley hated these moments. Interviewing family members in the aftermath of a gruesome murder was one of the toughest jobs a homicide detective faced, and Fagley had encountered some horrible situations during his time on the St. Paul force. From telling a single mother that her four-year-old daughter had been innocently shot during a drive-by near University Avenue to trying to interview a coked up dad about the murder of his teenage son only to hear pyscho-babble about needing another score, the detective had been in this situation too often.

The challenge was to make sure the questioning was gentle but thorough. Too often Fagley had seen incidents where police trying to understand the victim's family's feelings didn't ask the right questions or even overlooked clues and possible suspects within the family.

After interviewing Grady's brother Robert, he moved to other members of the family and finally Kyle Grady, the victim's nephew.

Grady sat across from Fagley at his family's kitchen table, wearing the same jeans and ratty black t-shirt he wore to school earlier in the day. Fagley observed the young boy was visibly shaken, but something in the body language seemed out of place to the detective, a manner he didn't usually see in these situations.

"Where were you today during the noon hour?" asked Fagley.

"A couple friends and I left campus to eat lunch down near the river," Grady answered.

"Isn't that against school rules?" the detective wondered.

"Only if you get caught."

"Is this something you often do?"

"Yeah, I guess."

"Have you ever been caught?"

"No."

"Did you go anywhere near your family's funeral home during lunch today?" Fagley asked.

"No," Grady replied, hesitating a little and looking away from the detective.

"Do you know who might have wanted to kill your uncle?"

"Nope."

"Any of your friends make any comments or call you this afternoon with some thoughts?"

"Nah, not really. Just a couple called to say they were sorry."

Fagley realized he wasn't going to get much out of this interview, and it didn't surprise him. Grady, like so many family members who've lost a loved one to murder, are usually rendered speechless or close to it. The detective thanked the teenager for his time, left his card with a phone number and asked him to call if he thought or heard of anything that might help the investigation. Fagley doubted he would ever hear from the young Grady.

Kelly's report went like many others. Quick lead in from the anchors, toss to Kelly, who narrated a short report that included a clip from the chief, and then back to the anchor.

"Sean, do the police have any suspects?" asked the perky anchor.

Kelly gritted his teeth as he tried to look thoughtful. He found this contrived question-and-answer banter between anchor and reporter abhorrent. The questions were scripted, flat, and there was little, if any, insightful dialogue between them.

"None yet, Candice, but we're expecting an update a little later tonight and hope to have more information at six and ten."

"Thanks, Sean, and try to stay warm. It looks really cold out there."

Well, no shit, thought Kelly, proof that even the most idiotic had a firm grasp of the inherently obvious on occasion.

At least in his own mind, many traits set Kelly apart from his competition, apart from people in general: how he spoke and how he looked, but especially his astute power of observation. As he surveyed the scene, Kelly took note of the other reporters either wrapping up or still in the midst of their broadcasts. None would offer much competition. He noticed a man standing off by himself in the deep shadows out of the bright lights of the TV crews. Of modest height, the man wore a dark overcoat. Characters—villians—from murder-mystery novels he'd read popped into Kelly's mind. Then Kelly noticed the Roman collar, and images of "ego-swabbing killers come back to the scene to view what they had wrought" pretty much imploded right then and there. *What would a priest be doing standing outside the police tape of a murder scene?* Maybe he wanted to comfort the people around the victims. Last Rites for the victims? Rubbernecker? At least it was something to consider as the story evolved. Kelly made a few cryptic notes.

CHAPTER THREE

Dinner at the rectory at St. Timothy's was served every night at 6:10. It had been this way for twenty years, since Father Fred Stanislowski, known as Father Fred to parishioners, became pastor. This allowed him to unwind with a bottle of wine during the CBS Evening News at 5:30, and he could also catch the day's local headlines on Channel 6 at 6:00. On good days, he'd be finished with his dinner by 6:20 and catch the sports.

At five-ten, his stocky body indicated he favored eating more than exercise, and his belly made an excellent resting place for his wine glass. His full, rounded face highlighted baby-blue eyes and a jovial smile, which gave nearly everyone who ever dealt with him or heard him say mass the feeling that he was just a regular guy, content with his role as a parish leader and not consumed by the power his position provided.

He gave his J. Lohr Estates Seven Oaks Cabernet Sauvignon a swirl, and a sniff for good measure and then a big sip. It was one of his favorite California Cabs, but it offered little help in dulling the pain of the day's big news, which, not surprisingly, led the Channel 6 newscast. Robert Grady, the victim's brother, had called him three times. Father Fred had worked closely with the Grady family since his arrival at St. Timothy's. Not only was theirs a professional relationship as morticians and pastor, but the Gradys were members of St. Timothy's. Phillip, in particular, had been active in the men's club and other parish organizations.

The backdoor to the rectory slammed shut, as Father Fred made his way from his den to the dining room. Father Joseph Birch, his young, opinionated associate, had arrived for dinner. His days were full, exactly what with Father Fred didn't always know, but somehow the younger priest always made it back to the rectory in time for dinner.

The young priest removed his black winter overcoat, revealing standard priestly garb. He almost never left the rectory without conventional black shirt and black pants or even the more traditional and conservative full-length black cassock. At a time when the Catholic Church was adapting to many of the current needs and trends of its flock, Father Birch was a throwback to another age.

"Quite a tragedy," intoned Father Birch.

"Indeed. Would you like some wine with dinner?" Father Fred asked without skipping a beat.

"Sure. What do you make of the situation?" Father Birch inquired. "I can't figure out why someone would want either of those men killed. It boggles the mind. I mean who? A despondent widower who thought his wife's make-up made her look too old in the casket last week? Doubtful."

Father Fred raised an eyebrow in acknowledgement of the ludicrousness of those scenarios as he poured the wine into Father Birch's glass.

"You should see the scene. All lit up, police and reporters everywhere."

"You were over there?" asked Father Fred with some surprise.

"Ah, just driving past," Father Birch answered reluctantly.

Father Fred found the admission strange, but didn't pursue it. Instead, he went back to his wine and food, pondering the week that lay ahead.

The things I do for you," said Detective Fagley.

"That's only because you admire and respect my top-caliber reporting," replied Kelly.

"Yeah, that's it," Fagley replied dismissively.

Somehow, Kelly had managed to convince Detective Fagley to take a quick break from the crime scene and meet him for a cup of coffee, something practically incomprehensible to most seasoned detectives. But Fagley, like Kelly, had his own drum banging in his head. While most marched to the tempo of a high school bass's beat, people like Kelly and Fagley preferred the all-out thumping of a John Bohnam or Keith Moon.

Fagley knew that a short break away from a crime scene always served him well. Looking at the same surroundings for hours on end, dulled one's perceptions; being around Kelly never dulled anyone's perceptions.

"Give me something that his Highness hasn't already spouted," demanded Kelly.

"Say 'Please' first," insisted Fagley mockingly.

"Sure. Please . . . fuck yourself!" exclaimed Kelly, grinning.

Fagley returned the smile, always amazed at how Kelly could make him laugh in the most dire circumstances. That was probably why he liked him so much.

"That's not very nice, but here's what we've got. Next to nothing."

"Nada?"

Both Kelly and Fagley took sips of their coffees and then, as if on cue, refrained from saying anything for about thirty seconds, and instead looked out the window of the coffee shop onto Second Street, where people in cars passed slowly.

"No prints yet," Fagley began. "No motive. No witnesses. The only small thing we have is that it appears some chemicals used for embalming might, and I stress might, have been removed from the basement."

"Embalming chemicals? Who would want that?" asked Kelly, realizing this was the first new angle he had heard, and he was most likely the first reporter to get this information.

"There's some speculation that it's the latest fad for high school gang members. Our pot has become their embalming fluid."

Fagley briefly explained that obtaining embalming fluid was the rage among high school gang members. They added the chemical to crop marijuana to make it stronger. As if some needed a stronger high, they were already ingesting the concoction.

"Nice," Kelly opined sarcastically. "Whatever happened to the days of kicking back with a friend or two, firing up a big fattie, drinking some beers and eating thirty White Castles? Now they're killing for embalming fluid? Innocence has most certainly been lost."

"No shit. But that's all I have right now."

The two again worked on their coffees. Kelly broke the silence, changing the subject to ask about Fagley's family. Keeping him busy, Fagley informed him. Both kids were in basketball, including a traveling team, which kept Fagley and his wife driving from practices to games and all places in between. Kelly smiled, feeling glad he was single.

"Any footprints or tire tracks that don't match employees?" Kelly asked, inkling for something Fagley might have overlooked or indeliberately forgotten to mention.

"Too many. They'd had a funeral this morning. The grieving family left the funeral home around 9:45. It was already sleeting."

"This embalming fluid angle, can I use it?" Kelly asked.

"Same rules as always: phrase it fairly, and don't use my name."

"Fair enough."

With that, Fagley turned the tables. It was not uncommon for Kelly to offer more information into an investigation than he got. The reporter always had something to offer, however poignant or insignificant. "So . . . do you have anything, Mr. Observation?" Fagely intoned with his usual sarcasm.

Kelly smiled. "Maybe, but I doubt it has any significance."

"Well?"

Kelly shook his head, considering how much to tell Fagley. He was nothing if not shrewd when it came to sharing observations, even with someone he'd known as long as the detective. Paranoia often forced Kelly to keep his mouth shut. He knew in this situation, however, that he had to offer something to ensure some future quid-pro-quo.

"I could have sworn I saw a guy standing off to the side of the cordoned-off area after I did my stand-up at five," Kelly explained. "It was dark, so I'm not sure, but it looked like he wore a Roman collar. Dark coat. Red scarf. Just standing there by himself. Probably nothing, but maybe just strange enough to take a look at."

"Okay," Fagley said, more confused than intrigued. He wondered why a priest would be standing outside the police line. Coming inside the funeral home to console family members was plausible, but standing on the other side of the tape seemed odd.

"If it turns into anything, I'll expect half your next check deposited into my Swiss bank account by the end of the month, or else . . ."

"You're a beauty. You know that? I gotta run."

"With that girth, I'm not sure you're running anywhere. Thanks for the help, and we'll be in touch."

Fagley chuckled to himself, as he headed back to the crime scene. Kelly, though a persistent ass at times, was a welcome respite from some of the dud reporters who struggled to put together two consecutive sentences that made sense.

Fagley and Kelly had enjoyed a unique relationship for almost ten years, since Fagley was a young detective in the St. Paul police department, and Kelly was becoming a minor reporter at Channel 6. The two ran into each other, literally, at A Fine Grind, an artsy coffee shop on Marshall Avenue in St. Paul. Though they had seen each other at various crime scenes, they had never really spoken until that chance encounter. The police had been two weeks into an investigation into whether the St. Paul chief of police was using city vehicles for his own carnal entertainment. There had been whispers for years that while it was the chief's job to serve and protect, he felt it was his secretaries' jobs to service him. To add to the mess, there were rumors the chief was adding to his own pension plan by dealing drugs and pimping. All part of serving and protecting, of course.

A delicate situation for obvious reasons, Fagley and his counterparts had trouble catching the chief in the act. That was until he ran into Kelly, who informed the detective of one of the chief's hot spots. But Kelly didn't just give up information like that for free. He wanted assurances from Fagley that he, and only he, would get a tip the day St. Paul's finest decided to bust their chief.

Fagley gave his word, Kelly got his scoop and a local Emmy, and the chief got more servicing in prison than he ever imagined. The bond between Kelly and Fagley was forged. Since then they had routinely traded information in a mutually beneficial professional relationship and one that came as close to a friendship as Kelly would allow with anyone.

CHAPTER FOUR

Kyle Grady sat on the bed in his room, dazed, his mind wandering aimlessly. The shock, the hurt, the uncertainty of what happened to his uncle all churning in his mind.

He was pulled out of sixth period Geometry shortly before two o'clock, the school's secretary using the inter-classroom paging system to request he come to the office. Not really sure why, he gathered his materials and casually walked out of the classroom, down the hallway and toward the office. Before he arrived, he could see his mom standing near the front doors to the school. Something was wrong; he could see it in the way she rubbed her eyes and was pacing.

At first, she said nothing and just hugged her son. Then eventually struggled through a few sentences that let the sophomore know his uncle had been brutally murdered. They needed to go to St. Tim's grade school, just across the street, to pick up his sister, June, and tell her the tragic news.

In his room, Kyle sat in near darkness. Blinds shut and daylight fading quickly, the teenager listened to the desperate strains of Nirvana that pounded through the ear buds of his iPod. Plagued by questions and paranoia, he still couldn't figure out a way to explain what had happened to his uncle. Why would someone commit such a senseless act? Who could be responsible? Did he tell his friends something about the funeral home that made them want to rob it? Was this the reason for the double murder?

Then there were questions about his own memory. He had skipped lunch in the cafeteria earlier in the day, opting instead to leave campus with a few of his friends for some recreation near the park that lined the river. A clear violation of school policy for underclassman, Kyle and his friends found ways to circumvent the lunch attendance system, which allowed them the chance to slip away without being noticed and return to school in time for fifth period.

The confused voice of Kurt Cobain grating through "Lithium" seemed to travel through Kyle's head, as he tried to put together a memory of the day's events starting with lunch. He knew he went with two friends and met two others at the park. They smoked some pot, which was their wont on the days they left for lunch, and then returned to school by one o'clock. At least that's what Kyle thought happened. As he sat on his bed, paranoia overtook his mind. He couldn't remember exactly what happened after the first couple hits from his favorite pipe. All he could recall clearly was being paged to come to the office, more than an hour-and-a-half after leaving school for lunch. Everything else was now a blur, a void of any hard facts, any concrete timeline.

What had really happened? He wrapped his arms around his knees that were folded in front of him on the bed and cried softly. Could it be as bad as he thought?

Kelly wrapped up his ten o'clock report without much fanfare, though he did make a short mention that authorities did suspect some embalming fluid might have been taken from the funeral home. On the return to the station, he spoke little to Benson, instead using the time to write some short stories for the morning's newscast on his station laptop. It allowed him flexibility to bolt, if desired, once he got back to the station.

Some of the ten o'clock news staffers were filing out of the station, as Kelly and Benson entered the underground garage. Based on

the time of night, they apparently had spent some time after the newscast discussing the latest station gossip over a couple pints at Brit's
Pub just down the mall from the station. Seeing Candice Wilson, his
favorite nightly anchor, Kelly instructed Benson to stop and let him
out of the van before they got completely into the garage.

"Hey, Candice, you dimwitted bitch," Kelly yelled, causing
some gawks from passers-by on the street. The rest of the staff took his
comment in stride; they expected as much and frankly were generally
entertained by Kelly's banter. "If you ever make a stupid comment
about the weather at the end of one of my reports again, I'll make you
look more stupid than you've ever appeared before on live TV, if that's
even possible. Got it?"

The perky anchor kept walking, ignoring her brash cohort.

Kelly made a quick skip through the newsroom to see if there
was anyone else worthy of his spite or conversation, though the two
were usually indistinguishable. He found no one to pester, and already
having checked his voice mail and email from the road, headed home
to St. Paul.

Kelly's drive from downtown Minneapolis to his home in the
Macalester-Groveland neighborhood of St. Paul took him about fifteen
minutes. At that time of night, he encountered little traffic on I-94, the
main thoroughfare between downtown Minneapolis and St. Paul, and
even fewer cars on the side streets of St. Paul once Kelly exited at
Cretin-Vandalia.

Kelly's house was modest but tastefully decorated. Television
had changed drastically in the three years he'd owned the house,
though the stories of murder, fires, and thefts remained remarkably the
same.

It was a Pete Townsend type of evening, dark and full of inner
demons, Kelly determined, putting the "All Good Cowboys Have
Chinese Eyes" album on the turntable. Not many people still had a
turntable, but Kelly cherished his old rock-n-roll record collection. He

also admitted to himself that he was too frugal to replace all the albums with CDs.

He opened a bottle of spicy tasting Gnarly Head Merlot, poured a glass and sat back to listen to Townsend's tortured voice. Kelly smiled slightly, realizing his demons were nothing compared to this musician's.

This had been one of the strangest first days of a murder story Kelly could remember. He went over the facts, closing his eyes to create a mental image of the crime scene. He revisited his conversation with Detective Fagley and the mention of a possible motive, though there was extreme doubt in both their minds that the quest for embalming fluid could lead someone to commit a double murder. Still people occasionally killed for much less. He thought of the priest. Something about his presence at the crime scene intrigued him. Why would he stand alone just watching the police and reporters go about their jobs? Was he somehow involved in the murders or did he have information about them? Ludicrous as that sounded, Kelly decided he should follow up on both.

Murder cases usually had a prime suspect within the first few hours. While tragic, their TV stories ran their course in two or three days, unless a high-profile individual was involved. This case was more complicated. Kelly wondered if police had any solid clues. A double homicide by nature was considered high-profile. The fact that it occurred in Hudson, a commuter suburb that averaged one murder every few years, usually bar brawls gone bad or domestic fights, added to its shock value.

As Townsend gathered steam in "Slit Skirts," Kelly savored the flavors of his burgundy. He made a mental list of people to talk to the following day. He would start with the police and then make his way to St. Timothy's church to see if he could learn more about Grady and perhaps identify the priest he saw at the funeral home. That image continued to stick with him as he turned off the stereo and made his way to bed.

Thirty miles east of St. Paul, two teenagers sat in a dimly-lit basement with the music of Green Day playing quietly in the background and enjoying their favorite form of exercise: rolling and sitting.

"This is some strong shit," said one, coughing slightly as he passed the lit joint to his friend.

As his friend took his first couple hits, the other teenager offered his commentary: "Wow, that fluid really makes the difference. Should help the street value considerably."

CHAPTER FIVE

The mood inside the rectory was simultaneously morose and kinetic. Father Fred knew he'd have to deal with both funeral arrangements for the family of Phillip Grady and also a shocked and grieving parish. How did one explain the presence of God in the midst of such a senseless act? It usually fell on the pastor's shoulders to find a way.

"I'll need your help not just with funeral arrangements but other duties as well, Joseph," Father Fred told his young associate, as the two sipped their morning coffee and looked over the newspapers. "This is going to be a long week for all of us."

"Are you meeting with the family today?" asked Father Birch.

"Yes. We're going to plan the funeral, which Heinrich and Sons Funeral Home will be handling. Strange, isn't it? This family grew up making a living out of other people dying, doing their best to comfort families who'd lost a loved one. And now, through the strangest circumstances, they can't even use their funeral home for one of their own family members."

The two ate their breakfasts, Father Fred enjoying scrambled eggs and three strips of bacon, Father Birch, more conscientious of his morning diet, opting for a bowl of Raisin Bran. Both read separate accounts of the previous day's murders in the two Twin Cities papers. The only difference between Kelly's TV reports and the print versions were more quotes from police and community residents in the papers. For all its glitz and glamour, TV could not surpass print when it came to painting a full picture replete with a border. Only so much could be stuffed into a thirty- or sixty-second report.

"It's a shame," said Father Birch, breaking the silence. "Let me know what you need me to do."

"For starters, plan on handling confessions tonight. It's the third Wednesday of the month, and the regulars'll be here. Someone has to be in the dark box, and I'm not sure where I'll be tonight. So, you get it."

"Okay."

"I'll let you know what else I need as we move forward," said Father Fred. "The funeral for Phillip is going to be Friday. I'd like your help con-celebrating and assisting with the overall flow. I'm sure the church will be packed. He had a lot of friends."

"I suppose he did," offered Father Birch, as his voice trailed off, suggesting he felt Phillip Grady was not viewed fondly by every-one.

Chief Walsh sat at his desk while his minions, including Detective Fagley, sat in chairs opposite. They were into day two of what was easily the most publicized case the Hudson P.D. had ever handled, and still there were no motives or suspects. The chief knew his force had to come up with something quickly or the pitbulls, otherwise known as the media, would become restless, not to mention the general public that would soon begin to fear that a cold-blooded killer was on the loose.

"What have we got, Fagley?" barked the chief.

"Nothing more than yesterday, Chief," replied Fagley, ducking.

"Dammit, why not? Haven't you talked to the families?"

"We've started to and will talk with them more today?" Fagley assured the chief.

"What about the drug angle?" wondered the chief.

"We've got two men following that, checking in with local high schools to get information about gang bangers, but that theory's tenuous at best."

"Tenuous is better than the shit you've got otherwise."

Everyone knew that even the weakest angle presented to the public was better than nothing at all. The drug angle at least could ease the public's concern that a serial killer or a madman was on the loose.

"BCA is expected to have some IDs sometime later today on the fingerprints that were lifted," May noted, speaking for the first time.

"What about a surveillance camera? Did they have one? Have you looked at the tapes yet?" bantered the chief.

"Geeze, Chief, I didn't even think of that. What'd we do without you?" said Fagley. "No, there were no surveillance cameras."

"I'm addressing the media at eleven this morning, and it'd be greatly appreciated if I could offer up some fresh info to give the appearance, at least, that we're trying to do our jobs, however incompetently that might seem right now."

"Aye, aye, sir." Fagley saluted the chief on his way out of the office, not bothering to look back at his boss's reaction.

The chief and Fagley usually got along well, though many officers who sat in on these meetings would never surmise as much. Fagley knew what the chief expected and how agitated he got if certain things weren't done as he liked. Knowing this occasionally made Fagley's job easier; not being able to come up with fresh info by eleven could make his job miserable.

Did you check with me before leaving with Benson this morning?" Watson asked Kelly over the phone.

"Let me see . . . no, I guess I didn't."

"Did it ever occur to you that I might want a different reporter on this story?" Watson asked.

"Listen, Julie," Kelly replied in a calming voice. "I know you're mentally slow but not disabled. Besides, if I waited for your blessing, all the other stations would be on the scene by the time you arrived in the newsroom. Be glad Benson and I are early risers."

"Call me with updates, and plan on a live shot at noon."

"I'll look forward to it. And do us all a favor, would ya?"

"What's that?"

"Get laid soon."

Kelly snapped his cell phone shut before waiting for Watson's reply and sipped his coffee, black, while re-reading the morning papers. Neither the *Star Tribune* nor the *St. Paul Pioneer Press* had any information different than he'd reported the previous evening nor did they include any reference to the embalming fluid motive.

The drive from downtown Minneapolis to Hudson could take anywhere from thirty minutes to an hour. At this time of the day, traveling east against rush hour traffic, it took about forty minutes to get to the funeral home. Police tape still surrounded the area, and some news crews had already arrived. A few police cars and the BCA van occupied the parking closest to the building, but Kelly saw no one. Most of the action seemed to be taking place inside.

Kelly made one trip around the premises on foot, sizing up the situation and determining that his competition appeared content to stand around and wait. That was enough for Kelly. He had already been in touch with Fagley earlier in the morning. In fact, that had been the first call he made when he woke up around six. Fagley had told him nothing else was new, that there would be a media briefing around eleven. The two had an understanding that if something big broke, Fagley would call Kelly's cell immediately.

Kelly got back into the van and told Benson to drive to St. Timothy's church. Always one for detail and preparation, Kelly had downloaded a map off Mapquest at home the previous evening, even though the news van had a GPS system.

They arrived at the church shortly before 8:15, just prior to the start of weekday mass. A daily communicant when his schedule allowed, Kelly rarely missed a chance to attend mass. *Oh?*

"I'm going into the church for a while," said Kelly, leaving Benson perplexed.

"And what do you expect me to do?"

"Hold down the fort. Call me if you need me. I'll set my cell to vibrate."

She rolled her eyes. "Some days I just can't figure you out."

"You never will, so stop trying."

Father Fred looked tired and morose at the altar. He used his homily to talk briefly about the funeral home murders, trying to put them into a religious context for the small group of parishioners. God had a reason for everything, Father Fred noted, but this one was hard to understand. He asked for the congregation's prayers for both victim's families and for members of the parish as well.

Kelly left church after taking communion and rejoined Benson in the white van in the church's side parking lot. News operations had switched to some plain, logo-free vehicles in the 1990s, when someone at some station suggested they could scoop the competition if their vehicles didn't announce their station's presence on a story. It wasn't much of a disguise, but Kelly, always concerned about his competition, felt anything that edged out other media was worth effort.

The reporter and his photographer went over a plan to approach the rectory and how Benson would handle the audio and video portions of any potential interview. Out of respect to Father Fred, Kelly told Benson to wait until the pastor agreed to an interview before she began rolling tape. Then they knocked on the door.

The priest recognized him upon opening the door. "Well, Mr. Kelly." As Kelly expected, Father Fred was not surprised by the television station's unannounced presence.

"I'm sorry about Phillip Grady's passing. I understand the two of you were quite close," said Kelly.

"Thank you. We were good friends. He's going to be missed."

"So, how I can help you?" Father Fred asked the reporter.

"I was hoping we could talk on camera—just five minutes—about Phillip, your memories of him, put a human touch to the story without invading the family's privacy," Kelly replied. Kelly used connections, but he was masterful at finding the right angles to get people, who otherwise might be camera shy, to talk.

"When would you want to do this?" asked Father Fred.

"We could do it right now right here outside or in your office, if you'd like. My camerawoman needs just a couple minutes to put a microphone on you and make sure the lighting is right."

Not waiting for an answer, Kelly nodded to Benson, who in turn held out the lapel mic. The pastor took the microphone and clipped it on his overcoat before even responding to the previous question. "Sure, I'll do it. Just keep the questions above board, as I know you will."

Then, feeling he had earned Father Fred's confidence, Kelly threw out a shocker, hoping to catch Father Fred off guard and measure his reaction.

"By the way, and I won't necessarily ask you this on-camera, but do you know of a priest who might have been hanging out near the funeral home around five last night? I could have sworn I saw someone in a Roman collar standing off to the side."

Kelly held eye contact with Father Fred, as the pastor considered his answer for a few seconds, first looking down, then looking back to make eye contact with Kelly. "No, I don't."

But there was something in the tone of Father Fred's voice that raised Kelly's interest. He was too deliberate in his answer. Instead of appearing completely shocked, his tone suggested he wondered the same thing. Then again, Kelly thought, it might just be all those murder-mystery novels acting up again in his head.

Chief Walsh addressed the media promptly at eleven. He spoke for about four minutes and then fielded questions for another ten minutes. He could have not spoken at all and accomplished the same. There was no new information, though he did his best to make it appear his crack staff was well on its way to finding the killer.

For most reporters, this story was turning into a nightmare. They were getting nothing to put on air or on paper, and were sitting around as other reporters got on screen or above the fold. Few of them filed stories for noon newscasts. Even the dullest knew the case wasn't an inch closer to being solved. Coming up with new angles that warranted airplay was difficult. Kelly knew his interview with Father Fred would offer something different than the other stations had, but he also realized there was a bigger story developing. But that didn't help him as news times rolled in. He had no new angles either. He wanted to talk to Father Birch, the associate at St. Timothy's, but figured that might be hard since Father Fred had already granted him an interview. Family members were all declining interview requests, and the man-on-the-street reaction Kelly left to the lazy reporters. Instead he began to gather information about embalming fluids and local high school gangs. A quick search on Google, plugging in the words embalming fluid marijuana, produced more than 35,000 results. Kelly scanned the first three, digesting the basic information that he could use in interviews and potential stories.

He called Hudson High School and scheduled an afternoon interview with the principal to discuss in general terms what types of gangs existed and how prominent drugs were in the area schools. If done right and without any fresh news, that could be the follow-up story for Wednesday or Thursday, the day before Grady's funeral. He placed one more call to Detective Fagley for an update. There was nothing new, except for the chief's increasing anxiety and rage.

CHAPTER SIX

udson High School, constructed in the 1980s, was the typical big box devoid of any personality. Kelly and Benson entered through the main doors and were quickly confronted by a rent-a-cop security guard, who asked their reason for coming to the school. "I forgot my diploma in my locker twenty years ago and wanted to see if they were holding it for me," Kelly offered with a grin.

"Oh, everyone's a comedian," said the guard, not amused.

"But not everyone is funny. We're here to see Mrs. Sherman."

"Sign in, then straight down the hall. Second door on the right."

There had been a time when school security consisted of locking the doors at night. The fact that a relatively small town like Hudson had stringent security spoke volumes about their youth. In some towns, the mere suspicion of teenagers involved in a double murder would be shocking. Kelly himself found it difficult to accept that they were looking for information about that very possibility, that a student or students of Hudson High School had something to do with the funeral home murders. He'd covered other murders that had involved high school students, but he had yet to accept the reality. He hated the idea of Columbine or even the killings in Cold Spring, Minnesota. In his day, Kelly and his friends settled disputes with their mouths, through pranks and once in a while with their fists. That was the extent of it. By the time it came to fists, most Ali-wannabes had forgotten what they were fighting about.

However, Kelly never liked high schools. Whether it was somehow related to his own experience or something else, he felt a stale stench permeated the hallways and infiltrated attitudes. Too much bureaucratic politics, burned out faculty members, and too few outlets for creativity and self-expression. High school clicks, mean meat-headed jocks, and apathetic losers—no wonder some kids turned to drugs as a cure to boredom.

Mrs. Judy Sherman emerged from her office to greet Kelly and Benson. Her plain, bureaucratic look had school principal written all over it. It would be interesting, Kelly thought, to see how she answered some of his questions.

"What can I do for you?" she asked curtly, leading the reporter and photographer into her office. The walls were decorated with diplomas representing lord knows how many different schools, degrees and thousand of dollars. Her desk was conspicuously clean of everything save for a phone. No notepads, no files, no nick-knacks or family photos. *What did she do all day?* Kelly wondered. Kelly made no attempt at small talk.

"As I mentioned on the phone, we're looking into doing a story about gangs in smaller school districts—"

"Before we go any further, let me state unequivocally that Hudson High School does not tolerate the existence of gangs. It's non-negotiable, and we make that quite clear to our students, who realize they will be suspended if there is any indication they are part of a gang."

Her statement sounded rehearsed. It was stern and fluid, as if she were reading out of the school handbook.

"I didn't suggest that you *condone* gangs," Kelly stated, "but we have had some reports that small gangs have cropped up, no pun intended, on some of the farms that border Hudson."

"Let me state again, Mr. Kelly: Hudson High School does not tolerate the existence of gangs."

"Right, you've established that, and unlike other reporters you may have dealt with, I do listen. I heard you the first time. In order to save time, I'd like to mic you and record our conversation, instead of having to ask you the same questions twice. Would that be okay? We'll keep the questions fairly generic and take no more than five minutes of your time. I think it'd go a long way in the final story of showing what you and your high school are doing to combat gangs."

As Kelly gently finessed Sherman's ego without her even realizing, Benson quickly set up her camera tri-pod and a light. Then, without missing a beat of her own, she asked Sherman to run a lapel microphone under her gaudy looking sweater. Simultaneously, Kelly held up a white sheet of paper that allowed Benson to get a white balance for her camera. All of this took place in forty-five seconds, leaving little time for Sherman to have second thoughts about doing the interview. Kelly and Benson were pros at a quick set-up. They boasted a near perfect record of getting desired interviews "on-camera." Already the tape was rolling.

"Now, we don't want to take much of your time, but I understand there's a gang by the name of Cropdusters growing, and some of the members might, and I stress *might*, attend this high school," Kelly began. "Certainly you keep close contact with law enforcement officials, who keep you apprised of the emergence of gangs and which students to watch closely. Is that right?"

Sherman looked at Kelly, then down at her desk, as if formulating what she would say next. It took a few seconds, probably closer to ten or fifteen, before she finally looked up, glancing first directly into the camera and then back at the reporter. "Yes, we have been advised on occasion that some of our students might be members of the Cropdusters. And, they . . ."

"One of their initiation rites allegedly," Kelly interrupted, "is to obtain embalming fluids which then can be used as a marijuana dipper, if you will, adding a powerful PCP kick to the traditional grass. You ever smoke weed, Mrs. Sherman?"

Benson had to contain her laughter behind the camera. She had worked with Kelly enough to know he liked to take the interviewee's mind, however abruptly, off the main subject matter and garner a response to a ludicrous question. Somehow, it helped him conduct a better interview.

"That question is totally out of line, and I don't know anything about this *alleged* ritual," Sherman stammered, visibly upset by Kelly's weed reference.

"Were two students suspended earlier this week after wearing t-shirts to school last Friday that supposedly contained the Cropduster logo?"

"Where did you hear any such thing?"

"Quite frankly, Mrs. Sherman, I think it's better if you let me ask the questions. Were two students suspended for such a violation?"

Again, the principal paused, weighing her options on what to say and how to say it. She was clearly regretting having agreed to the interview, and probably wished she had consulted the school district's attorney about being present to ensure she didn't say anything for which she could be held libel. "Ah, yes, I suppose they were," Sherman offered.

"How long was the suspension, and when was it served?"

"It's a two-day suspension and was served Monday and Tuesday of this week."

"Is this the first time there's been gang-related suspensions at Hudson High School?"

"Yes."

Kelly paused and pretended to consult his notebook, giving her time to think.

"What role have the police played?"

"They were the first to bring this to our attention and helped us pinpoint what to look for last week."

"What was the reaction from the students involved?"

Sherman's face looked disgusted. "I think they probably appreciated the days off."

Kelly had hit a stride now, insuring that Sherman's attention was on him and not the camera. Her tone had become conversational rather than official. "What about their parents? How did they react?"

"Jim Dorgan's parents are separated. Neither seemed to care too much. Frank Black's parents were mostly indifferent, too. Oops. I really shouldn't mention the kids' names."

The principal had unwittingly dropped a bombshell, and Kelly knew it. But instead of dwelling on the names she had just divulged, he kept his line of questioning rolling, hoping to elicit something more specific about the two kids and their families. "No worries. Have the police been here to follow up with the matter at all this week?"

"No."

"Are the two students back in school today?"

"Yes."

"Anything strange or out of the ordinary about them?"

"They seemed a bit more mellow, almost scared of something."

"Have either of the boys shown signs of violence in the past?"

"I'm not sure—"

Recognizing he had gotten about as much information as possible out of Sherman, Kelly chose to interrupt and cut Sherman short. "Do you think these boys might be suspects in the funeral home murders?"

"Okay, I think we've spent enough time—" Sherman began to work the microphone off her sweater.

"Do you think either one appears capable of murder?"

"That's enough. We're done."

Kelly had elicited more information, on-camera no less, than he thought he'd get prior to the interview. The two minutes it took to dismantle the camera and lighting equipment were marked by tension and silence. Sherman was angry and frustrated. This interview would not be good for future promotion prospects in the school system.

"Thanks for your time," Kelly said walking out the door, handing his card to Sherman in stride. "Don't hesitate to call my cell if you have any other information that you think we might find helpful for this story."

Sherman said nothing.

Showing signs of excitement, emotion that Kelly rarely displayed to co-workers, he dialed the station as soon as he and Benson got back into the van.

"Assignment Desk, Watson."

"I know where you live . . ." said Kelly in a hushed tone.

"All right, asshole, what do you have?" asked Watson, wasting no time at all on humor or small talk. Her day had been a struggle with the logistics of too many reporters and too few photographers on staff.

"First, that's Mr. Asshole to you," Kelly informed her. "Second, I've got more than I know what to do with. Fortunately for me, unlike others sitting at their desks in the newsroom or standing outside the funeral home in the cold, I can process a myriad of data in my brain and come up with a detailed story that makes sense. *Capiche?*"

Kelly explained to Watson the details of the Father Fred interview and his conversation with Mrs. Sherman. He suggested, unless anything else broke prior to five, they move forward with a story that quickly updated viewers on investigators' progress (none) and then looked more closely at the personal side of Grady through the words of Father Fred. He wasn't ready to go on-air with any suggestions that the two suspended students might be suspects. That was way too delicate. Other reporters wouldn't hesitate to make their own conclusions without a modicum of evidence to back it up. Kelly at least exercised professional prudence when dealing with stories like this one. He needed to talk with Detective Fagley to try to piece together what was a circumspect case at best.

CHAPTER SEVEN

Kyle Grady was the pride of his parents in his formative years. He was intelligent like his uncle and outgoing like his mom, impressing nearly all the teachers who had anything to do with the young Grady when he was a student at St. Tim's Grade School. He was an honor roll student, excelled at sports and occasionally charmed the young girls.

That all seemed to change overnight, when he matriculated at Hudson High School. A sense of rebellion pent up over years of doing everything his parents and teachers wanted manifested itself into a business venture. Grady realized quickly as a Freshman that there was money, good money, to be made by selling drugs, especially marijuana. It wasn't difficult to find people who grew it, add some intensifying chemicals and sell it to other students for a good profit. It was through this new venture that he forged a relationship with Frank Black and Jim Dorgan.

While police and others felt Black and Dorgan were the founders and leaders of the Cropdusters gang, it was actually the brainchild of Grady. None of the others had the smarts and savvy needed to run an operation like this.

By the end of his Freshman year, Grady's uncle sat his nephew down for a serious discussion at the elder's funeral home office. There was concern, the uncle stated, that something was amiss with his nephew and concerned his parents, who asked Phillip Grady to have the talk with his nephew. There was a sense of the boy's withdrawal around the house, saying very little to other family members and spending a lot of time in his room listening to music. There was concern on the part of some of his teachers at the high school, who expressed their opinions that the Freshman's work was sloppy and his potential unfulfilled.

A calm summary of concerns completed, the older Grady leaned forward, put both elbows on his desk, looked his nephew directly in the eye and spoke in a slow and clear tone.

"I'm worried you're using drugs. Are you?"

The young Grady, at that moment coming down from an afternoon high, felt his face become flushed, insecurity and anger welling inside him. He at first stared at the floor, shaking his head, and then looked back at his uncle directly in the eyes.

"Absolutely not, and I'm angry you would accuse me of that."

A verbal row escalated, audible to everyone inside the funeral home. An employee later joked that even the dead body on the gurney in the basement was moved by the heated exchange.

Their relationship, once close and friendly, was never the same after that day. The remaining seven months of Phillip Grady's life were plagued by acrimony and outward disdain from his only nephew.

The afternoon conversation that took place in the chief's office sounded nearly identical to the early morning meeting."All right, what have you got?" he asked his crack staff, again gathered in his office, as the sun began to set in the west.

"Next to nothing new," Fagley offered.

"Well, that's just not sufficient. Give me something, anything."

"Wasn't that a great Todd Rundgren album?"

"Okay, smartass," intoned the chief, "if that's the route you want to take then, hello it's me, and I'm about to kick your balls up into your throat if I don't get some movement. Does that help you see the light? And, yes, I liked that album, too."

Detective Fagley snickered at the chief's reply. Both were big fans of rocker and producer Todd Rundgren. To be able to share a bond and reduce, at least momentarily, the stress that came with this case was most welcome. Fagley made a note to tell Kelly about this, since Kelly was a bigger fan of Rundgren than the chief and Fagley combined. "The only angle we have is the embalming fluid," explained Fagley. "Two students at HHS were suspended last week for wearing gang insignias. They weren't in school on Tuesday, which means one or both could have been at the funeral home at the time of the murder. Their gang, the Cropdusters, apparently is into using embalming fluids to spike their weed. The PCP gives them an extra high, and converts them into lifelong Bob Marley fans on one hit."

The chief nodded, acknowledging that he thought this was a legitimate lead that could be pursued. "Have you talked to the students?" he asked.

"We have detectives en route to their houses as we speak."

"Why wait so long?"

"We didn't know they had been suspended until around three today."

"Okay, keep me posted."

Fagley left the chief's office as quickly as possible. He wanted to be present for at least one of the interviews with the students. What he didn't tell the chief is that the the police learned of the students' suspension and subsequent absence from school from a call Fagley got from Kelly just as the latter was leaving the school.

CHAPTER EIGHT

Hudson, bordered on the west by the St. Croix River, had farms just outside town in the other directions, though the town continued to push outward into the countryside. Just across the river in Wisconsin, the peaceful river town was now essentially another St. Paul suburb.

The Black farm was located three-quarters of a mile north of downtown just off Highway 35. What might have once been a thriving farm had become simply a piece of scruffy land with a dilapidated barn and an old farmhouse in desperate need of a coat of paint.

Fagley and one of his assistants, Jim Casey, approached the front door of the house together, hoping the lights turned on inside were an indication someone was home. Fagley pulled his pistol behind his back just in case they were met with a less than hospitable greeting.

They were in luck. A teenage boy answered the door, showing no indication of surprise or resistance.

"We're looking for Frank Black," Fagley said, as he flashed his badge with his left hand, his right hand still tucked behind his back with gun in hand.

"That's me."

"We're with the Hudson Police Department and would like to ask you some questions."

"'Bout what?"

Interviewing teenagers is always a pain in the ass, Fagley thought. They spoke in short sentences, sometimes just grunting one-word answers. They had little respect for any adults, including police officers. And they seemed unphased by any potential recrimination or punishment for their actions.

"I think it's best if we come inside," Fagley plainly stated, opening the screen door and walking into the house, as a gust of wind from the west blew shut the screen door.

"What makes you think you can just walk in?" Black demanded.

"We just did," Fagley said. "Now enough of the smart mouth. Where were you Tuesday around noon?"

"Sitting here playing X-Box."

"Was anyone with you?" Casey asked.

"No."

"Did your parents know you were suspended from school?"

"Do you think they care?"

A current of helplessness broke through the sullen tone in Black's voice and answered the question for the police. Fagley glanced around the lower level of the Black homestead. It was a fairly messy home in need of a good cleaning. A large television dominated the southwest corner of the room, but there were no signs of video games hooked up to this television nor were there any books or magazines. From a distance, Fagley took in the kitchen, which had outdated linoleum floors and worn-out cabinets. Unwashed dishes stood in the sink, and a jug of pancake syrup was on the counter.

Fagley had used a suspect's house in previous cases to learn a lot about the person in question. This house had potential to be very nice, but as is it was, it was devoid of any real personality and offered little, if any, clues into the Black family.

"Tell me about the Cropdusters," Fagley said.

"Not much to tell," Black replied with a shrug of his shoulder.

"Are you a member?"

"Suppose."

"Have you ever purchased or stolen embalming fluids like they use at funeral homes?" Casey asked.

"Why would I want to do that?" Black asked.

"Just answer the question, please," Fagley stated.

"No."

"Are you and Jim Dorgan good friends?"

"We're okay," answered Black with some reluctance and began to fidget with his hands and shift his weight.

"Why did you wear something with a Cropduster logo to school? Didn't you know you could get suspended?" asked Fagley.

"I wore it because I wanted to, and the two-day vacation wasn't bad either."

"Are your parents here?" asked Casey.

"No."

"What time do they get home?"

"Mom works until eleven, and dad usually stumbles in from the bar after that."

"Any brothers or sisters?"

"No."

"Have you ever been to the Grady Funeral Home?" Fagley asked.

"No."

"Would it surprise you if we told you your fingerprints were found there?" Casey inquired.

"Yes, because I just told you I've never been there." Black stated resolutely, with no increase of fear or concern. Black's lack of expression led Fagley to dig deeper and more quickly in his line of questioning.

"Do you have any guns in the house?"

"Just a couple hunting rifles," Black answered matter-of-factly, as if every high school teenager owned one or two. Then again, in states like Wisconsin, they probably did.

"Where are they?" Casey wondered.

"In the basement."

"Can we see them?"

"Suppose."

In the basement, Black showed the detectives two Remington Model 700 BDL rifles, easily one of the most popular hunting rifles in the country. Literally tens of thousands of deer hunters in Wisconsin alone owned this style of rifle. Fagley checked out both guns, looking for anything that might offer a clue to whether one of them was the murder weapon. He found no visible signs so continued with questions.

"When was the last time these were used?" asked Fagley.

"Last November."

"You clean them regularly?"

"Always."

"Ever shoot anyone with one of these?"

"Just deer. Hate to disappoint you."

"What type of ammunition do you use?"

"Here. Take some if you want."

Fagley's mouth dropped open for a moment, then he recovered and took the bullets from Black and turned his head to look at Casey. Without saying anything, the two had the same thought: either this kid had nothing to do with the murders that he confidently turned over bullets that could be seen as potential evidence or he was so stupid that he just offered the cops the key they needed to solving the murders. Fagley changed the subject.

"What can you tell us about Jim Dorgan?"

"I don't know. I told you. We're decent friends, hang out once in awhile. That's all."

"Does he own a gun?" asked Fagley.

"He's got a hunting rifle, too."

"You ever hunt together?"

"Sometimes."

"Is he good with a gun?"

"What do you mean?"

"Is he in control when he has a gun in his hands?"

"Yeah. Sure."

Fagley was on a roll and Casey let him handle the questioning, concentrating instead on Black's body language, which continued to appear limited at best. Fagley asked Black if Dorgan was into drugs, and if he knew what his friend was doing on Tuesday, the day of the murders. He asked if the two teenagers had spoken at all during their suspension from school on Monday and Tuesday. Black's one word, "Nope," was all he had to say to each of the queries.

After a pause, Fagley asked, "Do you have a cell phone I could use? I left mine in the car."

"Sure, here," said Black, handing the phone to Fagley.

"Excuse me for a second," Fagley said.

Fagley casually walked into another room in the basement. Once out of Black's view, he quickly scanned through some of the recently dialed numbers, committing to memory one number that appeared seven out of ten times. He then dialed his own cell number so he could have Black's cell phone number.

"Thanks," Fagley said, as he handed Black his phone. "Here's my card. Call me if you think of anything else you want to add. Okay?"

"Okay."

Black showed the detectives to the door, watched them get into their car and pull away. He sat down, took a deep breath and gathered his thoughts. *Strange*, he thought. He pulled his cell out of his pocket and dialed the number that Fagley had committed to memory.

"Hey. The cops were just here. They may be on to us."

CHAPTER NINE

Kelly was an efficient reporter when on a deadline. He could enter "the zone" and come out in a matter of minutes with a script, timecoded sound-bites he wanted to use, questions for the anchors, and some helpful suggestions for what video to use as b-roll. He was so immersed he didn't hear the phone ring until Benson spoke.

"It's Watson," said Benson, as she and Kelly sat in the mobile editing bay of the van. "She wants to know if you're all ready to go for the first story at five."

"Tell her if I wanted to fucking talk to her, I'd call her. Last time I checked, we have twenty minutes until air-time, and we'll be just fine. Tell her to worry about the incompetents."

What Kelly really had, he realized, were two strong angles to this story. When he had spoken with Watson earlier, he got her to agree to free up two-plus minutes for his story. Father Fred's comments, Kelly decided, would take up the better part of the second half, but the high school angle was still troubling Kelly. He knew he had something different but wondered what might actually be directly linked to the murder. Many local news reporters, especially those with a flair for drama, had a tendency to take an angle like this and either twist it into their own version of thriller fiction through selective use

of short sound-bites or combine so many unrelated facts that the viewer had no clue what was just said.

"Tonight's lead story deals again with the tragic double funeral
home murder in Hudson," read the perky anchor with her somber tone
reserved exclusively for stories like this. "We go live to Sean Kelly
with more. Sean . . ."

Kelly's live report was done not outside the funeral home,
where reporters from the other stations were gathered, but outside
Hudson High School, perfectly lit for the shot, as the sun had set just
prior to airtime. He appeared calm and serious in his dark colored
Brooks Brothers overcoat and colorful European wool soccer scarf. Not
traditional reporter fashion but one Kelly didn't mind inventing and
claiming his own.

"Within the past hour, Hudson Police have interviewed one
high school student," began Kelly. "While not officially a suspect,
police say they want to see if there is any connection to the murders.
The student, who we will not identify, was one of two students serving
a suspension on Tuesday when the murders occurred. Police say they
are also interested in the fact that the student questioned owned a
hunting rifle that uses the same type of ammunition that killed the two
victims. There has also been the suggestion that the two students are
members of a gang called the Cropdusters, which allegedly is into
obtaining through purchase or theft embalming fluids commonly found
at funeral homes. Police say they suspect some of those types of fluids
were missing from the funeral home, though they're not certain
whether they were taken during the murders.

"At Hudson High School today, principal Judy Sherman discussed the matter of the Cropdusters, whether there is indeed a gang
problem in this community and why the two students were suspended."

The sound-bite rolled, and Kelly looked over his notes for the
rest of the story. He had nailed it again, and he knew it. No other

reporter had the angles that he had just made public for the first time. He imagined the reactions of other newsrooms around town, where he figured producers were shaking their heads, wondering why Channel 6 was the only station not doing a live shot from the funeral homes. When they turned up the volume on Channel 6, they knew why.

But Kelly was never satisfied, even when he produced stellar reports—one of the inner demons that plagued him no matter how successful or happy he might be at a particular moment.

Kelly speculated from his most recent conversation with Fagley that the student link was worth exploring but, perhaps more than that, it was a way to keep the chief happy. Kelly could not get the image of the priest at the murder scene out of his mind. He wanted to talk with Father Birch, but knew from his conversation with Father Fred that the young associate was handling confessions and would probably not be available. He would have to try to get him tomorrow.

Kelly filed his six o'clock report live and then headed back to the station with Benson. It was rare for a reporter to leave a story like his without doing a live-shot for the news at ten. But Kelly had had enough. He was in constant contact with Fagley and played a hunch that nothing new was going to develop that night. He had successfully lobbied Watson to send a part-time photographer and one of the current interns to stake out the funeral home, just in case something broke. Unlike so many other reporters and producers in the newsroom, Kelly could spot capable interns and knew they would appreciate a shot at a stakeout, however cold and monotonous it might be.

"*Bless me Father for I have sinned. My last confession was just recently, and here are my sins. I sometimes get angry with those around me. I occasionally take the Lord's name in vain, and, recently, I have not always shown respect for life. For these and all my other sins, I am truly sorry.*"

Chapter Ten

Despite their public persona and quasi-celebrity status, many reporters have listed phone numbers. It is a good way to get an occasional tip, though the frequency of calls from drunken nutcases far outnumbered those with quality info. Kelly had one listed and one unlisted number. Though not a fan of caller ID, thinking it too obtrusive to the caller, he relented a few years ago and attempted to screen the calls on the listed number. The problem, he understood, was that any good information usually came from a blocked number; failure to answer those calls could mean a good story missed. The ludicrous calls usually came between ten at night and two in the morning, when the drunks still had enough energy to place a call even though their ability to speak in anything resembling a coherent fashion was dubious. The best calls, those with legitimate information and tips worth pursuing, often came early in the morning from people who'd pondered whether to call a reporter and then finally woke up early one morning and did it without further deliberation.

This morning, like most, Kelly had beaten his alarm, which he set for 5:25 on weekdays, and turned on WCCO-AM at 4:58. He liked to catch the CBS and local newscast first thing in the morning. It was an easy way, he figured, to know what main stories would appear that day in the *Star Trib*. He often joked loudly in the newsroom that the morning editor should send a royalty check to the *Star Trib* for all the stories that were lifted out of the paper.

Kelly was pleased to hear reports of the high school gang angle. Of course, there was no reference to his Channel 6 report that broke this part of the story, and he knew from monitoring the other television stations' ten o'clock newscasts and late night news that this angle belonged to him. When was his royalty check set to arrive?

The phone rang at exactly 5:08 A.M., interrupting the puke-sounding voice of the meteorologist hawking some new snake oil hair restoration product.

Kelly picked up on the first ring; he hated ringing phones.

"Hello," said Kelly, glancing at the caller ID as he picked up the phone. The machine listed, "Caller Unknown."

"Is this Sean Kelly from Channel 6?" asked a polite-sounding female voice.

"Yes. Who's this?" wondered Kelly aloud.

"I'd rather not say."

"Okay," said Kelly, putting the caller's voice in the above-fifty age bracket, though he knew that wasn't a certainty.

"You're wasting your time talking to the high school students," the caller said, clearly well aware of Kelly's report the previous evening.

"Why's that?" Kelly was intrigued by the caller's tone and matter-of-fact delivery. Over the years, he had developed a tacit internal skill of judging the authenticity of a tipster within the first minute of the conversation. His judgement was almost always accurate.

"They didn't do it," informed the caller, tweaking Kelly's interest even more.

"How do you know that?"

"The one who absolves sins needs to seek forgiveness."

"What . . . ?"

The caller hung up before Kelly could get out another question. He dialed *69. Predictably, though, he heard a computer-generated voice say that the number had been blocked at the caller's request.

The call had activated the conspiratorial voice inside his head, many coming from the mystery novels he read voraciously. He loved conspiracy theories and debating the merits of his arguments with friends over bottles of wine. For instance, he was convinced that U.S. missiles accidently shot down the TWA-747 off the coast of Long Island. With the same certainty, he felt MI-5 had something to do with the car crash that killed Princess Diana. He drew the line, however, with those who suggested the plane crash that killed Senator Paul Wellstone was the result of dirty Republican politics.

This call played right into Kelly's suspicion that a priest, whether Father Birch or the man standing at the scene, might have some information about the funeral home murders. This one he'd bounce off Fagley.

"Hey," said Kelly when Fagley's sleepy voice answered the phone.

"Do you know that it's fucking early in the morning and most normal human beings are still asleep?" asked Fagley, clearly annoyed by the early morning wake-up call, though he had come to expect calls from Kelly at all different hours of the day, especially with an unsolved case topping the day's news.

"Then what's your excuse?" said Kelly, enjoying the fact that he had awakened the detective.

"Very funny. What's up?"

"Anything new?"

"You call me up at 5:15 *in the morning* to ask if there's anything new? I'd call you. You know that."

"Of course. But did you ever consider that I might just miss you?"

Kelly described the conversation he had just had with the female caller. "The woman said I'm wasting my time pursuing the gang angle and instead made a veiled suggestion that a priest has knowledge. What do you think?" Kelly asked.

"Interesting. I'll say that."

"Has anyone from your department talked to the priests at St. Timothy's?" asked Kelly, knowing that someone from the Hudson P.D.

should have talked with the priests, at the very least to get some background on Grady's personality and perhaps find a theory or two why someone would have wanted him dead.

"We spoke with Father Fred briefly but no one else," Fagley acknowledged, sounding a tad sheepish. "I think you had everything and more in your interview with him."

"Does that surprise you?" Kelly said, chiding the detective.

"You know, I'm convinced you wake up earlier than most just so you can spend an extra ten minutes every day telling yourself how great you are," Fagley said, now clearly awake and alert enough to spar with Kelly.

"I'm the only one who realizes my greatness, so I have to remind myself," laughed the pompous reporter.

The two spent the next few minutes bantering about what insights either Father Fred or Father Birch might have to offer police. After trading some simple as well as ludicrous theories, both Fagley and Kelly admitted they felt it was doubtful either priest would have anything to offer with the exception of some background on Grady.

"I'll talk to the two guys again who did the interview with Father Fred and see if they noticed anything peculiar," said Fagley.

"I'll try to talk with the young associate, Father Birch," Kelly offered. "I'll let you know if he has anything of interest to say."

"I don't care what the rest of the media say, I think you're a pretty decent guy," said Fagley while laughing, knowing how to push Kelly's insecure buttons.

"Go back to your beauty sleep," said Kelly as he hung up.

Kelly skimmed the papers and watched the local morning newscasts, as he stretched for his morning run. He didn't like running in the morning, but with his schedule dictated by the murders, he had no other option. Running, among other things, allowed him to explore different story possibilities, especially when working a story like the current one. His route this morning took him from his home in the middle of the Macalester Groveland neighborhood of St. Paul through the Highland Village area, down Cleveland Avenue and then back

along the path that bordered Mississippi River Boulevard. His running
kept pace with the falsetto strains of Coldplay's Chris Martin, as "The
Hardest Part" played on his MP3. His mind pondered different ways
Father Birch might know something. Did he talk to Grady or the intern
shortly before the murders? It certainly wasn't uncommon for priests
to have regular conversations with people at funeral homes. Kelly
made a mental note to find out the most recent funerals to go through
the Grady Funeral Home and end up at St. Tim's. He already knew
from his conversations with Fagley that there was a funeral the day of
the murders, but he didn't know if St. Tim's handled the services afterwards. Since Grady was active in the parish, some other church official might be able to offer a perspective no one had yet considered.
Maybe someone said something to the priest in confidence before or
after the murders that might contain a clue. Whether in the confession
box or elsewhere, people regularly shared not only their sins but personal problems with priests, trusting that the conversation would not
be shared. The confessional guaranteed secrets; using a priest as a
personal confidant outside the confessional required personal trust.
Was Father Birch even the priest at the crime scene the night of the
murders, there because someone had said something to him?

"I want to talk to you about your interview with Father Fred," Fagley
said to Detective Jim Casey.

"What about it?" asked Casey.

"Was there anything strange about his behavior, anything that
he said that seemed out of the ordinary?"

"Not that I recall," said Casey.

"Did you ask him about Father Birch, what he's like?"

"Yeah," said Casey, giving pause as if trying to remember
something specific from the interview. "You know, now that you mention it, Father Fred did say something about Birch that now seems a
little strange. We asked him what Birch was like to be around, and
Father Fred said he was a little different. Very literal from a theologi-

cal standpoint, which naturally put him at odds with certain parishioners. He also, according to the pastor, had a bit of a temper and
could be short with people who didn't agree with him. Outside of that,
Father Fred said he was a fine priest."

"Okay," said Fagley, nodding and devising a plan, "Let's look
into this Birch a little more. I want to know what makes him tick and
what, if any, contact he had recently with Grady."

The weekday seven o'clock mass at Assumption on West Seventh
Street in downtown St. Paul was attended regularly by about thirty
people, not counting the dozen or two homeless who found refuge and
warmth in the pews in the back of the church. It was a quick, no-frills
mass, a perfect way to start the day. Kelly often attended four or five
times a week. Seven years before, he'd called the rectory, explained
that he wasn't a parishioner but attended weekday mass regularly and
then proceeded to ask if he could park for free in the church's lot during the state high school hockey tournament, which took place two
blocks away at the Xcel Energy Center. He got his parking pass and
also developed some relationships with Assumption's priests, namely
its pastor, Father Archer. It had been a week or two since the two had
spoken in person, so Kelly took the time after mass to duck into the
sacristy for a quick hello.

"Good morning, Father," said Kelly as he walked into the sacristy with his inimitable smile. His personality wasn't one that enjoyed
smiling often, but he learned through the years this smiling alone easily endeared himself to many and got a conversation off to a good start.

"Morning, Sean," said Father Archer warmly. "How are
things?"

"Busy. Thanks again for your help arranging the meeting with
Father Fred in Hudson."

"Glad it worked out," said Father Archer. The pastor enjoyed
using his many connections to put two friends together. In an odd way,
it gave him an added sense of purpose when the daily grind of running

a parish became too stressful or boring or sometimes a combination of both. In this particular situation, it almost gave the pastor a sense of being part of the story he saw on television. "I saw the story you ran on the news. Fred looked good. Such a tragic story, though. Any more leads?"

"Not really," Kelly admitted, getting straight to his next point. "But I need to learn more about Father Fred's associate, Father Birch. Do you know anything about him?"

"This is off the record, right?" Father Archer asked.

"Everything between us is off the record," Kelly assured him.

"Fred can't stand him," began Father Archer. "He's been a divisive force at St. Timothy's since the day he arrived. Fred says he's better suited for a pre-Vatican II parish, and, trust me, there are some of those still around. That doesn't sit well with most cafeteria Catholics these days."

The "cafeteria" moniker was in reference to the way many Catholics practiced their religion, picking and choosing what church tenets they wanted to follow and which ones they conveniently ignored. Most priests understood the rationale behind cafeteria Catholicism and, though loathe to publicly endorse this approach, were fairly comfortable with it.

"What else do you know about him?" asked Kelly.

"There's a rumor that he has a shady past, something that goes back to his time in the seminary at St. Mary's in Winona, but I don't know any details."

"Interesting. Let me know if you think of anything else," Kelly suggested. "There's something strange about him. I'm not sure there's any connection to the murders, but it's something I need to explore."

"Let's have lunch when you're done with that story," suggested Father Archer.

"Perfect. Have a good day," said Kelly as he turned and walked out of the sacristy.

The drive from downtown St. Paul to downtown Minneapolis via I-94 at 7:45 was still relatively easy. Only on rare occasions did it take longer than twenty minutes. Hit that same path after 8:00, and it could take twice as long. Kelly continued to think about his conversation with Father Archer, as he moved his Audi 100 from lane-to-lane, using the far right lane to get him to the Snelling exit and then timing his switch into the next lane just before that exit-only lane headed up the ramp to Snelling. This same move drove Kelly nuts when other drivers made it. That morning his concentration tuned out the horns of other drivers pissed off by his lane switching. He needed to get in touch with Father Birch and decide for himself if there was anything suspicious enough about him that could possibly be related to the murders. He recognized that Fagley and the other detectives were good at their jobs, but he approached interviews differently and consequently elicited stories and tidbits that the police didn't get out of the same subjects. He figured this would be a good day to contact the associate. The wake for Grady would warrant some coverage on the news, but outside of b-roll, there wasn't much of a story to tell about a wake.

Kelly listened with some interest to the discussion taking place on KQRS-FM. Today's topic of discussion was the funeral home murders. The host had already charged, tried and convicted the high school students. All the evidence, he suggested, pointed to them, namely the one who was cited in Kelly's report the previous evening. Suspended from school, no alibi, hunting rifle, member of a gang that had a penchant for embalming fluid—clearly a bad seed. It had to be this kid. Whether the host actually believed everything he said or whether it was just schtick, it worked. Kelly could sense the reaction of thousands of other Minnesota commuters, as they, too, listened— Kelly was one of the few listeners who took it all in as entertainment.

The newsroom was still relatively quiet when Kelly arrived, but to his relief, his favorite assignment editor was already at her desk.

"Good morning, Watson," said Kelly as he strutted past the assignment desk. "Did you get any last night?"

"You're such a pig," groaned Watson.

"And a damn good one at that."

"What's new with the funeral home murders?" asked the editor.

"There's the wake for Grady tonight," Kelly explained. "We'll need to cover it at least a little. I also have some other hunches I want to pursue."

"I'm sure you do," said Watson, shaking her head. From years of working with Kelly, she had come to expect he would have suspicions he wanted to follow. Finding the right balance and determining how long to let a photographer work with him was the challenge, knowing that many of his hunches resulted in nothing.

"Hey, you know you love me," said Kelly, flashing his smile, which even occasionally worked on Watson. "I'm the one reporter on the staff whose hand you don't have to hold or whose ego you don't have to stroke.'

"You do a good enough job stroking your own ego," said Watson.

CHAPTER ELEVEN

Detectives Fagley and Casey were waiting for Jim Dorgan when he arrived at Hudson High School just before the bell rang at 8:15. They had already cleared it with principal Sherman, not that her approval was even necessary, but they wanted to appear as inconspicuous as they could. The three went into an empty classroom not far from the main offices. Fagley handled the questioning.

"Are you and Frank Black good friends?" Fagley asked.

"Not really," said Dorgan, not making eye contact with either detective and instead alternating between looking out the window or down at his hands, which were resting on the table in front of him. "We hang together once in a while."

"Then why has he called you so much this week?"

"I don't know," Dorgan said with a shrug. "Maybe he was just bored on his days off."

"Are you a member of the Cropdusters?" Fagley continued, hoping to get some type of reaction from the teenager. So far, the answers had been direct, and Dorgan showed no other visible signs of fear, surprise or agitation.

"You could say that."

"Have you ever purchased or stolen embalming fluid?"

"No."

Fagley continued to ask more questions about the Cropdusters, and Dorgan explained that he joined the "club," as he called it, the previous year. He told the detectives that the Cropdusters consisted of about a dozen members, all Hudson High School students who did not participate in any extracurricular activities. Like other teenagers, the gang's members were into cars and video games, often meeting at someone's house for PlayStation or Xbox tournaments.

"Do you own a gun?"

"A hunting rifle, if that counts."

"It does. Where is it?"

"At my dad's house."

Fagley paused, looked at his partner and nodded. Casey then took over and asked Dorgan a little more about his family, how he divided time between his divorced parents, trying to get a feel for Dorgan's personality. It was difficult, the teenager admitted, having divorced parents, especially when he sensed neither really cared that much about their son. He told the detectives that he was an only child, and his parents divorced when he'd been in the second grade. Since then, he admitted, he floated through life, making just a few friends, Black among them, but none who he considered a best friend. He told the detectives he enjoyed hunting with his father. Deer hunting was Dorgan's favorite, though he and his father also hunted birds and squirrels.

"Where were you on Tuesday around noon?" Casey asked.

"At my mom's house," Dorgan said.

"Was there anyone else there at that time?"

"No."

"Did you talk to Frank Black at that time?" asked the detective.

"I don't know what time we talked," said Dorgan

"Did you go anywhere Tuesday?" Casey continued, attempting to establish a way Dorgan could have gone to the Grady Funeral Home and back and who might have seen him. Dorgan had not yet established any solid alibi for Tuesday.

"I went to Wal-Mart that morning," Dorgan said.

"Did you buy anything?"

"Just some candy and a new game for my PlayStation."

Dorgan explained he had driven himself back and forth to Wal-Mart, had not seen anyone he knew, and to his knowledge, no one he knew had seen him. He paid cash for the purchases and didn't think he had the receipt but said he'd look for it when he went to his mother's house after school. What he told the detectives about his day on Tuesday offered nothing to eliminate him as a suspect in the murders.

"Did you see Frank Black at all on Tuesday?" Fagley chimed in.

"No," said Dorgan while shaking his head.

"Well, here's my card. Call me if you think of anything else."

"Yeah. Okay."

Dorgan headed back to class and, en route, sent a text message: "Just talked to the cops. Think it went good."

In his conversations with police, Dorgan had been collected, appearing unconcerned that he was the focus of questioning and perhaps a suspect in a double homicide. This didn't really surprise Fagley. One of his cohorts, earlier in the week, reviewed police records to see if Dorgan or his friend, Frank Black, showed up at all on police records. They both had. Black had been cited twice, once for loitering in a restaurant where he apparently wasn't welcome and another time for petty theft. Dorgan, on the other hand, had a long list of violations, dating back to grade school. There was theft, disturbing the peace, and two incidents of underage drinking. A third violation in that category would result in the possibility of a short jail stay. Not good for a sophomore in high school.

Something didn't add up. Literally. Kyle Grady scoured his financial records of the Cropdusters' marijuana business. When he wasn't stoned, he was detailed-oriented and managed his business with acumen most MBA's couldn't muster. He knew how to make his suppliers feel appreciated and his customers happy not to mention providing both with confidentiality necessary to ensure business continued to flourish without interruption. His people skills were second only to his inventory and cost management abilities. And that's what troubled him, as he scoured his profit and loss sheets, disguised as Fantasy Football statistics if they were to ever fall into the wrong hands.

He knew adding embalming fluid to the marijuana crops he purchased increased not only the strength of the high but could also make the drug more addictive. After all, he knew what the addition of addictive chemicals meant for the cigarette business throughout years of denial. What bothered Grady was he could not account for the purchase of four bottles of embalming fluid. His records showed the four bottles had been in his inventory, but there was no records of outgoing funds.

He admitted to himself, pouring over the books, that he occasionally took a full or half-used bottle from the family funeral home, when he was working there doing odd jobs like cleaning. But he was wise enough to know he could never get away with taking four bottles and have it go unnoticed. Something didn't add up.

CHAPTER TWELVE

Chief Walsh gathered the troops in his office at 9:00 a.m. sharp. He had already met with Hudson's mayor for coffee earlier that day. The mayor had made it seem as if the invite was just for coffee, but both men knew better. It was a thorough verbal ass-kicking. The mayor, who was up for re-election later in the year, was clearly starting to worry. High-profile case. No suspects. City residents angry and ready to blame the mayor. Take out anger at the polls in November. It didn't matter the size of the city. A killer on the loose was never good for business or politics.

"All right, folks," began the chief. "The mayor just reamed me a new one, and I'm ready to do the same to you. Give me some good news before I'm forced to fire the lot of you."

"We've talked to both students," Fagley said. "Neither has an alibi for the time in question. Both have access to hunting rifles. Any connection stops there. We're going to follow up with Wal-Mart and take a look at the surveillance video. Dorgan, one of the kids, said he bought some candy and a PlayStation game there late Tuesday morning. There's a chance he bought something else that might implicate him. We're going to get a search warrant for their homes to get their hunting rifles and look for any traces of embalming fluid. Beyond that, we have nothing."

"Well, nothing sucks," Walsh barked.

"We're doing the best we can," Fagley said.

"That's what the Packers say every time they lose to the Bears or Vikings," said the chief. "Let's review a list of people we've interviewed, and go back and talk to them. You need to find more people who might have been in the vicinity of the funeral home at the time of the murders. Let's increase our Crimestoppers reward to $50,000 for any info that leads to catching the killers, and make sure the media get that info. We need them to play up that angle a little more."

With that, Walsh pointed his finger at the door. Everyone stood and left in silence. With every hour that passed, their jobs became more difficult. Most clues and suspects are found within a day or two of the murders.

Can you tell me what happened?"

"No."

"You can't or you won't?" Kyle Grady asked his friend Frank Black, as the two sat off to a side of the school's lunchroom away from the throngs of noisy students. It was the first time they spoke at any length since the murders at the funeral home.

"I don't know nothing about the murders," Black replied. "I'm sorry. I know it's tough for you, and if I had something that might help, I would be the first to tell you, even before I tell police. It's just that I don't have nothing. Neither does Jim. We were both at home that day, as you recall."

Grady was momentarily silent, pondering what he just heard while taking a small bite of his peanut butter sandwich.

"Have you heard anything on the street?" Grady asked. "Anything from any of the other Cropdusters? Someone must be saying something."

"Nothing."

"What happened to those bottles of embalming fluid? Who got them?"

"I don't know."

Again Grady paused, this time eating some of his Doritos and taking a few sips of a Coke.

"Kyle, buddy, we're friends," Black said, trying to break the tension. "I know this is a tough time for you, and I'm sorry. But we all have to be extra careful. With the police sniffing around, it could open a whole new can of worms. You understand, don't you?"

Grady just nodded in agreement.

Sean Kelly thought about calling Father Fred out of courtesy to let him know that he wanted to speak with Father Birch, but he thought an unexpected approach might work better. After quickly stepping inside the back of the church at 8:20 a.m., just far enough inside to see the altar but strategically out of the way to avoid being seen, Kelly saw what he wanted: Father Fred was saying mass. Without as much as a pause, he exited the church, nodded to Benson, who had her camera gear already in tow, and headed for the front door of the rectory. He rang the doorbell and fortuitously was greeted by Father Birch.

"Hi, Father. I'm Sean Kelly from Channel 6," said Kelly. "We spoke with Father Fred the other day, but we're hoping we could talk with you for a few minutes."

"About what?" asked Father Birch, who was wearing a long dark robe he often favored.

"I just wanted to get your reflections on Phillip Grady and what his untimely passing means for the parish, maybe a little about how you as an associate pastor help parishioners heal during this difficult time," Kelly explained, doing his best to make the interview sound innocuous.

"I'll talk to you, but no film," stated Father Birch.

"Okay." It wasn't what Kelly wanted, but he could at least have a shot at getting some new information.

"Come on inside," said Father Birch, gesturing for the reporter to follow him into the rectory.

Kelly motioned for Benson to follow him, too, even though she wouldn't be shooting at this point. It was always good to have another observer to compare thoughts and observations after the conversation.

"Did you know Phillip Grady well and work closely with him?" began Kelly.

"Well, yes, we did work closely together on a number of occasions both related to parish activities and funerals."

Father Birch spoke in a very deliberate manner, appearing to measure his answers before and while he was giving them. His voice was soothing but firm, what might be considered a classic preacher's voice full of careful enunciation and varying inflections.

"Did you two get along well?" Kelly asked bluntly.

"I suppose, for the most part. Yes."

"Did he have any enemies that you were aware of?"

"No."

"Was there any reason, to your knowledge, that someone might have wanted to kill him?"

"I can't think of any."

Father Birch asked Kelly and Benson if they wanted coffee. Both said yes, and the priest left the room, which was just off to one side of the main hallway, and headed to the kitchen. It was a good strategy, Kelly thought, on the part of the young priest to disrupt the line of questioning just as they hit a sensitive topic. Kelly was impressed.

Father Birch returned within minutes, carrying two coffee cups on saucers. He hadn't bothered to ask Kelly and Benson how they liked their coffee, and neither had requested anything special. Kelly thanked Father Birch and took two sips. It wasn't Starbucks, but it wasn't bad. He waited for the priest to sit down and then proceeded. "Did you ever have any disagreements with Phillip?" asked Kelly.

Father Birch didn't answer immediately. When he finally did, his delivery was even slower than normal. "Well, I suppose we had a couple."

"What about?"

"Usually they were related to my role with various youth groups within the parish," admitted the priest. "I think he thought I was too much of a friend to some of the kids. I think his nephew perhaps was jealous of the fact that, in his perception, I liked some of the other kids in the youth groups more and paid more attention to them."

Father Birch told Kelly that he and Grady never actually discussed their differences in detail. It was merely the priest's explanation based on a couple brief conversations the two had had. And, Father Birch said, Father Fred never discussed the situation with his young associate, which in Father Birch's opinion, indicated there was nothing really wrong.

"What do you enjoy most about being a parish priest?" Kelly asked in hopes of learning more about this strange individual.

"I like the responses I get to my homilies and teaching religion class one day a week at the school," Father Birch said.

"What type of subject evokes the greatest response?"

"I don't know. I suppose when I talk about the traditional aspects of the church. People really like that. I think there's a renewed desire to take a more traditional approach to Catholicism that we haven't seen for a long time."

The young priest launched into a speech about many of the things that bothered him with the current state of the Catholic Church. His diatribe ranged from small matters, like how people dressed for Sunday mass, to issues on a larger scope like abortion and a literal interpretation of various aspects of the Bible. As he spoke, his voice crescendoed, his faced reddened, and his emotions overflowed. Kelly felt as if he and Benson were among thousands at an Al Sharpton rally. Kelly had never heard or seen a Catholic priest speak like this but now understood why this priest had devout followers as well as detractors. He was like anchovies: one either really liked them or found them offensive.

"Do you like the new pope?" interjected Kelly as the priest took a breath to regain his composure. Kelly feared without a question, the priest might take a breath and pick up where he left off.

"I'm hopeful he will recognize that the American church needs some reform," admitted Father Birch still somewhat out of breath from his impassioned speech. "There's a liberal wing to it that just doesn't fit with God's message."

"What do you mean by that?" Kelly asked, clearly as curious as he was puzzled by the priest's statement.

"Well, for one, we need to reaffirm the traditional tenets on which Catholicsim was founded," Father Birch said, learning forward in his chair and visibly beginning to gather steam for another rant. "There needs to be a stronger push for respect for life, not just anti-abortion elements but anti-birth control as well. We need to expect our Catholic politicians to adhere to their faith when they formulate polit-ical positions. I love what the bishop of LaCrosse did, when he declared politicians who were pro-choice could not receive commun-ion. That took a lot of guts, but it was the right thing."

The priest paused, as if preparing to launch into other topics, but Kelly filled the gap with another question. "When was the last time you talked to Phillip Grady?"

"Let's see," said Father Birch, tilting his head in a way as if searching for an answer. "We spoke on the phone earlier this week, but I can't remember what day. Obviously it had to have been Monday or Tuesday morning."

"Do you remember the conversation?" asked Kelly.

"I believe we spoke mostly about plans for the upcoming win-ter camping trip for the parish youth group. That's scheduled to take place in late February."

"Was it a friendly conversation?"

"I suppose, though we disagreed a little on how many parents were needed to chaperone."

Father Birch admitted he like to have only a few parents accompany him and the youth on these outings. It allowed him, he said, the opportunity to discuss religious matters freely with the youth group and not be interrupted or contradicted by parents who might not fully agree with the priest's teaching.

"When was the last time you went to the funeral home?" Kelly inquired.

"I'm not sure. It was probably a week or so ago, whenever I did the last funeral that Grady's handled."

Kelly asked Father Birch if St. Tim's was the church for the funeral that Grady handled on Tuesday morning. No, the priest said, the parish had not had any funerals yet this week.

"Did you drive past there or anything on Tuesday?"

"No," the young priest replied tersely.

"Well, you must be very busy with the preparations for tomorrow's funeral as well as other business. I appreciate your time and insights. Here's my card. Feel free to call me if you think of anything else that might help us tell Phillip's story. And thanks for the coffee, too."

"You're welcome. If I think of something, I'll call. God bless you."

Kelly and Benson walked in silence to the van. The conversation with Father Birch, by design, had taken less than fifteen minutes, which meant Father Fred was still saying the 8:15 mass. Not that there would have been a problem, but it was probably better, Kelly thought, if Father Fred didn't walk in on the meeting. Once in the van, Benson broke the silence.

"What are your thoughts?"

"God forgive me as I say this, but that dude is one fucked up individual," said Kelly shaking his head and looking at Benson for her reaction. "Did you hear some of the shit he said? What's next? Is David Duke going to start preaching from the pulpit of Father Birch's church. Let's hope to God that he never gets a position of leadership. Man, oh man."

"He *was* strange," Benson agreed. "Do you think he was the priest you saw Tuesday?"

"I know he was."

"Now how do you know that? And yet he said he didn't go near the funeral home. Curious, isn't it?"

"Newsflash: priests can lie, too."

What Kelly didn't mention was that a unique looking pocket watch that Father Birch pulled out and consulted during their conversation. The priest at the funeral home Tuesday night also had a pocket watch.

CHAPTER THIRTEEN

Detective Fagley secured warrants to search both Dorgan's and Black's homes. When police arrived at all three homes unannounced shortly after ten o'clock, parents were home at all three residences. The detectives explained their reason for coming to the house again, asked to search, and the parents all readily agreed, voicing no concern either when police asked if they could take the hunting rifles to run some tests back at headquarters. It was strange, thought Fagley. There was no resistence, no skepticism, no anger. Usually police could at least count on one angry individual who's spent too much time watching *CSI: Miami* and thinks his rights are constantly being violated. Not so this morning.

The ballistics crew from the state crime lab in Madison had been alerted and promptly dropped other work to thoroughly examine the hunting rifles when they arrived. Forensic scientists determined quickly that all the rifles were properly registered to the teenagers' dads. They then performed tests to see if any of the guns had recently been fired. All tests came up negative or inconclusive. Finally, lab technicians attempted to determine if any of the slugs removed during the victims' autopsies could have possibly been fired from the guns in questions. The answer: possible but unlikely.

Just as the balllistics crew was completing its paperwork and looking over the conclusions, getting ready to prepare the rifles for return to their owners, Fagley burst through the doors of the lab, cell phone to ear.

"Great work. Thanks," said Fagley, as he ended his conversation and snapped shut his RAZR phone. "Guess what? That was Casey. He just scanned through the surveillance video at Wal-Mart from Tuesday morning. On it is a boy, almost certainly Dorgan, at the checkout. True to his story, he bought some candy and a new game for his PlayStation. What he failed to mention is that it appears from the video that he also happened to purchase ammunition for a hunting rifle. We also checked the Wal-Mart computer system, which tracks sales and inventory flow. It showed that one box of bullets, and, get this, the same type of bullets that were pulled from the victims, was purchased at 10:38 Tuesday morning. The transaction was cash, so we unfortunately don't have any more data to link Dorgan to the purchase."

"But how was a minor able to purchase ammunition?" asked one of the techs. "Did no one ask for ID?"

"Here's the kicker," Fagley explained. "Dorgan had an adult with him. So even though it appears the purchase was made with Dorgan's own money, that very well might explain failure to check any ID either at the check-out counter or in the hunting department. Now the strangest thing of all is that the adult with Dorgan, at least as best as we can determine from the video, appeared to be a Catholic priest."

"Assignment desk, Watson."

"I've got two angles to cover at noon. Set aside two minutes for me."

"What have you got, Kelly?" she asked.

"The police are running some ballistic tests on the hunting rifles that belong to the families of the two high school students they questioned," Kelly explained, writing part of the story in his head as he dictated the facts to Watson. "The second student was questioned this morning. I can't get out of my contact what, if anything, the lab has found. We can also make mention with some b-roll that the public wake for Grady begins at four this afternoon, and funeral home officials are planning for a couple thousand to pass through."

"Not bad," admitted Watson. "By the way, the network called and said they might be sending a reporter from Chicago and were hoping you could brief her if she arrives today."

"Tell them to get fucked," Kelly growled. "I'm not getting paid to do their legwork."

"I'm sure they'll appreciate that."

Kelly hung up the phone and pondered a few things. He hated being on a story when the network sent in one of its own. It was probably rooted in jealousy. He figured he was better than whatever reporter would arrive, yet they had a national audience and got paid more. He had tried unsuccessfully on two previous occasions to get a network correspondent job. His reputation for being demanding and high maintenance preceded his applications, however. The network brass, finely tuned in broadcast mismanagement skills, wanted reporters and producers who would kiss their fat, under-exercised asses. Good reporting skills were secondary, at best.

The other notion whirling in Kelly's head was that Fagley had something he wasn't telling. When he last spoke with him within the hour, Fagley was brief and terse, forthcoming only with the fact that the rifles were being checked out. At one point in the conversation, Fagley seemed almost ready to add more to the conversation but instead ended it quickly. The two agreed to meet later that afternoon at the St. Croix Cigar Company on Second Street.

Kelly had one more call to make before putting the finishing touches on his noon report.

"Hello?"

"Hey, it's Sean," said Kelly. "Are you making any progress on the information I wanted you to get?"

"Some, and I expect to have more by 12:30. I'm waiting back on one call."

"That's what I like to hear. Don't let anyone give you any shit."

"Don't worry. I won't."

Fagley and his posse split up. Four detectives went to the high school, where they were going to question Dorgan and Black separately. They agreed, at least for the moment, not to bring them in for questioning, hoping instead to make the teens feel as comfortable as possible. Fagley and Casey went to St. Timothy's, where they found Father Birch finishing his lunch. This time Casey led the questioning.

"We know you're busy with the Grady wake and funeral, so we won't keep you long," the detective said.

"That's okay," Father Birch acknowledged. "I have a few minutes."

Casey cut right to the chase. "How well do you know Frank Black and Jim Dorgan?"

"Fairly well," the priest said. "They're members of the parish, and I have them in the teen youth group that's preparing for Confirmation."

"How would you describe the two boys?" Casey asked.

"They're normal teenagers," explained the priest. "Quiet. Reserved. Not what I would consider social outcasts, but neither will win most popular sophomore this year."

"Do you ever see them outside of class?"

"Yes, on occasion we've done things together, gone out for lunch and such."

"Where were you Tuesday morning around 10:00 or 10:30?" asked Fagley.

"Let's see. I was here until about 9:00 and then went to run some errands."

"Where did you go?" Fagley asked.

Father Birch explained that he filled up his car with gas at the local SuperAmerica, went to Target to buy some socks and made a stop at Walgreens to pick up a prescription. After that, he told the detectives he returned to the rectory. His errands lasted about fifty minutes.

"Do you own any guns, Father?" Casey asked.

"Yes, I have a hunting rifle," the priest acknowledged.

"When did you last use it?" Fagley asked.

"Last week. I did some skeet shooting at a friend's farm."

"Have you ever gone hunting with Black or Dorgan?"

"No."

Fagley considered for a second whether a pause would help the interview process but decided otherwise and kept rolling with questions. "Why did you help Dorgan buy bullets Tuesday at Wal-Mart?"

"What?" asked the priest, looking confused. "I already told you where I went, and Wal-Mart wasn't one of the stops."

Father Birch's tenor began to show signs of surprise and agitation. He clearly did not expect this line of questioning and gave indications, both with his voice and body language that his comfort level had just faded.

"We have reason to believe that you were at Wal-Mart Tueday with Jim Dorgan and helped him purchase ammunition for a hunting rifle."

Father Birch's face began to redden, and he began to nervously twiddle his thumbs in his folded hands. His disgust with the detectives was palpable. "That simply isn't true. Now if you don't have anything else to ask, I'm going to have to wrap this up. I have a lot of work to do."

"I'm sure you do. Thanks for your time. We'll be in touch. We can see ourselves to the door."

Detectives Fagley and Casey compared notes with the four detectives who talked with Dorgan and Black. Their stories all checked out, as if they had rehearsed what they would say. Any evidence indicating that either of the boys or Father Birch was involved in the murders was circumspect at best, nothing firm enough to justify an arrest. But police had no other suspects, not even the tiniest of leads. And without such, they were forced to concentrate on what little information they had, however tenuous, that might possibly link the teens or the priest to the murders.

The police strongly suspected Dorgan and Father Birch were lying about the ammunition purchase at Wal-Mart, but the video surveillance by itself was not enough to confirm that, much less finger them for murder. There were doubts as well about whether the three had ever hunted together. But again, Fagley told his cohorts, that fact alone was not enough to bring up murder charges. Add to that the fact that earlier searches of the three homes turned up no traces of embalming fluids, and the detectives were left with imaginative theories that even Jerry Bruckheimer would find too far-fetched.

CHAPTER FOURTEEN

The St. Croix Cigar Company was a new addition to Hudson's historic Second Street. During the summer, the street and surrounding areas were filled with people, many of whom were boaters on the St. Croix River, just to the west of Second Street. In the winter, it was much easier to find a parking space.

The cigar shop offered a wide selection of popular cigars, a comfortable smoking lounge and wireless Internet. Kelly appreciated the fact that there were still a few places where he could enjoy a smoke indoors. While not a regular smoker, he certainly was not a supporter of government-imposed smoking bans. His first exposure to the realities of a smoking ban came four years earlier, while on a trip to San Francisco, which had just imposed a smoking ban on all restaurants and bars. It seemed the only type of smoking that could legally take place in one of these establishments was a different form favored by Hugh Grant. Tired of watching a lopsided Super Bowl between the Tampa Bay Bucs and Oakland Raiders, Kelly ventured from his motel room near the Presidio and walked down Union Street. The new anti-smoking law, he quickly learned, protected the health of people inside the bars and restaurants but not pedestrians. He figured by the end of his forty-minute walk he had secondhand-smoked a pack of cigarettes thanks to all the people who had escaped the comforts of the indoors to persevere the cold rain and smoke legally outdoors. A sarcastically brazen letter from Kelly to the Mayor of San Francisco followed, suggesting he was going to file a class action lawsuit against the city on behalf of all pedestrians that don't smoke and whose health was now in jeopardy. The letter went unanswered.

Kelly was well into his Avo No. 2 and checking his email on his laptop, when Fagley walked through the door shortly after two. It was clear from his facial expression that the pressure was getting to Fagley. He bought a Fuente 8-5-8, lit it and plopped down in a leather chair next to Kelly. Fortunately, they were the only two in the smoking lounge.

"You look like shit," Kelly began.

"Thanks for the compliment," said Fagley in between puffs.

"You cut me off on the phone earlier," Kelly began, "which leads me to believe (a) there were too many people near you, so you couldn't share anything that might be considered confidential, (b) you censored yourself, choosing not to share any information or (c) you really had to take a piss."

"Funny," said Fagley smiling and rubbing his forehead. "We're getting nowhere. We've interviewed the two students and Father Birch to no avail. There are a few weak links that could tie them to the killings, but that's it. Not enough to hold them, and a prosecutor would laugh at us with our lack of evidence. We're missing something with them, or they're just not the ones who dunnit."

"Well, maybe I've got something to help you," Kelly said in his pretentious voice. "Father Birch, I have learned, has a penchant for young boys and guns. At his previous assignment, a church in River Falls, the word is he angered some parents by getting a little too close to some members of the youth group. Nothing was ever made public, and it's difficult to say, at least from what I've heard, that there was any conclusive evidence that he did anything illegal. But his normal tour of duty was cut short after the church's pastor got tired of hearing complaints from vociferous parents. That's how he ended up at St. Timothy's last year."

"That doesn't make him a murder suspect," Fagley said. "What about guns?"

"When he was in the seminary at St. Mary's University in Winona, he was charged with possessing an unlicensed firearm. Apparently he got into an argument with another driver on Gilmore Avenue, a case of road rage. According to the police report, Birch, I guess, not quite satisfied with the direction his discussion with the other driver was taking, unlocked his trunk and pulled out a sawed-off shotgun. Fortunately for everyone involved, the police arrived at about the same time and calmed Birch down. Some of his classmates also say he kept two or three hunting rifles in his room at the Seminary. I think the classmates were a little freaked out by it. And according to Wisconsin and Minnesota records, he has purchased no fewer than ten different guns, a combination of rifles and handguns, over the past five years.

"I'm going to use this information coupled with the fact that he's been questioned by police on the news tonight," Kelly continued. "Is there anything else I should know?"

"No, it seems like you have more information than we do."

"And that surprises you? I'm going to personally contact Chief Walsh for my commission. Whose wages should he garnish?"

"Very funny," Fagley said. He appreciated the fact that Kelly shared this information with him before putting it on the news. It gave Fagley a chance to share it with the chief immediately. The last thing the detectives needed was their boss seeing a news report that contained much more data than they had on Father Birch.

"Now that I've given you more information than anyone on your staff is capable of finding on their own, I need a little favor. There's a young woman named Shelly Rosen, who was arrested outside a bar down the street last weekend for disorderly conduct. She had been a little overserved and got into a cat fight with some chick she thinks stole her boyfriend. It would be appreciated if you could find a way to make the charge disappear."

Fagley did a double-take. "What? Why the interest on your part? Are you boning her?"

"Let's just say she had something to do with getting the information I just gave you, and with that info you should be able to at least make it appear to the chief that you and your fellow detectives are not all incompetent fucks. Okay?"

Fagley sighed. "I'll take care of it." He got up from his chair and prepared to leave.

Kelly nodded and then said: "Thanks. Stay in touch."

Fagley left his cigar to burn out on its own in the ashtray and walked out to his car. He now had more info to process without really knowing how to possibly pin the murders on the priest or his teenage buddies. Kelly, meantime, stayed behind, took another puff of his Avo and dialed a number on his cell phone.

"Hello?"

"Hey, it's me," Kelly said. "The charge'll be dropped later today."

"Thanks. I appreciate it," said Rosen, offering a sigh of relief for good measure.

"Thank you for your help. You're not so bad for a USC grad. Now before you hurt your arm patting yourself on the back, look into those other matters I told you about. Okay?"

"Got it."

Kelly hung up the phone without saying good-bye, a trait that bothered many. Why waste time with an extra word or two, he maintained, when it should be clear either from the silence or dial tone that the conversation had ended. He enjoyed working with Shelly Rosen, ever since she'd been hired late the year before as an associate producer, which in television newsrooms was often just one step above an intern. Reporters rarely talked to interns or associate producers unless they needed coffee or help picking up their dry cleaning. Kelly was different. He engaged new hires in conversation, challenging them on one subject or another and determining within about two minutes if he would ever talk with them again. The answer was usually no. He often marveled at how so-called reputable colleges and universities could churn out such boring and intellectually-devoid graduates.

Rosen was different, though. He quickly called her on the fact that she attended the University of Southern California, a longtime rival of Kelly's alma mater Notre Dame, and with the exception of the band and cheerleaders, he felt everything else about USC was subpar. He loved to talk about Notre Dame, finding creative ways many would think impossible to work into a conversation the fact that he attended school under the Golden Dome. He especially enjoyed sparring with people who hated Notre Dame. At a party earlier in the month that featured the Fiesta Bowl between Notre Dame and Ohio State, a neighbor who arrived late opined to anyone in earshot that he couldn't figure out the fascination so many people had with Notre Dame. Why was it, this neighbor wondered, that every ND grad found a way within the first ten minutes of a conversation with someone they've just met to mention the fact that they'd attended Notre Dame? Already agitated by the fact that the Buckeyes were kicking ND's butt and fueled by at least a bottle of Kendall-Jackson Pinot Noir, Kelly let the neighbor know that he should get his facts straight. The ND alumni office had done extensive research, Kelly spouted sarcastically, and determined that it took an average of 5.6 minutes for a Domer to work such a mention into a conversation. Take that, you dipshit Johnnie.

Rosen won Kelly's respect in the first minute of their conversation by quoting stats about recent ND-USC games, lauding the Trojans' recent national championships and wondering aloud whether Notre Dame would ever again win a bowl game in her lifetime. Kelly paused, nodded his head and walked off without saying a word. Rosen had passed his test by showing more than a modicum of intelligence and, more important, the ability and willingness to come right back at him in conversation.

Not all their discussions over the past months displayed such a hostile tone, though most of the newsroom flunkies who had witnessed one or more of their colorful exchanges, figured the two hated each other. Kelly schooled Rosen on how to handle her duties as associate producer in a timely manner that would allow her to spend time learning other aspects of the newsroom. He gave her some investigative research projects that most producers found tedious, demeaning or simply impossible to accomplish. Rosen thrived on these requests and produced more information than needed. When Kelly asked her Wednesday to look into the history of Father Joseph Birch, he had little doubt she would uncover some nuggets. He was right. Now he had to find a way to prove this priest was the killer.

CHAPTER FIFTEEN

A s promised, the network sent Becky Lewis, one of its Chicago reporters, to cover the funeral home murders. She phoned Kelly from the Minneapolis-St. Paul airport shortly after noon, indicating she was coming to Hudson to cover the story and was hopeful she could meet with Kelly for a few minutes to get some background on the story. She was forewarned about his cantankerous ways, especially when he felt other reporters were asking him to do their work. Somehow she managed to charm Kelly just enough to secure a five-minute meeting, or as he abruptly informed her, shorter than five minutes if she started to bore him or piss him off.

Kelly had never met Lewis but obviously had seen her work on the network news. He thought her reporting style was decent, though he couldn't remember any report of hers that really stood out as unique or groundbreaking. Curious as always, he took time after Fagley left the smoke shop, to search the network's website for a biography on Lewis. Two words jump off his screen: Boston College. If there was one school Kelly detested, it was BC. Ever since they spoiled Notre Dame's title chances with a huge upset in 1993, he had despised the school, taking every opportunity to hurl insults to BC grads he met.

His research revealed that Lewis had graduated from Boston College in 1991. Upon graduation, she landed a general assignment reporter job at a Providence station and then moved to Boston two years later. Five years into her Boston gig, she was hired by the CBS-owned station WBBM in Chicago. While there, she won numerous awards for her coverage of city politics, which in Chicago was often more entertaining and followed more closely than some of the city's sporting teams. Lewis' style and success in Chicago impressed the network brass, who made her part of the Chicago bureau three years ago. She was now part of the younger generation of reporters that Katie Couric apparently favored. Kelly learned from the bio that Lewis was single, or at least there was no mention of a spouse, and enjoyed running, biking, and music in her freetime.

She arrived, as promised, promptly at 2:34 to meet Kelly at the St. Croix Cigar Company. Kelly liked to use strange meeting times to determine how much attention people paid to detail. He picked the cigar shop as a meeting spot not just because he knew he would be there for his meeting with Fagley, but he wanted to set the tone and test Lewis. This meeting was going to be on his terms, and he then could gage from her reaction to the cigar smoke, how their relationship might proceed.

Kelly studied Lewis as she walked through the doorway. She was dressed in light-blue blouse and black skirt, not too short but short enough to show off her slender legs covered by black nylons. She wore just enough make-up to enhance her glossy black hair and deep-blue eyes. Her high heels seemed to complement her confident gait.

Kelly glanced at his watch, nodded in acknowledgement and rose from his leather chair. Keeping the lit Avo in his left hand, he offered his right hand to greet her.

"Right on time," Kelly stated firmly. "I'm impressed."

"Becky Lewis," she announced. "Nice to meet you. Thanks for making time."

"I gather you're not filing a report tonight based on your arrival time," Kelly said. "I, on the other hand, have to keep moving, so, as I said on the phone, we'll have to keep this short. Do you want anything from the humidor?"

"Sure. I'll take a Petit Corona," said Lewis, displaying a firm grasp of cigar sizes that truly surprised Kelly. He didn't wait for her to suggest a brand and walked into the humidor, selected a Partagas, told the man behind the counter to put it on his tab and walked back to sit next to Lewis. Her interest in meeting, Lewis explained, was not to be brought up to speed on the investigation; she had already viewed Kelly's reports on Channel 6's website. She told him she wanted instead some of his observations and insights into any of the possible suspects. Kelly played coy, claiming to not know too much more than what he'd reported. He did offer a preview to what he planned to report on today's evening news and made cursory mention of both Father Fred and Father Birch.

"Do you think the whacko priest did it?" Lewis asked.

Kelly shook his head and puffed on his cigar. "I don't know. I don't think so, but I just don't have any proof that he didn't."

"Listen," Lewis snapped. "I'm a network reporter, but I'm not a bitch, I know you probably don't like me coming here and asking all these questions. But if there's anything you can do to help me out during my stay, it would be much appreciated, even if you are a Notre Dame grad."

Both laughed at her comment.

"I'll see what I can do," Kelly replied. "Where are you and your illustrious crew staying?"

"We're at the Hilton in downtown Minneapolis," Lewis said. "Wanted to be close to your station, if we need to do any feeds from there. Though I suspect we'll do most our feeds from here in Hudson."

"How long do you plan to stay?" Kelly inquired.

"Probably just a few days," Lewis said. "We're scheduled to file a report tomorrow after the funeral and then see if there are any new developments."

Kelly stood and pulled one of his cards out of his front shirt pocket. Lewis reciprocated and thanked him for the time.

Kelly considered Lewis, as he walked down Second Street to meet Benson at a prearranged spot. He couldn't help but smile at his own thoughts, however lascivious. There was something he really liked about Lewis, and he wanted to talk with her again. Maybe over dinner if their schedules allowed. He hadn't lost sight, however, of the fact that professionally at least she was still a competitor, and her presence, he understood, would challenge him to work harder to avoid being scooped.

Phillip Grady's wake wasn't scheduled to begin until four o'clock, but a line began forming outside the funeral home at 3:30. By 3:50, the line wrapped around the corner and extended the length of a city block. Media crews had moved their "homebase" from the Grady funeral home to this location. The police made no attempt to hide their presence, presumably hoping to find some clues and knowing it's not uncommon for a killer to attend the wake and funeral of his victims. Just ask O.J. Simpson.

While the focus of the investigation had been on the two high school students and lately Father Birch as well, police had also found a few minutes to talk with Grady family members, most notably the victim's brother, Robert. They had managed to get twenty minutes with him on Wednesday, searching for any possible motives he might consider. A botched robbery was the best Robert could offer. He made it vehemently clear that his brother was well liked by fellow parishioners, well respected by members of the community that had used the funeral home's services at some point in their lives and practically revered by family members, especially his brother. Police would have liked more time and had Robert more focused during the twenty minutes they spent with him, but understandably he was wracked with grief, at times unable to speak more than a few consecutive sentences without breaking down. The brutal circumstances of the deaths made it even more difficult to comprehend and accept. Police realized they got little but wouldn't get more from him right then. They would have to wait until after the funeral to get some more time with Robert and other family members.

Meantime, Chief Walsh had called upon an old colleague in Woodbury, Minnesota, the hometown of Charles Illsmere, the other victim. He asked his friend, a deputy in the Woodbury Police Department, to talk with Illsmere's family and friends. There was certainly a possibility that the killer had targeted Illsmere, and Grady had been killed because he was a witness, though investigators dismissed the theory as remote. Illsmere was a young college student. With the exception of a few family members and close friends, few people even knew Illsmere was working at the funeral home. The fact that his schedule was irregular compounded the difficulty in establishing a motive or suspect with regard to Illsmere. Still, Chief Walsh realized all angles had to be pursued, especially given the minute progress his department seemed to be making.

Kelly observed the masses gathering around the funeral home. He knew how difficult this could be for the people waiting to pay the family their respects. There were some people, Kelly noted, who knew the family well and felt devastated for them. There were others who knew only the victim but felt it necessary to pay a visit to the funeral home anyway. And there were a select few who felt their status, or perceived status, in the community made a quick visit mandatory. Though there would be no quick visits tonight. Some people stood outside in line for more than an hour, as the temperature dipped below twenty. There was something cruel about this situation, Kelly thought.

He had written his five and six o'clock stories after meeting up with Benson. Barring any major new developments, he was set. But he was still troubled by what, if any, role Father Birch had in the murders. Loose connections continued to point to the priest as a suspect or at least an accomplice, which made interesting copy for the evening newscasts. Kelly went over the facts in his head, replaying his conversation with Father Birch that morning and recounting the other pieces of information he had discovered about the priest. What would move a priest to kill two people? A simple disagreement? A threat to make public damaging information? A temporary insane rage?

The Catholic Church in America had been severely damaged in recent years by allegations and admissions of sexual abuse by the clergy dating back decades. After denying the problem for years, the Church finally acknowledged that transgressions occurred and were often covered up. While the Church had taken great steps to avoid similar scenarios after that, there was still the chance the problem could persist. Could Father Birch somehow be a perpetrator of sexual abuse with some of the youth at St. Tim's or anywhere else? Just the thought turned Kelly's stomach.

There was also the issue of impatience and a short temper. Kelly saw signs of the former at the end of his discussion with Father Birch earlier that day. A temper had manifested itself during the incident in Winona that Rosen had found. Could this lead to murder? Under unfortunate circumstances, maybe.

The contemplative mood was interrupted by the tones of the Notre Dame "Victory March," the ring tone Kelly had downloaded to his phone. He quickly glanced at the incoming number, which was blocked, and answered.

"Hello."

"Is this Sean Kelly?" asked a woman's voice at the other end.

"Yeah, who's this and how did you get my cell number?" barked Kelly, who went to great lengths to keep his cell number as private as possible.

"Don't worry about that," said the woman dismissively. "What's important is that you keep after Father Birch."

"What do you mean?" asked Kelly.

"He was scheduled to meet with Phillip Grady at two o'clock Tuesday afternoon at the funeral home," the caller noted.

"And how do you know this?" he inquired.

"That doesn't matter. I thought you might want to look into it."

"Why . . . ?"

Kelly realized the caller had already hung up. The connection hadn't been the best; it sounded like the caller was in a moving car, but Kelly felt fairly certain it was the same voice that called him at home earlier that week. He wondered who this person was, how she would know so much about Father Birch and why they were calling Kelly. Anonymous sources could present precarious situations. They usually targeted one reporter and then determined if that reporter was making good use of the tips. If it was determined the reporter was doing a good job, the anonymous tips kept coming on an exclusive basis. However, if the tipster felt the information was not being put to good use, they often chose to send future tips to a different reporter. It was difficult to determine the motives that drove an anonymous source, at least those who presented what turned out to be legitimate information. Some were simply altruistic and felt the best way they could help was to make sure someone in the media told the story. Other unidentified sources took a perverse pleasure in feeling they were part of a story as the result of their tip. Still others might just be pissed at the world or a particular company or individual, and their way of attaining satisfaction or retribution was to operate a smear campaign through the media.

Kelly prided himself on his ability to size up an individual within a minute or two of meeting them in person. Even though he was good at spotting a legitimate anonymous source through phone calls alone, a personal assessment of that individual over the phone was a little more difficult. He never trusted people who smiled too much. Life was good, but not that good to be constantly smiling. He could promptly identify people he felt were simply full of shit, big talkers who rarely said anything of substance. He felt the same as he did after the woman's first call. There was something about the lady's voice over the phone that sounded firm and genuine. He appreciated the fact that her calls were brief but still contained useful information. There wasn't any fake attempt to make small talk or even really appear friendly. He liked it that way, and that was the main reason he felt he was getting some interesting leads.

Pursuing this latest angle would be the challenge. It was doubtful, Kelly felt, that Father Birch would willingly admit he had a meeting scheduled with Grady and even less likely Kelly could get his hands on Father Birch's calender. Grady's datebook or the secretary at the funeral home might be the best source.

The police should have already looked at Grady's schedule and talked with funeral home employees, but Fagley had not mentioned anything. To be fair, Kelly reasoned, he and Fagley did not always share every single bit of information immediately. There was also the possibility that one or more of the detectives saw Father Birch's name on Grady's calender but chose not to follow up on it. A Catholic priest was usually not the initial prime suspect in a double murder.

"Bless me Father for I have sinned. My last confession was last week, and here are my sins. I sometimes swear. I don't always get along with others, and recently I did something very wrong. For these and all my other sins, I am sorry."

CHAPTER SIXTEEN

Kelly beat his alarm, waking up at 4:52 a.m. It was always good to avoid hearing the buzzer sound when you're in a deep sleep, but nonetheless he was still a little pissed he had missed out on a few minutes of sleep. On days when he was more sluggish, he wouldn't hesitate to attempt to hit the snooze button for an hour or more. Today, though, his mind was racing. He turned on WCCO and caught the CBS and local news. The world was still spinning and no WCCO reporters had dug up anything new on the funeral home murders. He would ponder theories that were nagging at his murder-mystery-novel steeped conspiratorial brain during his morning run in a few minutes, but first he made the obligatory phone call to Fagely's cell.

"Has anyone told you lately that you're really an asshole?" asked Fagley before Kelly could even say a word.

"Not lately, but a little affirmation before the sun rises never hurts. Anything new?" Kelly asked.

"Yeah. We arrested the killer last night and he confessed. Then we all went out and tied one on. I guess I forgot to call you," joked the detective.

"You're a beauty. Anything new or do you need me to find some fresh clues for you?" Kelly inquired.

"I hate to ever give you credit and boost your already super-sized ego, but we're at a loss for anything new," admitted Fagley. "I'd be happy to entertain anything you might have."

"I'll let you know. Now get back to your beauty sleep. You need it."

"Fuck you."

Kelly's run this morning took him down Cleveland to Summit. At the University of St. Thomas, he turned right on Summit and proceeded past some of the grandest homes in the state for the next mile and a half. Through his earbuds pounded the beat of Steve Earle's "The Revolution Starts Now," from the MP3 player, a good song for running. As he ran, Kelly went over the myriad of unanswered questions regarding the murders.

Had Father Birch become the prime suspect and was he capable of killing two people? If he was capable of murder, what could Phillip Grady have done or said to move the priest to kill? Why was Father Birch supposedly scheduled to meet with Grady at two the day of the murder? Who was the lady who called him with the tips and what was her reason for calling? Were the teenagers involved in the murders? Was there some other completely different angle that had yet to be explored? Could Father Birch have some knowledge of the murder but not be the actual killer?

Kelly took a right off Summit and onto Hamline then crossed Grand and hung another right on Lincoln. He began to wind his way through the quiet neighborhood streets back toward his home. As he did, he attempted to formulate different theories, however preposterous.

What if Father Birch had showed up early for his meeting with Grady and actually saw the killer leaving the funeral home? The time-line didn't quite fit, because the secretary supposedly returned around one and discovered the bodies, and that would have been really early for a 2:00 p.m. meeting. But what if Father Birch had showed up early or the secretary had taken a longer lunch than she admitted.

Or there's the possibility that Father Birch and Grady disagreed on the way something at the church was being run. Grady requested a meeting away from the church to discuss it, but Father Birch blew a gasket before the scheduled meeting time, grabbed one of his guns and went Waco.

Or there was still a reasonable possibility that Father Birch was at the rectory eating lunch and both teenagers were lounging around their homes while some other individual was pulling the trigger.

That brought Kelly back to the obvious: keep looking at Father Birch and gather as much information about him, his relationship with Grady and his whereabouts on Tuesday. Yeah, it was as easy as that. Not.

Kelly dialed his cell phone from his Audi in the parking lot of Assumption. It was just after morning mass. He knew based on the hour and circumstances that reaching a live human voice would be a longshot, but he thought he would call the Grady Funeral Home nonetheless. He had spent at least part of this morning's mass thinking of exactly what he would say if, in fact, someone answered this early.

"Grady Funeral Home," answered a male voice after two rings.

"Hi, is this Robert Grady?"

"Yes. Who's this?"

"I'm sorry to bother you this early. This is Sean Kelly from Channel 6. I want to express my condolences."

"Why are you calling so early?" asked Grady in an even, somber tone.

"Under normal circumstances, I wouldn't," Kelly explained. "But while I know the police are working diligently, I think I might be in the process of uncovering some additional information that I might be able to put together and pass along to the authorities to help them catch whoever killed your brother."

Kelly was a master at assuaging anyone's anger at an early morning call from a reporter, especially at a time of such grief. There were times when the person on the other end of the phone would simply hang up or salute him with a string of profanities, but generally he was able to get people to talk with him for a few minutes.

"What sort of information?" wondered Grady.

"Robert, did your brother and Father Birch have any run-ins at the church?" Kelly asked, wasting no time getting to the meat.

"Well, yeah, you could say that."

"About what?"

"It usually had to do with Father Birch's role with the youth group," explained Grady. "My son was involved in different aspects of the group. Kyle's been very involved because he's going through Confirmation class."

"What, exactly, did Father Birch do that upset your brother?" asked Kelly.

"I really don't know. I . . . I just don't know for sure."

"Did you know Father Birch was supposed to meet with your brother Tuesday at two at the funeral home?"

"Who told you that?" he demanded, with surprise in his voice.

"What do you think the agenda was?" Kelly said, evading his question.

"Who told you anything about that?" asked Grady again.

"An unidentified caller gave me that info," admitted Kelly. "I have no clue who it is or if they were even telling the truth. Is it true? Have police asked you anything about it?"

"Phillip mentioned he had a meeting but didn't mention with whom. And I can't seem to find his calendar, even though he almost always kept it on his desk."

"All right. Thanks. I hate to impose and want you to know that I would only use this kind of information in rare circumstances and not share it with anyone else, but could I possibly get your cell phone number to contact you in the future?" Kelly requested.

"Sure. If it helps police find the killer, then so be it."

The two exchanged numbers and said good-bye. Kelly hung up his cell phone and just stared at the two bell towers on Assumption. He really hated stories like this. Contacting family members of the victims as he had just done was never easy; in fact, he found an element of it despicable. But he also knew, doing his best to put aside whatever modesty he might possess, that he stood as good a chance as the police in some cases of finding the perpetrator.

As he started his car and put it into gear, he noticed one of the other daily mass regulars still sitting in her Mercedes CS Coupe, a hot car for an older woman who had previously driven a Jaguar XJ6. This was odd, Kelly thought, because she often beat him out of the parking lot immediately after mass and sometimes right after communion.

CHAPTER SEVENTEEN

Weather, especially during the winter in the Midwest, can add to the suffering of funeral goers. As if mourning the loss of a loved one or friend isn't difficult enough, a severe cold spell can make matters all that much more unpleasant. Such was the case on this Friday in January, as the Grady family prepared to say good-bye to Phillip. The cold air that Kelly felt during his run earlier in the morning had not warmed as evidenced by the bulky winter coats and scarves people wore as they entered St. Timothy's Church.

Father Fred had anticipated a full church for the funeral and planned accordingly. He and the funeral director ensured there were the proper number of pews reserved for family members that would process in with the casket. The family agreed to let the media film portions of the funeral mass from the choir loft, tapping into an audio box located next to the organ. The media were also instructed in stern terms that they were to remain on one side of the choir loft and not attempt to access shots from anywhere else in the church. Police requested and were granted two pews, one near the front and another in the rear of the church, where Fagley and other detectives would sit ostensibly as mourners paying their respects but in reality looking for any possible clues as well.

Father Fred and Father Birch concelebrated the mass, neither displaying too much emotion until Father Fred delivered his homily.

"It's impossible to find a logical answer for this madness that took Phillip from us much too early," Father Fred stated. "But in our time of grief and mourning, we must remember that God has a plan for each of us. Sometimes we might not agree with his plan or question his plans for those close to us. That's okay, but in the end, we need to accept his plan and move on with our lives in a way that Phillip would like."

As Kelly watched and listened from the choir loft, he marveled at Father Fred's voice. There was, Kelly noted, a certain calming manner to it, as he attempted to put the brutal murder into some type of religious perspective that those left behind could grasp. While the pastor sounded reassuring, Kelly wondered whether Father Fred actually believed what he was saying. Certainly priests must question God in the same manner the average person sitting in a pew on Sunday did on occasion. Where was the good of God to be found in the seemingly senseless murders of two innocent human beings? By all accounts from the conversations Kelly had had over the past four days, Grady was a man devoted to his family and his Catholic faith, active in his church. And this was how God determined he should leave the planet? Then again, Kelly reasoned, for Grady and Illsmere, death was quick and relatively painless. Perhaps that was their reward from God. But what about those family members and friends left behind? They had to endure the suffering.

Robert Grady delivered the eulogy. Unlike Father Fred's homily, Grady's voice was full of emotion. "I remember summer days when Phillip and I would sneak away from the funeral home, leaving unfinished chores for my dad. We would ride our bikes to the banks of the St. Croix, where we would fish for two or three hours. We literally did this hundreds of times, and never once caught a fish. Never. One day I said to Phillip, 'Why do we keep doing this when we never catch anything?' And he said philosophically, as any ten-year-old would, 'It's through the journey that we find what we really need and can savor, even if it's not the catch we're looking for.'

"And that summed up Phillip's life. He was always looking forward for something better, the eternal optimist. When we think of him in the days to come and feel sad for ourselves, we must remember his approach to life and find solace in the needs we discover in our journeys."

Even the members of the media, cynical by nature, were visibly moved by Grady's words. And if just for a minute, they weren't just on a quest to lead the newscast or beat their counterparts.

Kyle Grady, dressed in an ill-fitting dark suit, sat in between his mom and sister in the front pew. Along side them were his dad and grieving aunt. His mind wandered, as Father Fred talked about his uncle. Feelings of sadness, despair and guilt plagued the young high schooler. His eyes roamed the church, looking at the pastor at the pulpit, the statues on the altar and eventually Father Birch, the young associate he knew fairly well from the work the priest did with the youth group.

As he looked around, taking in little of his dad's eulogy, Grady thought about the short interviews he had with police the previous days. Still numb from his uncle's death, the young Grady felt he did a good job answering the questions. Straight-forward, short answers. He watched too many re-runs of *Law & Order* to know how people who talked too much during an interrogation often talked themselves right into the role of suspect. Yet Grady knew he had nothing to fear. At least he attempted to convince himself he had nothing to fear. There were just enough doubts in his mind, the residual of too much marijuana over the past two years, to make him feel completely safe. He still couldn't recall precisely from the time he left school and was summoned to the school office to meet his grieving mom, part of which corresponded to the time his uncle and Illsmore were killed. The possibilities were enough to drive a young mind crazy.

"Do you think the killer was at the funeral?" Kelly asked Fagley, as the two stood off to the side outside the church.

"That's what I love about you," Fagley noted. "Your compassion, your ability to offer just the right feeling. It's beautiful."

"And so are you. Okay, I'll admit some parts of the funeral were moving, especially his brother's tribute. But last time I checked, you incompetents still hadn't found a prime suspect, which means there's a killer on the road, if I may quote Jim Morrison."

"Any new insights or leads we should follow?" asked Fagley.

"There you go again," Kelly said. "Waiting for me to do your job. And what makes you think if I had anything substantive that I would share it with your sorry ass? Huh? Let's just say I have questions about Father Birch. Something doesn't seem right."

Fagley told Kelly police were considering bringing Father Birch into the station for a formal interview, even though there were serious doubts among the detectives that the priest was involved. But, Fagley reasoned, if it became public knowledge that Father Birch was brought in for questioning, the police would be under even more pressure to produce enough evidence to warrant an arrest. Anything short of that, and the public would consider the police guilty of pointing the finger at an innocent priest. Not a pleasant dilemma.

Kelly's Friday reports focused almost exclusively on the funeral proceedings and little on the police investigation. He saw Lewis at the funeral and spoke with her briefly outside the church. They conversed a couple times via phone later in the day, and Kelly told her he looked forward to seeing her report. After watching it, Kelly phoned Lewis, told her he thought Katie Couric showed a look of approval when she came out of the report and then asked Lewis to dinner. She paused, somewhat shocked, and then said she would enjoy that. They agreed to meet at seven at Manny's Steakhouse in the Hyatt Hotel, just a short walk from the Hilton where Lewis was staying. Kelly already had spoken with the station and convinced them he did not need to do a live report for the ten o'clock news. Live shots at five and six would suffice.

Manny's was one of the most popular steakhouses in the Twin Cities, not necessarily one of Kelly's favorites but one of the better options in downtown Minneapolis. The dark-paneled rooms of the restaurant and photos of celebrities who had eaten there offered character, a welcome respite from the cookie-cutter chains that populated the suburbs.

Kelly convinced Benson to stop at his house on the way back from Hudson, so he could change clothes. The photographer only acquiesced to the request after Kelly promised her two bottles of Kendall-Jackson Vintner's Reserve California Chardonnay, one of her favorites, from his cellar. He opted for a gray Brooks Brothers suit with a single vent, a white shirt with French cuffs that allowed him to show off his Notre Dame cufflinks and a pink and white striped tie—dignified and sensitive at the same time.

Lewis had changed from the quasi-business suit that she wore while reporting earlier in the day to a chic black dress from Ferragamo. Not the best choice for January in the frozen tundra, but with the Skyway system in downtown Minneapolis, she was able to make the three-block walk from her hotel without going outside too often.

The two enjoyed a bottle of a deliciously tannic Kunde Estate Cabernet Sauvignon, a perfect complement to Manny's signature steaks, and shared stories from their careers. In the course of the conversation, Lewis admitted that she had been accepted at both Boston College and Notre Dame, eventually turning down the latter, a rare occurrence among applicants to both schools. Kelly just smiled as she related the story. His normal brash and caustic demeanor seemed to have taken the night off, which perplexed even him. He blamed it on her blue eyes.

They worked their way through the salad and dinner courses but passed on dessert, settling instead on espresso.

"When do you go back to Chicago?" Kelly asked.

"Early tomorrow," Lewis said.

"Bummer. I was just starting to overlook your Boston College handicap and beginning to like you."

"You'll just have to look me up next time you're in Chicago," Lewis said with a flirtatious smile.

Kelly spent most of Saturday in Hudson, talking to anyone he could about Father Birch and the teenagers, trying to find any connections to the murders. He found none and did follow-up reports on Saturday and Sunday. These stories were necessary to indicate the station hadn't forgotten or fallen behind the story, but in reality, these reports contained little, if any, fresh information and were by Kelly's own high standards weak, at best. No other media outlets had anything new either, and the story died one week after it began. There were the obligatory follow-up calls to Fagley and others, some on a daily basis, but with no fresh information about any potential suspect, reporters moved on to other stories. The resources didn't exist to allow an investigative reporter the opportunity to work full-time on the funeral home murders. There's an old adage in television news that "if it bleeds, it leads." But once the blood was dried and cleaned, the story often becomes as dead as any victims.

"*Bless me Father for I have sinned. My last confession was within the last week, and here are my sins. Well, really, there's just one sin I want to talk about. I know information about who killed the two men at the funeral home, but I'm in a precarious situation that doesn't allow me to talk to the authorities without potentially doing damage to myself and others. For this sin, I am sorry.*"

PURGATORY

CHAPTER EIGHTEEN

Spring's arrival that year in the Midwest was fickle, a teasing temptress. The initial thaws of March were followed by more snow and then a long, gradual transition into warmer weather. In Minnesota, it was easy to recognize spring's arrival, as temperatures topped fifty-five, bikes and cars came out of winter storage, and the paths along the Mississippi River and city lakes filled with people, pent up inside their homes for months like bears in hibernation, finally given a reminder that winter wasn't eternal.

Kelly loved this time of year. Like many others, he could only take so many cloudy, cold days. On this particular day in mid-April, Kelly decided to join the crowds that were welcoming back spring. One of his springtime rituals included taking the dust cover off his 1984 Jaguar XJ6, which sat inside his garage protected from the elements for the past six months. He'd charged the battery the previous day, and the old jalopy had started again. A new spring could begin.

The afternoon sun shone bright on Mississippi River Boulevard, as Kelly steered the Jag south off Summit and onto the boulevard, an area of St. Paul that contained some of the most unique and coveted homes. It was, Kelly reasoned, a perfect day for driving and thinking. The last two months seemed a blur in retrospect, filled with the reporting of one mundane story after another. At times like these, Kelly had to remind himself that he had a job that paid fairly well and wasn't manual labor, even if the hours could be long and grueling. But the stories that Watson and others at the assignment desk chose each day was something beyond Kelly's comprehension. Did the average viewer really like seeing that shit? Unfortunately the answer was probably yes.

Kelly thought more about the funeral home murder case, as he navigated over the Ford Parkway Bridge and into Minneapolis. After his follow-up reports the week of the murders, he had not filed one single report about the case. Other television stations attempted to appear as though they had fresh information but reported nothing substantial either. The same could be said for the daily newspapers. That didn't stop Kelly from thinking about the case, however. In fact, he realized he had become obsessed with it, pondering different clues and scenarios on a daily basis. He still spoke regularly with Detective Fagley. Sometimes the conversations were brief, the two just checking with each other to see if there were any breaks in the case. Other conversations, usually later at night and aided by some California Zinfandel or other potent red, were extensive, with both Kelly and Fagley sharing their theories on the case. And still, there was nothing new. That was until two nights before.

Kelly's Jag cruised along Minnehaha Parkway, which traveled almost the entire distance west from the Mississippi River to Lake Harriet. As he passed under the eight lanes of 35W, filled with the start of rush hour traffic and seemingly a world apart from the serene scene along Minnehaha Creek below, Kelly replayed in his mind the phone conversation from two nights ago.

"It's been a while, hasn't it?" asked a woman's voice at the other end when Kelly picked up the phone just before the ten o'clock news was about to begin. Kelly did not mistake the voice for one second; he knew it was the same individual who had called him the week of the murders.

"How have you been?" asked Kelly.

"The better question is what have you been up to?" asked the caller. "I thought I gave you enough clues to follow up on, but I haven't seen you report one story on the case since that first week."

"Not for a lack of trying," Kelly admitted. "I followed your leads, and the police did the same. What we found wasn't worth much."

"Then you haven't looked hard enough or asked the right questions," the woman informed him rather flatly.

"Why should I believe you? What's your role in this whole thing?" asked Kelly with a touch of derisiveness in his voice. After all, he felt he had followed the leads she had provided.

"You know I can't tell you everything, because it would reveal my identity, which I can't let happen."

"Why are you so concerned now to call me months afterwards?" Kelly asked.

"That's a good question."

"It is my job to ask good questions," said Kelly pompously before he started laughing. He used the line often and marveled at the different responses it elicited from others.

"Ah, touché," said the caller, clearly in tune with Kelly's wit. "Well?"

"I don't like what Father Birch is doing at St. Timothy's," the caller said. "He's not a good man and certainly not a good priest."

"What does that have to do with the murders? Do you think he killed those two?" Kelly asked.

"It's not my place to judge. I just know his life offers clues that could lead you to the murderers."

"What specifically about his life? Haven't we been over much of this before?"

"You haven't explored his past or how that might lead you to other clues," suggested the caller.

"What about his past?" Kelly wondered.

"Let's just say part of his history could be part of hundreds of other priests' histories. You're smart; you should be able to figure it out." And with that she clicked off the line.

Why now? Kelly wondered as he drove around Lake Harriet, making his way north toward Uptown. Why would she contact him after more than two months? Through his obsessions and musings, he had never really considered Father Birch the prime suspect. He found it hard to believe that he could actually kill two people. But Kelly reasoned it was something more complicated, especially if Father Birch was involved. Did the priest have firsthand evidence or knowledge about the murderer? And what about his past?

He wanted to explore these mysteries more, but was struggling to convince anyone in the newsroom that the story warranted more of his time. Many of the news executives viewed time spent on investigative reporting as a glorified leaves-of-absence sans any real productivity. They wanted results, a cheap story about people enjoying the nice weather or what they thought of the Twins' prospects early in the season. Hard-hitting news. He had to find a way to pursue what angles might exist.

"This is Shelley," said Shelley Rosen as she picked up her cell phone in the newsroom.

"Hey, hot stuff," said Kelly. "How would you like to go out for a drink with a man who gets better looking every day?"

"I'd love to, but what are you going to do?" Rosen replied.

"Fuck you."

"Only in your dreams."

"Perhaps."

There was that element of sexual tension between Shelley Rosen and the veteran reporter. But both viewed it as harmless, fun verbal entertainment to see who could outwit the other, the greater the sexual innuendo, the better. Kelly had been cited by the station on no fewer than four previous occasions in his career after co-workers complained about his language, sometimes mean and derogatory and other times filled with sexual references and overtones. He managed to escape each time with a written reprimand that ended up in his official file and the promise that he would apologize to the person who filed the complaint. Fortunately, his verbal abuses never resulted in lawsuits, not yet at least.

Rosen understood his need to spar verbally and appreciated his ribald manner, finding it charming in a perverse sort of way.

"Seriously, do you have any time to meet?" Kelly asked. "I want to talk with you about Father Birch."

"Are you still fixated on him?" Rosen inquired. "When are you going to give it up, Perry Mason?"

"After I find Grady's killer." Kelly stated.

"Yeah, you and O.J.," joked Rosen.

Rosen was one of few people in the newsroom who realized Kelly obsessed over the funeral home murders. He occasionally shared some theories with her to get feedback, and whenever she mentioned the story in passing, his demeanor changed immediately.

"Let's say twenty minutes at Willie's. Okay?" Kelly said.

"Sure, because I wasn't really doing anything important at work right now, and none of the bosses will miss me if I suddenly leave."

"That's one of the things I love about you—you're so perceptive and realize that no one in that newsroom is really aware of anything, even if it happens right under their nose. Besides, this is official work."

"Oh, really? Drinking wine is part of the job description?"

"It is in my book. I'll see you in a few minutes."

"Bye."

Willie's Wine Bar and Cuisine, a cool little venue on Harmon Place in downtown Minneapolis just across the street from the Minneapolis campus of The University of St. Thomas Law School, had a wide, sometimes eclectic, selection of wines from around the world.

Kelly found a parking space at a meter on the same block as Willie's. He couldn't stand paying the high price that parking lots charged. His friends couldn't stand his penurious ways when it came to parking. He put George Constanza to shame.

He strolled into Willie's and took a seat at his normal table located toward the back of the restaurant next to a window. People watching, one of his favorite laid-back pastimes, was perfect from this vantage, yet he remained just far enough away from the action at the bar to remain relatively undisturbed. Rosen joined him within minutes.

"Did anyone even notice you were leaving?" Kelly inquired.

"Nope."

"See what I mean? What are you up for? How about a French Hob Nob Pinot Noir? Will that work?"

"If you think so, then that'll be just fine."

Kelly ordered the wine and an appetizer. Then he quickly got to the case.

"I want to share something with you in confidence," Kelly said.

"I'm so honored," said Rosen, struggling to contain her sarcasm and laughter.

"Shut up."

"You're so eloquent when you're obsessed with something."

Kelly spent the next five minutes sharing the details of his source, the female caller, recalling the initial phone call and those that followed. The only thing that interrupted Kelly's rant was the waitress bringing the wine and appetizer. Kelly swirled the wine, sniffed it and took a sip. He told the waitress it was just fine and let her pour more into his and Rosen's glasses. After another sip, Kelly resumed his monologue, ending with the story of the most recent call a few nights past.

"And?" Rosen asked, not quite sure where Kelly was headed.

"Well, why would she call now?" wondered Kelly aloud. "Is there something new about to break? Am I missing something obvious?"

"What did Detective Fagley say about it?" Rosen asked.

"I haven't told him about the most recent call yet. I want to consider how to handle it and how to pry a little before I call him."

The two paused, both taking sips of their wine and eating some of the bruschetta.

"So what can I do?" asked Rosen, finally breaking the silence.

"Where do you want me to start?" Kelly replied with a sly grin on his face.

"You're such a pig!"

"Yes I am, but a good one," Kelly said. "Remember the checking you did to find out about the guns and traffic stop in Winona? I want you to revisit those sources and see if you can learn anything else about Father Birch's past that might be suspect."

"I can do that."

"Good, and remember to keep this between us."

"You're so paranoid," she said.

"Well, at least I'm good at something," he surmised.

The two finished their wine and appetizer while enjoying some casual conversation about things unrelated to work. Kelly did not mention anything about the caller's mysterious clue that Father Birch's history could apply to hundreds of other priests. Were there sexual abuse allegations in the priest's past? That certainly would not come as a surprise when the list of priests involved in such actions or accusations seemed never-ending. Though supposedly the Catholic Church had finally publicly recognized the problem and begun to take proactive measures to prevent it around the time Father Birch would have been in the seminary. So, if he was suspected or guilty of any such incidents, how could he be a parish priest working so closely with youth? Kelly vowed he would talk to his bosses in the morning and ask to spend more time to revisit the case.

"What's on your mind, Mr. Kelly?" asked news director Jon Ashbury, as Kelly sat down for a meeting in his office.

"Don't patronize me." Kelly had disliked Ashbury from the first week he arrived at the station two years before.

"I see you're happy as usual," replied Ashbury, who had made his disdain toward Kelly known shortly after his arrival at the station.

Kelly had embarrassed his boss, who during his first meeting with the entire newsroom staff, was at a loss to name both of Minnesota's U.S. senators. When Kelly filled the pregnant pause in Ashbury's speech with the names Mondale and Humphrey, Ashbury proceeded with his speech using the names Mondale and Humphrey. Much to the boss's chagrin, the entire newsroom struggled to contain its laughter, except Kelly. He simply stood off to the side grinning and staring at Ashbury, wondering how someone so stupid could end up as a news director in the market the size of the Twin Cities.

"I want to take a few weeks and do some more investigating into the funeral home murders in Hudson," Kelly explained.

"I thought we'd already been over this," Ashbury said curtly. "Nothing new's appeared since the first week, and even the police have no leads. You've said as much. What makes you think you can find something of relevance more than three months after the crime?"

"Let's start with the fact that I'm good," Kelly said as he leaned forward in his chair and stared at his boss. "Add to that the fact that most other reporters, and the police as well, have trouble finding their butt with both hands. And finally, I received a new tip."

"Oh, is that so? One tip, and you want me to set you free for what could very well amount to a two-week vacation with pay."

"You know, I try to offer you some respect because you are, after all, my boss." Kelly stated. "But then you spout such dimwitted, ill-informed garble that it pains me to think the University of Minnesota ever gave you a degree. How is that?"

"Now you listen here. Many others and myself . . ."

"No, to be gramaticallly correct, it's 'many others and I.' But, please, continue."

"We're fed up with your bullshit. Always in people's faces with your asinine comments and commentary. Not a team player. If it weren't for the union, I'd have fired you long ago."

"Well isn't that nice?" said Kelly."I guess you're forgetting that I contribute more to this newsroom in a given day than most other staff members will in an entire month. Or maybe you're forgetting that your predecessor fought me over my request to investigate the St. Paul Police chief and nearly killed the story. She, of course, had no trouble taking credit at all the award ceremonies that honored that report. Do yourself a favor. Get me out of your hair and away from the newsroom for two weeks. I won't need a photog every day, but when I do need one, I want Benson. I also want Shelley Rosen to work with me when I think it's necessary."

"You ask for a lot," Ashbury said.

"Yes I do, and I always deliver. So, what do you say?"

"I'll give you one week. Next Tuesday. I want some assurance that you'll have at least two follow-up reports ready for May sweeps. If you don't have enough info by next week, you're back to your normal work. Fair enough?"

"That'll work. I don't care what everyone else says. I think you're a great guy."

Kelly rose and exited without shaking hands. It wasn't his custom to be so rude, and he hadn't planned for this meeting to become so personally confrontational, but his loathing of Ashbury was so intense he feared he might break his hand if the two were to shake. Anger management was not Kelly's strong suit.

He spent all of two minutes gathering materials from his desk and casually informed Watson at the assignment desk that he was officially "on-assignment" and not to be bothered for at least a week.

CHAPTER NINETEEN

The St. Croix River displayed the most welcome sign of spring, as Kelly drove his Jag east over the Minnesota-Wisconsin border. There were just a few chunks of ice remaining, floating sporadically through the main channel and offering just a slight reminder of the winter that had passed, when the river was completely frozen. The sunshine and morning temp indicated spring was here, at least for another day.

Detective Fagley had already arrived at the St. Croix Cigar Company ahead of the meeting he and Kelly had scheduled for eleven o'clock. Though they had spoken daily on the phone since January, this was the first time they had gotten together since the week of the murders. Fagley was enjoying a Hoyo de Monterey and a fresh cup of coffee with his required cream. Kelly grabbed a cup, straight black and strong, to go with the Punch Corona he had selected from the store's well-stocked walk-in humidor.

"How you been?" asked Kelly as bit off the end of his cigar, wasting no time on the ritual of clipping, sniffing and lighting that many serious cigar smokers had turned into an art form.

"Not bad," Fagley said. "Not too good either. The chief is grilling us daily on whether we've found anything new."

"And, have you?" Kelly inquired.

"Not much."

"Well, I'm here to help," Kelly informed the detective. "I'm spending the next week or more to see what I can dig up. What's the current reward for a tip that leads to the arrest of the suspects?"

"Very funny," remarked Fagley.

"Seriously! I have reason to believe that we've all overlooked something."

"And what gives you that feeling, Holmes?"

"I got a call the other day from a lady who called me a few times right after the murders occured. She didn't say much, but she did indicate we're missing something with Father Birch. When was the last time you talked with him?"

"About a month ago," Fagley acknowledged.

"How many times have you and your staff interviewed him since the murders?"

"Four."

"Do you still consider him the prime suspect?"

"Yes, but without enough evidence to charge him."

"Do you have a motive yet?"

"No."

"Well, that poses a problem."

"Have you talked to the high school kids recently?"

"No. They're either innocent or have their stories so well-rehearsed that we can't break them. They've offered nothing."

"What about Father Fred? Have you spoken much with him lately?"

"Not lately. We talked to him three times since the murders, and he offered very little information about Father Birch or anything else. I think he's more interested in his pending retirement later this year."

"Well, I can see you guys have been very productive."

"I don't see you leading the ten o'clock news."

"Not yet. I'll keep you posted on anything that might interest you. Same rules as always, right?"

"You betcha."

The midday sun shone brightly on the Grady Funeral Home, as Kelly pulled his Jag into the parking lot, making sure, as always, to park as far away as possible from other cars that could potentially dent his. It was strange, if not eerie, Kelly thought, that on such a beautiful day he was going to talk to the brother of a victim of what still seemed to be a senseless murder. The best and worst of God's creations intertwined. He headed inside.

"Hi. I'm here to see Robert Grady. My name's Sean Kelly."

"I'll let him know you're here," said the receptionist.

The secretary, whose name was Shirley Hennan according to the nameplate on her desk, quickly rose and made her way down a hallway where the offices were located. Within a minute, she returned with a man wearing a white shirt, dark pants and non-descript tie.

"Hello. I'm Robert Grady."

"Sean Kelly."

"Let's go to my office."

The office was simple yet comfortable. A desk, a sofa, and a couple chairs. On the wall hung the standard diplomas, while behind the desk were family photos. Kelly recognized Robert and Phillip in a number of them.

"Thanks for taking the time to see me," Kelly began.

"Well, I'll do what I can to help," replied Grady.

"I want to go over some questions," Kelly said. "I'm sure the police have asked you many of them before, but I have my own leads that I'm following, and your answers could be helpful. So, please bear with me if this seems redundant. You told me when we first spoke on the phone that your brother and Father Birch didn't always get along. Why was that?"

"Oh, I think it was a few different things," Grady explained. "My brother and many others at the church didn't like Father Birch's conservative ways. He was very polarizing, invigorating some parishioners and alienating others. He's more of a throwback to pre-Vatican II than what we might think of as a modern-day priest."

"Was there anything specifically they disagreed over?" Kelly asked, searching for some common thread.

"I really don't know. I know, as I told you, that my son was part of Father Birch's confirmation class, and I think there were some issues during one of the youth group's overnight camping outings. I'm not sure what those issues were but they might have had something to do with alcohol."

"How long ago was this outing?" Kelly asked.

"Last summer."

"Did your brother go on the trip?"

"No."

"Was your brother involved with any specific groups or committees at the church?"

"He was an active member in the men's club, and he was part of the finance committee for a number of years."

"Did Father Birch have any role in the men's club or finance committee?" Kelly inquired.

"As associate pastor, he would attend some men's club events and would sit in on some of the finance committee meetings," Grady explained, "though I don't think the money side of the church was of much interest to him."

Grady appeared uncomfortable behind his desk. He had a pen in his right hand and tapped it against the notepad on his desk. He occasionally made direct eye contact with Kelly, but more often looked down at his desk as if debating internally how much he wanted to reveal. He seemed to Kelly to be a no-frills individual, not necessarily devoid of any personality but very focused on business.

"You confirmed that Father Birch was scheduled to meet with your brother the day of the murders. Did they meet at any other time here or elsewhere prior to that?"

"Not to my knowledge," noted Grady.

"Did they talk on the phone at all?" Kelly asked.

"I recall one conversation a week before the murders. My brother's office is next to mine, so I could hear his raised voice."

"What did you overhear?"

"It was something like, 'Listen, Father, we've been over this before. If you don't address this in a proper way by the end of next week, I'm going to take it to the archbishop's office.' Then the call apparently ended then because I didn't hear him say anything else."

Kelly considered what Grady just told him. It was the first he'd heard of a possible threat, something that could conceivably be viewed as a motive. This was interesting.

"Did he talk to you about the call at all?" Kelly asked.

"No, but I could tell he was upset. Not just the day of the call but for days after."

Grady explained that his brother was the more garrulous one in the family, quick with a light joke to brighten what could be an otherwise dreary occupation. His brother, Grady suggested, was the type of person that people enjoyed being around because of his energetic personality. That's why Robert Grady suspected something was wrong after the telephone exchange. He couldn't recall ever seeing his brother so subdued, practically angry, for such a long time.

"Does Father Birch have a reputation for having a temper?" Kelly asked, following up on what others had told him and what he had seen firsthand.

"His critics would suggest he can be very short with people who disagree with him."

"Have you had any encounters with him?" Kelly asked.

"Nothing outside the ordinary. You know, seeing him at the back of church after mass on Sunday and on funeral home business, nothing more than that."

"What's your take on him? Honestly." Kelly questioned.

"Honestly?" said Grady. "I think he's a little whacked. I don't like his ultra-conservative views toward religion, and I don't really like the way he seems to be polarizing segments of the parish. But what can you do? Certainly some parishioners have already made their concerns known to Father Fred. It's tough to get rid of a priest, especially with such a shortage these days."

"No kidding, but there should be some place the archdiocese could send the bad eggs."

"How about the archbishop's office?" Grady suggested sarcastically, peaking Kelly's interest.

"Oh, really? Not a big fan of Archbishop Malone." Kelly asked.

"Not really."

"Am I forgetting to ask you anything relevant? Anything you want to add?"

"What made you contact me this week?" Grady wondered. "I mean it's been more than three months since my brother's death."

"Well, let's just say I'm curious, and I have some hunches," Kelly said. "So, I thought it would be worth my time to look into the matter again. Feel free to call me if you think of anything else I should check out. Okay?"

"Will do."

"Thanks for your time."

Kelly's cell phone rang just as he got into his car. He glanced at the phone and recognized the number instantly.

"What's up?"

"Is that how you always answer the phone?" asked Shelley Rosen. "Whatever happened to polite manners? Something like, 'Hello, this is Sean. How may I help you?'"

"How about, 'What the fuck do you want?'"

"I can see you're in your normal pleasant mood," Rosen observed. "Well, here's something that might interest you."

"Fire away."

"I did some more checking today and found that while Father Birch was at the seminary at St. Mary's in Winona, there were two incidents involving the youth group at St. Mary's grade school."

"What type of incidents?" Kelly asked.

"I wasn't able to confirm the details, but they allegedly dealt with improper contact with two of the fifth-grade boys," Rosen explained. "Seminarians apparently spend some time in Catholic grade schools as part of their training."

"Anything else?" Kelly wondered.

"Isn't that enough?"

"How did you get this info by the way?" he asked.

"I have my sources," she said.

"Yeah, don't we all? But what does this mean? Do you have any theories?"

"Not really," she admitted.

"Okay, Einstein, let me know when you do. By the way, good work."

Kelly disconnected the call. This was an interesting development that had not been made public or discussed privately, at least to his knowledge. While once again intriguing, though, it shed little evidence on whether Father Birch was capable of murder. But Kelly was beginning to see common themes running through the background of Father Birch: propensity to anger and fondness for young boys, if the stories were true. Left with little else, Kelly decided to work backward from the murder, trying to devise a reason, however outlandish, that Father Birch might have been driven to kill Grady and his intern.

CHAPTER TWENTY

Either inspired by or fearful of Kelly's renewed presence on the case, Detective Fagley spent the rest of the afternoon reviewing the transcripts of the interviews he and his counterparts had had with Father Birch. The interview he had done with the priest one week following the murder was the most extensive. Fagley sat at his desk, transcript in hand, but did not read it. Instead he stared out the window, into the blue sky, and conjured an image of Father Birch during the interview. The priest, Fagley recalled, seemed unusually calm, practically unphased by nearly every aspect of the interrogation, even parts that seemed to imply that he was the prime suspect. Then Fagley realized what he might have missed or overlooked. He thumbed through the transcript until he found the passage he wanted to review.

> Fagley: "How would you describe your relationship with Phillip Grady?"
> Father Birch: "It's okay."
> Fagley: "Did you have much contact with him through the parish?"
> Father Birch: "We worked on some funerals together. I would see him at Men's Club meetings occasionally. But we never socialized beyond that."

Fagley: "Did you have much contact with his nephew?"

Father Birch: "I knew his nephew through the youth group that was preparing for Confirmation. He's a good kid."

Fagley: "Did you ever have any disagreements with Mr. Grady?"

Father Birch: "No."

Fagley: "Did you know of anyone who didn't like Mr. Grady or might have had any reason to kill him?"

Father Birch: "That would be a very strong statement that requires speculation. I don't think I'm fit to offer such an opinion. But it just seems so senseless that someone would be willing to kill two people just to take four bottles of embalming fluid."

That was it, Fagley realized. How did Father Birch know the precise number of bottles that had been removed from the funeral home? Then again, he wondered, how could anyone be exactly sure how many bottles were removed? Police had never made public the number four, and the media had never reported an exact number of bottles either. According to Robert Grady, he and his staff kept a detailed inventory on a daily basis, and through that, they determined that four bottles were missing. They weren't on the shelves, they weren't in the garbage, and they weren't found anywhere else on the funeral home premises. Ergo, it would reason that four bottles had been taken the day of the murders. And even if it was possibly a number other than four, why would the priest be so matter-of-fact about the quantity? Fagley was embarrassed that he had overlooked the comment during the interview, since it clearly suggested that Father Birch either had firsthand knowledge of the scene or at least what was taken from it. He looked over the rest of the transcript to see if he had missed anything else.

Fagley: "How did Father Fred and Phillip Grady get along?"

Father Birch: "Fine. I think they were decent friends. They certainly had known each other for years."

Fagley: "Do you know if they ever had disagreements?"

Father Birch: "No, I don't think so."

Fagley: "Is there anyone else in the parish who might have had a disagreement with Mr. Grady?"

Father Birch: "Not that I can think of."

Fagley: "Okay. Will you give me a call if you think of anything else that might be helpful?"

Father Birch: "Most surely."

Fagley still couldn't believe that he had missed an opportunity to follow up on the comment about the missing bottles. He decided at that moment that he needed to review the photos and the report from the crime scene and then schedule another interview with Father Birch. This one would have to be more formal, at the police station and videotaped, something that was standard procedure for prime suspects.

CHAPTER TWENTY-ONE

One of the challenges of an investigative reporter was to contact the right sources at the right time. If a reporter approached the wrong person at the wrong time, that individual might become suspicious and alert others of the reporter's intention. Background, information generally given to a reporter with the promise that the facts would not be attributed to the source, was the backbone of many investigative reports. There was a certain technique to obtaining background, and that was the primary reason Kelly was traveling without a photographer. It allowed him to present an image that ideally made potential sources comfortable. That was not to say they would always divulge all the information the reporter was seeking, but it assured that they would not freeze up once the camera's light went on. Kelly was masterful when it came to getting people to open up. Most people, whether talking to reporters and just in general conversation with friends, tended to love to talk about themselves. The key was to ask just the right questions, and let the session roll from there. He rarely took notes, though he'd often record the conversations, usually with the other person's permission. Sometimes he just kept his small digital audio recorder tucked in a pocket inside the jacket of one of his expensive Savile Row suits.

Getting his next interview turned out easier than expected. A couple phone calls, and Kelly was able to secure the name and home phone number of Cindy Hughes, the director of the St. Timothy's Youth Group. He explained to her over the phone his reason for wanting to meet, and she immediately invited him to her house that afternoon, greeting him at the door before he even had a chance to ring the doorbell. Kelly sensed there was something she wanted to say.

"Thanks for taking time to see me," Kelly began.

"No problem. But you did say this is off the record, right?" Hughes asked.

"Yes, though I'll record it just so I don't have to take any notes," Kelly explained. "But your name won't be used in conjunction with any information you give me."

"What is it exactly you want to talk about?" she asked.

"In your role as director of the youth group at St. Tim's, how closely do you work with Father Birch?"

"Oh, he's pretty involved, especially with the kids preparing for Confirmation," she explained.

"What do you think of him?" the reporter inquired.

After a slight pause, she said, "Well, my mother always said if you can't say something nice, don't say anything at all."

"So did mine, but I obviously haven't heeded her words as closely as she'd like," Kelly joked.

The Hughes' house was a modest rambler with indications in the living room and kitchen, where the two were seated, that it was home to kids. Toys were scattered everywhere, and fittingly a sign on the wall read, "Please don't mind our mess. The kids are busy making memories."

"Father Birch is a very passionate individual. He seems to love being a priest, and he has inspired many of the youth to take their faith more seriously."

"But . . ."

"But not everyone is as gung-ho as he is about various aspects of the Church."

"Did you go camping with the Confirmation class last summer?"

Hughes blinked, clearly stunned at Kelly's knowledge of so much of St. Tim's and some of the activities. She took a sip of her bottled water before responding. "How did you find out about that? Yes, I did," she said.

"Was Father Birch part of outing, too?" Kelly wondered.

"Yes."

"What went wrong?"

Hughes again hesitated, looking troubled by the line of questioning and maybe what might be made public in the media. "It's something I'm not comfortable talking about," Hughes admitted.

"But it might be important."

Slowly she said, "It was suggested that Father Birch provided alcohol to three of the boys and shared a tent with them. There were also some suggestions that he may have attempted to fondle them, but, of course, there was no proof."

"How was the matter handled?" Kelly asked.

Hughes explained that there was never a formal complaint filed. She heard rumors from hers and other kids who were either part of the trip or heard about it in school. She never directly confronted Father Birch about the suggestions nor did she take the matter to Father Fred immediately.

"Do you know which three boys were involved?" Kelly inquired.

She nodded. "Frank Black, Jim Dorgan, and Kyle Grady."

Now it was Kelly's turn to pause and gather his thoughts, doing his best not to act too surprised.

"I see," he said slowly. "Have you ever seen Father Birch get angry or raise his voice with anyone?"

"Once or twice. There was one time when he seemed to get very angry with a parent during a youth group meeting. They were arguing outside the school gym, where we were having an activity night, but we could clearly hear their voices get louder."

"Do you remember what they were discussing?"

"I couldn't tell exactly what the topic was, but I do remember hearing Father Birch practically scream, 'If you threaten me with this again, I'll take this matter into my own hands and settle things that way.'"

"Do you know who he was arguing with?"

"Phillip Grady."

"When was this?" Kelly asked.

"About three weeks before Phillip Grady was killed."

What began as a friendly, informal discussion had evolved into a tension-filled kitchen. Kelly realized he had just been told enough information to possibly finger the priest for the murders, and Hughes understood the potential ramifications of what she just uttered. Neither felt comfortable.

"Have police talked to you at all since the murders?" Kelly asked.

"No."

"Okay, well this helps a lot. I hope you'll call me if you think of anything else. Also, it would be best, I think, if you keep our conversation between us for now."

"I'll do that."

Images of the previous summer's youth group camping trip continued to haunt Kyle Grady, as he lay on his bed of his darkened room. The blinds had not been opened since the day his uncle was killed. His room became his retreat, a place to think and sulk and try to piece together what happened to his uncle not to mention why. Many of his thoughts focused on the youth group's trip.

The outing was intended to be a fun way to bond with fellow students, their young priest and Christ in preparation for Confirmation the following Spring. What teen wouldn't want to get away from his or her parents for a day or two with minimal parental supervision? It was a rite of passage toward adulthood as much as it was a religious experience.

Grady and his two closest friends – Jim Dorgan and Frank Black – prepared meticulously weeks in advance for the camping trip.

They knew, or at least thought they knew, precisely how they could sneak alcohol and drugs into their camping gear. Father Birch and the few parents who were slated to accompany the group of 28 were smart, the teens realized, but not clever enough to find the "goods." Father Birch was insistent that only a few adults chaperone in hopes that the teens would feel more comfortable and open about their spirituality that way.

The first day and night went by without any problems. Grady and his two friends managed to get far enough away from the campsite during one of the breaks and smoke some weed. Their highs lasted into the early evening hours, and when they retired to their tent, they were able to enjoy a night-capper of straight vodka, which they knew allegedly couldn't be detected on one's breath. Too naïve to know the difference, they each put back a few shots, talked in hushed tones and eventually passed out.

Grady stared at the posters on his bedroom wall, which included Kid Rock and Pamela Anderson, as his thoughts turned to the second night of the youth group camping trip. He and his two friends followed the same routine, sneaking away for an afternoon pot break, each enjoying a high that lasted well past the mass the group celebrated at five o'clock. Later, after returning to their tents for another nightcap, everything seemed to change. Father Birch took time on his rounds of goodnights to stop at the tent Kyle shared with Dorgan and Black.

Stunned, at first, at the appearance of the priest as they were passing around what appeared to be a bottle of Sprite, Black and Dorgan seemed to invite the young priest to join them. Something was amiss.

Grady never liked the young priest. Though his two friends seemed to have forged a unique bond with the dramatic priest, Kyle found Father Birch annoying, too over-the-top with his views on Catholicism and antics from the pulpit. He watched with feigning interest as his two friends talked openly with the priest about their thoughts on the camping trip, their views on the Catholic church and hunting. He noticed not only did his two friends continue to drink from the Sprite bottle, but they poured a glass for Father Birch, too. Too buzzed to really be shocked, Grady just sat, watched and listened.

Revisiting that night in his head as he lay on his bed, Grady now realized what happened next changed all four lives irrevocably in a short period of time, even if there were still some unanswered questions.

CHAPTER TWENTY-TWO

Father Fred was in the middle of enjoying a good bottle of Gnarly Head Old Vine Zin and watching Katie Couric stumble through her intros, when the phone rang. He waited three rings and, realizing no one else was going to answer, picked up the phone himself.

"Hello," Father Fred answered.

"Father, just the person I was looking for."

"Archbishop Malone, how are you?" Father Fred said, trying to conceal the fact that the archbishop was just the person he didn't want to hear from.

"I'm fine, thanks for asking. And yourself?" asked the archbishop in what best could be described as a faux friendly voice. It always bothered Father Fred that the archbishop could be such a phony, even in a one-on-one conversation.

"I'm well. Thank you."

"I just wanted to check in with you to see how things are going with our . . . situation," said the archbishop, his voice taking on a sterner tone.

"Things seem to be okay, though I understand a reporter has begun to look into the funeral home murders once again. I doubt he'll find any of the details of our situation," Father Fred admitted.

"He better not. I'm counting on you with this one. Make sure you take care of all the details to ensure nothing gets out, if you know what I mean."

"I'm doing my best," Father Fred said, struggling to contain his disgust with the topic of conversation and the archbishop's lecturing.

"Let's just hope your best is good enough," the archbishop said tersely and then added without sincerity: "Have a good evening, Father."

"You, too, Archbishop. Thanks for the call."

There were few things that could spoil a good bottle of Zinfandel, but the call from the archbishop provided the antithesis of the wedding at Canaan effect, turning the Zin into something foul. Father Fred stared at the television, taking in nothing of the report airing but instead contemplating his life. Here he was just a few months from retirement, and he was faced with moral dilemmas he had never encountered in his nearly fifty years in the priesthood. He couldn't recall having a class in the seminary on how to deal with anything like this. He was left to his best judgement and whatever other obstacles extraneous circumstances might present.

The drive west from Hudson on I-94 during evening rush hour offered Kelly a chance to sort through the day's meetings. A consummate button pusher on the car radio, he worked his way through the FM rock stations, finally settling on the alternative station blaring Foo Fighters' song "Hero," which always reminded Kelly of the late NASCAR driver Dale Earnhardt ever since one of the television networks had used the song as part of a tribute to the man in the black number three.

Kelly was convinced that there was ample evidence that Father Birch and Phillip Grady did not get along well but still doubted that he had enough to prove the priest was the killer. He had to devise a way to get a sit-down with Father Birch and learn more about him. He also wanted to talk with the three high school students that Hughes had mentioned who were allegedly involved in the camping incident. Just the thought of it was appalling, and he shook his head as he pondered how he could address the allegation with the students. It's not something where you just pick up the phone and say, "So, I hear the priest gave you some booze and then grabbed your balls."

One advantage to having teenagers involved a criminal investigation is they tend to talk a lot among themselves, which leads to more discussions, which sometimes leads to helpful tips. Sorting through the bountiful fruits of gossip can become quite a headache for police.

Within the first few months of the murders, Lori Newman logged more than 200 anonymous tips that were phoned in to police. She told detectives that most of the callers sounded young, mostly likely how an average teenager's puberty-aging voice might sound. Some of the calls, she explained to Det. Fagley, were outlandish, so absurd they were barely worth discussion, though she knew the detective wanted to be briefly apprised of every call. There were two calls recently, she noted, that came in consecutive days, both around four o'clock and both from a male who sounded like he was the person behind both calls, which she recounted lasted a mere twenty seconds each.

"He said the Cropdusters hold the key to the murder investigation," she explained.

"Well, there's something new," Fagley said, displaying a rare moment of sarcasm with office staff he knew was already stressed from the murders. "How would you describe the tone of his voice? Serious?"

"Yes, there was something about his voice that made me stop and take notice during both calls," she said. "No giggling like I've heard in others. Very serious. Very matter-of-fact."

"What else did he say in addition to the Cropduster reference?"

"He quoted two songs. In the first call, he said something like, and we can go back and listen to the tape to hear the exact words, but it was something like, 'To find the killer, listen to Robbie Robertson's song "Fallen Angel."'

"That's it? That's all he said in the first call?"

"Yes. Then he hung up. And then in the second call, I remember it vividly because it was so strange. He said, 'Like Pete Townsend sings, 'Give blood, but you may find that blood is not enough,' and then he continued after a short pause with 'So give love, and keep blood between brothers.''"

"So we have a rock-n-roll aficionado on our hands. Great. That's going to get us far. I don't suppose there were any solid leads on tracing the telephone the calls were made from?"

"Both pay phones in town, but not in places that are visible to security cameras. I already checked."

"Not bad. It might be something. But now I think I'm going to have those songs running through my head all night."

"Beats Brittney Spears," said Newman, as she broke into a dance mocking the crazy pop singer. A brief, though much needed, humorous respite that even Fagley appreciated.

Kelly had entered into one of his blue moods, when nothing was quite terribly wrong but so much seemed to be missing. He sat alone in his house staring at the day's financial news on CNBC but not really paying much attention to it. High gas prices and jitters on Wall Street. What else is new?

He savored a sip of his Gnarly Head Zinfandel, one of those fabulous value-driven wines with a good spicy kick to it. This vintage recently received an 89 from *The Midwest Wine Connection* newspaper.

The reporter was bored, a demon that plagued him more than he wanted. The funeral home murder case seemed to be have hit a dead end. Even his secret caller had quit phoning. As much as he was personally torn by the tragedy of two murders, he loved the adrenaline the story provided. However he knew without any fresh developments, he would be relegated to meaningless general assignment reporting about happy news, something he despised.

It also occurred to him as he took another sip of his Zin and brooded, that he really liked Becky Lewis and, in the aftermath of her short stay in the Twin Cities, realized he wanted to pursue something more with her. What that something was he wasn't quite sure, but he knew that Lewis was one of those women who could reach into his chest and tug on his heart without much effort. Beautiful and smart, the network reporter had an air about her that Kelly loved. It wasn't overconfidence or a high maintenance attitude but one which seemed to both challenge him and attract him. Oh, who was he kidding, he wondered. He struggled enough with relationships and with four hundred miles between them, it would be even more difficult. Besides, he reasoned, she was after all a BC grad.

The shrill of the telephone ringing roused Kelly from his romantic dreamland.

"Hello," said Kelly without looking at the caller ID.

"What's up?" Adam Fagley asked.

"Oh, just sitting here wondering how someone as intelligent as I and one who gets better looking every day doesn't fare better with women."

"And you need to wonder?"

"Fuck you. What's new in your world?"

"I was just discussing some of the phone tips we've received over the last week or so and wanted to get your thoughts on two of them," the detective said. "A couple musical references."

"Well," Kelly said and then paused for dramatic effect, "I am the self-proclaimed Patriarch of Music."

"And full of shit as always," Fagley quickly retorted. "Anyway, our lady at the front desk said she got two calls on consecutive days mostly from the same individual based on the sound of his voice. In the first call he referred to Robbie Robertson song "Fallen Angel."

"Freshman year of college."

"What?"

"That album came out my freshman year at ND."

"So? Who cares?"

"I thought you might."

"Anyway, in the second call, he talked about Pete Townsend's "Give Blood.""

"Senior year in high school," Kelly replied. "Give blood, but you may find that blood is not enough. Now that's interesting. And what about the verse that says keep blood between brother? You think Grady's brother offed him?"

"Doubtful," Fagley remarked. "But possible, I suppose, though he has an alibi."

"How much did you question him?" Kelly asked. "Did you follow up on the alibi and confirm it? Is it airtight? I mean he inherits the whole business now. Maybe older brother was trying to push him out or caught lifting something from the coffers."

"I doubt it."

"Well I don't see you and your cohorts moving this investigation successfully in a different direction. Maybe I'll follow up on it. Can I use the info on the songs?"

"Yeah, I suppose, but same rules apply."

"Thanks."

"Thank you. Now you've given me some theories that'll keep me awake tonight."

"One of the things I do best."

They both hung up their phones without an official good-bye. Kelly took a long sip of wine from his Riedel glass, a wine chalice of sorts since the bowl of the glass was so big, and thought about the caller's references to those specific tunes. He reasoned there might be something there to pursue. It would at least add a little color, and music for that matter, to his report tomorrow. And, he realized, it took his mind off Becky Lewis at least for a few minutes.

CHAPTER TWENTY-THREE

Fighting sporadic insomnia for yet another night, Kelly gave in at 4:30 and decided if he couldn't sleep, he'd have a little fun at his friend's expense.

"You have to be fucking kidding me," mumbled Detective Fagley as he answered his cell phone. "You know I have a family that likes to sleep normal hours."

"Please say hi to them for me," said Kelly, already laughing at his own prank. "Did I ever tell you the story about when my parents owned a stock car track outside Fountain City, Wisconsin?"

"No," Fagley groaned, "but somehow I suspect you're about to regal me with the tale right now."

"One night, points leader Karl Frey was black-flagged in the feature, which cost him a lot of points with only two weeks to go in the season. Now Karl was a feisty individual who couldn't stand losing, especially if the flagman had something to do with it. So, he stewed for a few hours, probably consumed a couple beers, and finally decided to call my parents at home at three in the morning. When my mom answered, Karl said, 'Judy, I can't sleep, and I'm not going to let you sleep either.' And my mom responded in her always friendly voice by saying, 'I hate to disappoint you, Karl, but we're still up counting change.'"

"And you called me to tell me *this* story?" asked Fagley.

"No, I called you because I couldn't sleep, and I didn't want you to either," Kelly replied. "Aren't I generous?"

"You're a fucking asshole, that's what you are," noted Fagley.

"I wanted to see if you had any new information on the funeral home murders."

"Any new information in the last, what, fourteen hours since we last spoke?"

"Come on," Kelly said. "I know you better. Now that you know I'm devoting more time to look into the case, I know full well you went back to your office and spent all afternoon going over different angles in hopes that I won't find the killer before you do. Spare yourself that worry because I'm certain I'll beat you to it. But rest assured I'll make you look good in the process."

"You're so humble."

"I try," offered Kelly, though neither believed it. "So what did you find? I think you should bring Birch in later today, and let me sit behind the glass. I might be able to offer some lines of questioning that could be helpful."

Fagley thought about the proposal and waited before answering. It was one of the stranger requests Kelly had ever posed, since most law enforcement officials view the mere existence of reporters as an obstruction of justice.

"I'll think about it," Fagley offered. "But how am I going to justify it with the others in the office? They don't like media mingling in their cases, and I know some of them don't like you."

"They're just jealous of my brilliance that they lack."

"You might be right," Fagley agreed, realizing his cohorts did not see Kelly in quite the same vein that he did.

"I usually am. So give me a heads up when you want me at the station, and I'll be there. I'm going to be around your town today any way."

"I'll see what I can do. Now go away. I still have a few hours to sleep."

The thought of seeing Father Birch interviewed by police and having the opportunity to offer some insights to those doing the questioning was intriguing to Kelly. He knew that the chances were slim that Fagley could get permission; cops were very territorial, especially when they felt someone outside the force might have better information than they did on a particular case. But leads and clues in this case were so scarce that they might capitulate, knowing that anything that led to an arrest was better than a bruised ego or two within the department.

The Partridge Family's "It's One of Those Nights (Yes Love)" blared through the headphones connected to the MP3 player, as Kelly meandered the neighborhood streets during his morning run. He was one of the few people willingly to admit that he enjoyed the Partridge Family and would go so far as to suggest that the arrangements on some of the songs were pure genius, at least as far as pop music was concerned. Not to mention that this little ditty even includes the words "ya betcha," a true Midwestern saying if ever there was one.

Strange thoughts came to Kelly when he ran. As he made his way along Edgecumbe Road, where it lined the Highland Executive 9 Golf Course, he wondered how many Catholic priests were homosexuals, either knowingly or unknowingly. He had certainly seen a number that displayed the typical gay tendencies. Priesthood had to be a strange lifestyle, Kelly reasoned, giving up sex for your adult life. It didn't seem natural, though he knew many of his married friends had complained they had done the same once they got hitched.

The sex abuse scandal that wrecked havoc on the Catholic Church raised many questions, not least among them was the recurring debate over whether the Vatican should allow priests to marry. A shortage of priests would certainly suggest that married priests would make sense and that strong consideration should be given to ordaining women priests. In some ways, Kelly felt the Church was still stuck in the Dark Ages. In addition to sullying the Church's image, the sex scandal presented the Church with a hypocritical dichotomous dilemma: the Church continued to oppose homosexuality, deeming it sinful, but the actions of the priests involved in the sex scandal clearly acted on those tendencies. There was a story two years ago about a parish priest in St. Paul who became involved with a married woman who was a teacher at the parish school. Kelly remembered remarking to one of his priest friends that the archdiocese should have thanked that priest—for once a priestly sex story didn't involve a boy. Joking aside, Kelly and many other American Catholics felt that the Church need-ed to address the homosexual issue with a more open mind. Gays, after all, were God-created people as well. Why should they be denied the rights of heterosexual Catholics because they were born with a differ-ent gene or something? The issue of gay marriage and the state's role in the matter generated more vitriolic hatred than any other political issue from Catholics and other religious-right zealots who supposedly preached love and understanding. The irony, Kelly thought, was that gay couples seemed to have a lower divorce rate than heterosexuals. Maybe they knew something the straights didn't.

Kelly always believed the number of homosexual priests was small, but the problems created by the Church's longstanding inabili-ty to deal with the matter effectively were immense. The fact that Father Birch was gay was probably a certainty, and it sounded as though he had managed to skirt severe punishment or condemnation for improprieties. What role any of these actions might have had on him being capable of murder was still tenuous. It bothered Kelly, the further he got into this investigation, that the Church still had so many internal problems and, in some cases, unresolved contradictions. Nor was it comforting for the reporter, who took certain aspects of his Catholic faith very seriously, that he might be on the trail to exposing some ugly truths about the Catholic church.

Father Birch made it clear that he was not pleased having to spend part of his day off with the police and was even more displeased with having to go to the police station. Detective Fagley tried to reassure him, as they drove to the station, that the questioning should not take too long and the police appreciated his willingness to cooperate.

It took some prodding, and eventually the chief was called on to make a final decision, but Detective Fagley prevailed with his request to let Kelly sit behind the glass during the Father Birch interview. Fagley decided to have Lieutenant Sam May, one of the officers who had been involved with aspects of the investigation from day one, work the interview with him. Father Birch sat by himself at the table in the interrogation room facing Fagley.

"Thanks again for taking time to come down," Fagley began. "This shouldn't take too long."

"I hope not," Father Birch replied.

"We want to know more about your relationship with Phillip Grady," Fagley began in a calm, reassuring voice. "What were the two of you arguing about outside the gym a few weeks before the murders?"

Fagley decided he would use the information Kelly had shared with him and get the interview moving right away.

"It was nothing much," the priest said, gesturing with his right hand to emphasize his point and attempting to play down any hint of malice. "We had a slight disagreement about how he thought the youth group should be run."

"Did you threaten to take the subject of the argument to someone else?" Fagley asked.

"I might have," admitted Father Birch. "I don't really recall."

"Why did you call him the week before the murders?"

This question shocked Father Birch, and for a moment he seemed visibly shaken. "What? I never called him."

Fagley stood up from his chair with notes in hand and began walking around the small table at which the priest sat. He paced around twice, watching the priest's reaction the entire time, before asking another question. "Why do phone records show there was a call from a number at the church rectory?"

"It wasn't me," Father Birch protested.

"His brother Robert would suggest otherwise."

"Well, he's just not right."

"Are you lying to us about this call?" demanded the detective, who had stopped pacing.

"Absolutely not. I resent that suggestion," the priest responded loudly. "I've cooperated with you whenever you've asked, and this is how I'm treated?"

Lieutenant May entered the room and nodded to Fagley without exchanging any words. The detective left the room. May had observed the entire interview thus far with Kelly and others behind the mirrored glass.

"There are some people who suggest you and Phillip Grady had a tumultuous relationship," May began. "Why would they think that?"

"Because Phillip Grady was a conniving weasel," the priest opined, displaying feeling about Grady he had not yet expressed to the police. Everyone watching the interview, including Kelly, realized they might be close to that moment when the prime suspect slipped. "He wanted things done his way, and if they weren't being done to his satisfaction, he would play people against one another and spread vicious rumors."

"Can you think of anyone who might have been the victim of these rumors?" wondered the Lieutenant.

"No one in particular."

"What happened on the camping trip with the youth group last summer?" May asked.

"What do you mean what happened?" stammered Father Birch with a tone of disbelief. "We had a wonderful time. It was a retreat for those preparing for Confirmation."

"I'll be back in a minute."

May left the room and joined Kelly and Fagley behind the glass. It was planned that they would take periodic breaks, so they could share their thoughts and also watch to see if Father Birch displayed any nervous tendencies while sitting alone in the room. Alone, he sat without expression, as though he was enveloped in prayer.

"I think you need to pound him about the sexual-abuse allegations," Kelly suggested. "See if there's any truth to him providing alcohol to minors. I have a feeling that if this guy's your suspect, it might be because Phillip Grady had some incriminating evidence on Birch and was about the blow the whistle."

"Where did you hear anything about sex, alcohol, and minors?" Fagley asked, these being points Kelly hadn't discussed with him prior to that day.

"Just ask him about it," Kelly demurred. "I think you should pound him some more on the argument with Phillip Grady, too. And why is he lying about the phone conversation?"

Fagley and May returned to the interrogation room together. May took his seat, but Fagley remained standing just off to Father Birch's left and began his questioning immediately.

"Have you ever given members of the youth group alcohol?" Fagley asked.

"No."

"Have you ever had inappropriate sexual contact with a minor?" May inquired.

"Certainly not. Where did this come from?"

"Was Phillip Grady threatening to turn you in for giving booze to some members of the youth group and then trying to get them to have sex with you?" Fagley added.

"That's preposterous," said Father Birch, throwing up his hands in disbelief.

"Then what specifically was your argument outside the gym about?" May asked.

"He didn't like some of my conservative approaches to the Church nor the fact that I was sharing it with the youth group. That's all. Nothing more, nothing less. But you know how religion can be a hot button topic. I'll admit that."

"That sounds like a weak reason to get into a shouting match," Fagley suggested as he began to pace the room once again.

"I suppose it was," agreed the priest.

"Really, Father, something doesn't fit here," May stated. "Either I'm not getting it or you're not telling the whole truth. What, specifically, did you mean by taking matters into your own hands and settling things that way?"

"I don't know."

"How did you know that precisely four bottles of embalming fluid were removed from the funeral home the day of the murders?" Fagley asked.

Father Birch gaped at him. "Where did that come from?"

"During one of our previous conversations, you made reference to four bottles being taken," Fagley recalled. "That information was never made public. How did you know that? Were you inside the funeral home the day of the killings?"

"No, I wasn't," Father Birch pronounced, pounding his right fist on the table. "Are we done here, because this is making no sense?"

"We'll be done when I say we are, okay?" Fagley said. "I'm getting more than a little upset with you, Father. You're hiding something. Let's go back to your relationship with Phillip Grady. What was the reason for the shouting match? There had to be more to it than just a disagreement over your conservative views."

"There wasn't, and I resent you suggesting I killed him."

"I never made any such suggestion. Why do you bring that up?"

Kelly watched as Father Birch grew increasingly agitated, wringing his hands and sweating. Since Fagley had returned to the interrogation room, the priest spent most of the time squirming while attempting to answer the questions. From behind the glass, Kelly studied Birch's body language. He had seen similar expressions countless times from people he had interviewed for stories. The sweating and clutching hands was generally a sign of discomfort but not guilt. The guilty ones were usually more emphatic with denials and steered conversations in directions they wanted to take. Father Birch seemed content to answer most of the questions, at least until the line of interrogation became more confrontational. Kelly wanted his own shot at asking the priest some different questions, which obviously wouldn't happen under these circumstances. But watching the interrogation gave Kelly some other ideas about how to pursue an interview with the priest and what angles he might take to elicit some fresh information. He was convinced the priest had more information that he was willing to share with the cops, and there was a good chance some of that information could help uncover the killer. If only it were that easy.

"Was there anything else that you and Phillip Grady disagreed over?" Lieutenant May asked, taking over the role as "good cop," as Fagley paced around the table.

"No. There wasn't."

"Did you have any other confrontations with him?" May queried.

"No."

Fagley left the room, while May finished up the questioning. "Now think hard. Are you sure you didn't talk with Phillip Grady on the phone the week prior to the killings?"

"No. I know I didn't."

"Well, I think that's about all we have for now. Thanks for coming in. I'll give you a ride back to the rectory."

Lieutenant May escorted Father Birch out of the interview room, through the hallway and out the back door of the station to the parking lot. Fagley and Kelly remained in the room behind the glass to compare thoughts.

"You think he did it?" Fagley began.

"Nope," said Kelly with a shake of his head.

"Really?"

"Really. I think he's one fucked-up dude," Kelly noted, "but I don't think he offed the two. What do you think?"

"I don't know," admitted Fagley. "I thought we could get him to crack a little more, but he didn't. What about this temper you told me he has? I didn't see it. I thought we would get a glimpse if we pushed him, but he didn't budge."

"Maybe you just didn't push the right buttons," Kelly said.

"Oh, and you would have."

"Of course. Keep me posted if you hear anything new. I gotta run."

CHAPTER TWENTY-FOUR

Kyle Grady's business continued to thrive. In stoned moments, he found energy to pat himself on the back. When lucid, questions lingered about what exactly he did that cold day in January his uncle was killed. He kept close to Jim Dogan and Frank Black, using the two as business associates and to get updates on their conversations with the police. After a few initial interviews in the days that followed his uncle's murder, Grady had little contact with police, much to his relief and satisfaction. Still, he worried what Dorgan and Black, no longer two people he considered friends, might know and tell investigators. The more police suspected the two teenagers, the more Grady worried.

He was careful not to email his two cohorts, knowing even deleted could sometimes be retrieved off a computer's hard drive and offer motive. He rarely called or texted their cell phones for the same reasons. Most information was shared during lunch at school. The din of the lunchroom loud enough to cover anything the teenagers shared with each other, which generally wasn't much.

"We need a bigger cut," explained Dorgan in between sips of his Red Bull.

Grady studied the face across the table from him, looking for clues about how to proceed with the negotiation. There was more at stake than just a few percentage points on sales.

"We talked about this, and we agree it's fair if we get another ten percent commission," Black said, looking away from Grady as he spoke to make sure no one was walking toward them.

"Gimme a break," Grady retorted. "I'll consider five, but definitely not ten."

Dorgan and Black, as they rehearsed, sat silently, letting Grady make the next move before they said anything more.

"Okay, six, but that's as high as I can go. I'm already getting pinched."

"We get ten or we share your secrets," Black warned.

"And what secrets do I have that you don't?" Grady asked, the disgust at being blackmailed rang through.

"Let's just say we know all your shortcomings, even the ones you might not remember because you were too fuckin' stoned at the time."

Now it was Grady's turn for silence. Were they right, he wondered, or just bluffing? Fear enveloped Grady, as he calmly stuffed his uneaten sandwich and chips into the brown lunch bag, crumbling it for the garbage.

"Okay, ten it is."

Grady stood up quickly and walked away from the table without another word, without even looking at his cohorts. The ghost of uncertainly attacked him again, this time more intense than in previous visits.

Kelly despised idle time when he was working, but he had a few hours to kill before Hudson High School let out for the day. Today, instead of hanging out at the cigar shop, Kelly quickly checked his email and voice mail and then went for a long walk along the St. Croix River. He always marveled at the money people had and how many of them displayed their wealth in the form of boats, especially in this climate when there were only about six months of nice weather to enjoy watercraft. The harbors along with the St. Croix were filled with boats big and small. As he walked, he saw a woman emerge from one of the boats and begin walking along the dock straight toward him.

"Sean Kelly, right?" she said, extending her hand. "I'm Shirley Hennan. I work at the Grady Funeral Home. I've seen you on the news."

"Hi, Shirley, nice to meet you" Kelly responded, grasping her hand.

"Strange meeting you here," she said with a slight smile.

"I'm just out for a walk, trying to clear my head and kill some time before my next meeting. And you?"

"I took the day off, so I could work on my boat a little," she admitted. "Just put it in last week. Probably a little early, but we've got spring fever."

"Care to join me for a little walk?" Kelly inquired, jumping at the opportunity presented. "I'd like to ask you a few questions."

"This isn't going to land me on the ten o'clock news, is it?" she asked again with a smile.

"No, of course not," Kelly assured her.

The two walked for a couple blocks, passing the time with questions about how things were at the funeral home, how Robert was handling everything. Hennan told Kelly that things were about as good as possible, that Robert Grady had days when she felt he found it difficult to function, almost as though he was clinically depressed. Yet other days, he plowed himself into his work so much that it practically therapeutic.

"What kind of person was Phillip Grady?" asked Kelly.

"He was a nice man, a tough boss, you know, pretty demanding to make sure things were done the way he wanted them," admitted Hennan. "Much more buttoned down than his brother Robert. But he was fair, even when he seemed a little demanding."

"What about his relationship with Father Birch from St. Tim's? Did you ever get a glimpse into that?"

"The two didn't like each other," she said. "That's for sure. But I'm not certain why. It's not something Phillip discussed. There was one time when I walked in on a heated discussion the two were having. It was at St. Tim's prior to a funeral. Phillip had forgotten something, and called to ask me to run it over to the church. When I got there, the two were in the back of the church practically in each other's face. You know, pointing fingers at each other."

"Do you know what they were arguing about?" asked Kelly.

"Hard to say for sure, but I remember hearing Phillip say he had enough evidence to prove it wasn't him, but I'm not sure what he was referring to."

This was news. Kelly reiterated what she had just said for clarity. "He said he had evidence to *exonerate* him, to exonerate Phillip himself?"

"That's what it sounded like," she said.

"What was Father Birch's response?" Kelly wondered.

"I couldn't hear everything clearly, but it really sounded something like, 'But that doesn't change the fact that there is money missing.'"

"Interesting," said Kelly slowly as he attempted to process the conversation and keep the questions flowing without too much interruption. "You found the bodies that day in January, didn't you?"

"Yes."

"I know this might be difficult to talk about, so stop me if you don't want me to keep asking questions," Kelly cautioned.

"No, to be honest, it might be good for me to talk about it," she admitted. "I talked with police that day and in a follow-up interview, but I haven't discussed the murders with anyone else since. It was truly a nightmare I'd like to forget and wish never happened, but obviously that's not going to happen."

"Was there anything strange about the funeral home when you came back from lunch?" he inquired. "Did you notice anything missing or out of place either near the murder scene or elsewhere?"

"There was one thing I've thought about a lot over the past two months, but I can't seem to think why I keep obsessing over it," she suggested.

"What is it?"

"There was a gray Buick sedan parked about a half block down from the funeral home, and I passed it coming back from lunch. Normally, I'm not that observant, but it was the only car along that part of the street, so when police asked me to recount as much as I could, that image came to me."

"What's so strange about a gray Buick?"

"Well, it wasn't just the car but who I saw inside it. Now remember I was driving and not paying too much attention, but it certainly appeared that the driver was wearing a Roman collar."

Electricity went through Kelly. "So it might have been a priest? Did you get a good glimpse of the driver? Did you recognize him from St. Tim's or elsewhere?"

"No," she said.

"Did you tell police this?" Kelly asked.

"Of course."

"Was there anything else out of the ordinary?" he wondered.

"You mean other than two dead bodies inside the funeral home? Sorry, sometimes I have to be a little caustic or I'll go nuts from what I saw."

"I understand."

"There was one other thing that I keep mulling over," Hennan said and then paused. "When I dropped some letters I had typed on Phillip's desk right before I left for lunch, I noticed there was a file marked 'St. Timothy's 2006 Audit.' When I went through his office with police after I found the bodies that afternoon, there was no trace of that file. It was gone."

"Was Phillip in his office when you dropped the letters on his desk?" Kelly wanted to know.

"No, he and Charles were in the basement working on a body that had come in. I suppose he could have come up to his office and removed the file or perhaps given it to someone if they stopped by over the lunch hour, but that seems a little strange. I don't know. It's probably nothing, but you asked."

"That's interesting."

"I need to go, but I enjoyed our conversation," Hennan said.

"Thanks for your time. Let's stay in touch."

Kelly's mind whirled, as he walked back to his Jag, parked on a side street off Second. This chance encounter with Shirley Hennan had proved quite beneficial. Why hadn't Fagely discussed the gray Buick or the audit file with him? Was he deliberately keeping something from him or had the police explored the issues as much as they thought they warranted and dropped the matters? It wouldn't be the first time in history that police had failed to prioritize clues properly, especially in a high profile case where every nutcase, wanna-be informant calls with tips so ludicrous even the mental institutions would laugh at them.

Kelly made a note to talk with Fagley about the car and whether police suspected a priest might have actually been in the driver's seat. It was certainly possible that the killer would have parked some place other than the funeral home's parking lot, though concealing a hunting rifle while walking a half-block could prove challenging. The medical examiner's office put the time of death sometime between 12:15 and shortly before Hennan discovered the bodies just after one, so it was feasible that the driver of the Buick could have whacked the victims and then ambled back to his car, getting situated in the front seat just as Hennan drove past on her way back from lunch.

What intrigued Kelly more than the car was the issue of the audit file coupled with the conversation that Hennan recounted from the church. This was the first time, to the reporter's knowledge, that there had been any reference to money when people talked about the strained relationships between Father Birch and Grady. But from the conversation Hennan recalled, it was difficult to determine who was accusing whom of financial improprieties. Sex, money, religion, and murder. Kelly reasoned some Hollywood producer could find a reality show concept somewhere amid this tangled web.

"Hi, I'm looking for Jim Dorgan," said Kelly as he stood on the front steps to Dorgan's dad's house.

"Yeah, that's me," the kid said. "You're the guy on Channel 6, right?"

"Yeah. I wanted to see if we could talk a little."

"About what?"

"Can I come in first?" Kelly asked.

"Sure," said Dorgan, holding open the door for the repoter.

Kelly surveyed the interior of the house, as he walked through the door. Minimalism, he suspected, was the theme. All the walls were painted white, though they seemed discolored, most likely the result of cigarette smoke, the smell of which lingered in the air. There were no photos or paintings on the walls and just a few framed photos on the mantle above the fireplace. There was a large-screen television, a flat screen suspended against the northeast wall. Kelly did notice some signs of athletics, something he had not seen at Black's house. In addition to a basketball hoop on the garage outside, there was a bucket next to the front door that contained a basketball and a LaCrosse stick. LaCrosse, Kelly realized, was on the verge of becoming the next big sport in America, much faster and more exciting than soccer. Who could ever have predicted that the rape charges brought, and dropped, against three Duke University LaCrosse players would have done so much to raise the visibility of the sport?

"I know police talked to you and your friend Frank in the days that followed the funeral home murders in January," Kelly explained, as the two stood in the entryway, "but there are some things I wanted to ask you."

"Okay," Dorgan hesitated. "I guess. Is this off the record?"

"I suppose you could say that. If we want something for a report, I'll arrange to have a photographer come, and we'll do the interview on tape. But for now, this is just you and me talking casually. Okay?"

"Sure."

Kelly had already set his small digital audio recorder to tape the conversation. He kept the piece of equipment in the side pocket of his overcoat, out of sight but able to detect and record what was said. He did this not to trick his subjects but so he could review the conversation later if he needed to. The laws on secretly recording someone varied from state to state, and Kelly didn't really care to waste time checking out what Wisconsin law said on this matter.

"I understand you and the youth group from St. Tim's went camping last summer with Father Birch. What happened on that trip?"

"Oh, not much," Dorgan explained, looking directly at Kelly as he did. "You know, we prayed a lot, had camp fires. It was a two-night deal. Kind of fun."

"Did Father Birch have any alcohol with him?"

If this question shocked Dorgan, he showed no signs of being disturbed by it.

"How would I know?" asked the teenager.

"Well, he might have offered you some," Kelly suggested.

"Nah, didn't offer me any."

Kelly asked Dorgan about what he thought of the young priest, and the teenager said he found him okay, nothing spectacular but no one to get overly annoyed at like others did. Kelly then asked Dorgan if he had ever seen Father Birch get angry.

"Oh, yeah," Dorgan said, laughing a little as he continued. "Couple times, in fact once on that camping trip, he just lost it, went nuts, yelling at some of the kids."

"What made him mad?" Kelly wanted to know.

Kelly sat down in one of the chairs and Dorgan flopped himself onto the sofa. He seemed almost flattered that Kelly wanted some time. Kelly had seen this effect in some interviewees; they hoped they might end up on the TV news.

"Oh, I don't know," Dorgan said about Father Birch anger. "You'll have to ask the person who made him mad."

"And who was that?" Kelly wondered.

"Kyle Grady, I think," Dorgan replied.

"Why did you go to buy bullets at Wal-Mart with Father Birch the day of the murders?" Kelly asked.

"How did you know that?" asked Dorgan, clearly surprised.

Preening, Kelly said, "Oh, I have my ways."

"We were planning to go skeet shooting one of these days," Dorgan admitted.

"Isn't it a little odd that a priest would go and buy bullets with you on a day when you're supposed to be sitting out a suspension from school?" Kelly asked.

"Nah, Father Birch's like that. He understands kids, gets what we're about."

Dorgan explained that he, Father Birch, and Frank Black had forged a relationship and often went skeet shooting. He admitted that he and Black never felt odd being with the priest, though others in their class looked at them strangely when they would talk about hanging out together, particularly when they all shot guns. It just wasn't something most teenagers did.

"Skeet's not cheap," Kelly stated. "Did Father Birch pay for it?"

"Yeah," Dorgan nodded. "He always seemed to have money. You should see his gun collection. He must have eight or ten different hunting rifles."

"Is that so?" Kelly said. "Anything else I should know?"

"I don't think so," Dorgan offered.

"Well, thanks for your time. Can I give you a call if I have any other questions?"

"Sure, I guess."

Father Birch stewed, walking back and forth in his room at the rectory. The interview with the police hadn't gone as well as he had hoped. They didn't have information that could charge him, but he was worried they were closing in on that. What was the big deal about the camping trip and who would have said something to the police? The altercation was ludicrous, a misunderstanding that had seemed to escalate into something so much bigger.

The day had taken its toll on him, so Father Birch decided to skip dinner with Father Fred, wanting to avoid any further scurrilous round of questioning the pastor might decide worthy. Instead, the young priest kept to his room, opening a cabinet inside his closet in which he kept a collection of his favorite single-malt scotch. Tonight, Father Birch chose an unopened bottle of Laphroaig, ten years old, full of smokey flavors and intense sensations. After pouring his first dram, he logged onto his laptop computer. The advent of the Internet during his seminary days had created another universe for the lost priest. It was here that he could email friends in confidence, sharing some of his innermost thoughts too embarrassing to divulge in standard conversation. He enjoyed surfing the net to read what various websites with an ultra-conservative Catholic bent had to say, often taking notes that he would sometimes work into his own homilies on Sunday. Through the Internet, Father Birch found a unique form of companionship, the ability to escape some of life's hardest trials and feel that there were others facing the same challenges as he.

Chapter Twenty-Five

The drive back to the Twin Cities was at once peaceful and disturbing for Kelly. During his radio button pushing, he settled on the music side of Public Radio, which was playing Brahms' Violin Concerto, serene and placid until the final movement, which began with a bang and continued to pound from there. A beautiful piece of music. Kelly couldn't help but smile and shake his head whenever his car radio ended up on this station. He marveled at what beautiful music was played, yet hated pledge drives. Whenever they came on, he tuned out.

As violinist Nigel Hamilton's bow and fingers dug in for the final movement, Kelly's mind went back over the conversations from the day. For all the speculation, theories and supposition that the involved parties, including Kelly, brought to the table, the interview with Father Birch offered little, if any, new information to suggest he was the killer. Kelly knew Fagley disagreed. The detective, Kelly could tell, was even more convinced that they had the killer and just needed another piece or two of damning evidence. The priest's contentious relationship with Phillip Grady, which seemed to be pretty well accepted, and a propensity to flip out when pushed, as he did toward the end of the interview, alone were not enough to convict him, let alone charge him.

During the conversation with Dorgan, Kelly had noticed something on the screen of Dorgan's laptop computer sitting on the dining room table. He hadn't realized its possible significance at the time because the image was not constantly on the screen, and Kelly had to view it out of the corner of is eye to avoid appearing too obvious as he walked past the table on his way out of the house. What appeared to be a screen saver had a photo of Father Birch, Dorgan, and Frank Black, standing together with smiles on their faces and wearing sunglasses, each holding a hunting rifle. Under the photo, a quote taken from the original "Blues Brothers" movie with Dan Akroyd and John Belushi read: "We're on a mission from God."

Shirley Hennan had difficultly sleeping that night. She felt, at least at first, that her conversation with Sean Kelly was helpful, almost a catharsis of sorts. Yet as she pondered the different points they'd covered and the observations she'd shared with the reporter, she became concerned, worried that she had revealed too much information. She also knew there was something she hadn't told anyone because she wasn't completely certain she was correct, though if put on a scale of one to ten, her certainty would weigh in at 9.9 and then some. She hadn't mentioned anything to Robert Grady, nothing to the police during the short period they interviewed her after the murders and now today she'd stopped short of offering her poignant observation to Kelly. Like others involved in the case, Hennan was a member of St. Tim's.

She enjoyed the parish and attended mass regularly. She and her husband weren't overly involved in church activities but enough so to know many parishioners, not to mention the priests and school faculty. As she rolled over in bed and looked at her digital alarm clock, which now read 2:12, she contemplated her options. She knew the information she had, if absolutely correct, could drastically affect the lives of many in the parish, some of whom she considered friends. But her dilemma, which had haunted her since the day of the murders, was whether to tell police or someone else. And what happened if she was wrong?

"Bless me Father for I have sinned. My last confession was last week, and here are my sins. At times, I have become angry with people around me and chastised them in ways my Maker would not approve. I have not always lived up to the religious ideals I have preached to others. And most troubling is that I have come into knowledge of some improprieties where I work. I know I should make public the information I have discovered, but I'm scared. For these and all my sins, I am truly sorry.

CHAPTER TWENTY-SIX

K elly's phone rang just before five o'clock, minutes, if not seconds, prior to his alarm setting up its roar. He figured it was Fagley taking a moment to get back at him for yesterday's early morning call. Kelly hated people who looked at their caller ID and then answered as if in mid-conversation without even bothering to say hello. Skipping good-bye was one thing, but there was still a place for a modicum of manners on the phone, despite what all of the so-called technological advances had wrought. He didn't even bother looking at the caller ID and just answered the phone, as he flipped on the light next to his bed and shut off his alarm.

"Hello," Kelly answered.

"Hi," said a female voice at the other end of the line. "I'm sorry to bother you so early, but I know I can usually reach you at this hour and not run the risk of your wrath from waking you up."

It was the recognizable voice of his secret source, someone who, with the exception of being female, had kept her identity to herself. She offered no clues during their conversations and either blocked the number from which she was calling or, more likely, simply rotated from one safe phone to another. Kelly was beginning to wonder if the information she was providing was even worth pursuing.

"What's on your mind this morning?" Kelly asked.

"I'm glad to see you're finally following some of my advice," she stated bluntly.

"And what advice specifically are you referring to?" the reporter wondered.

"Did you ever see the movie *All the President's Men*? Of course you have. Every journalist worth anything has seen that. Well, as I'm sure you recall, there's a key piece of advice that one of the sources offers Woodward and Bernstein. Do you remember what that was?"

"Let me see," Kelly said, thinking. "Katie Graham was going to get her tit in a ringer if she wasn't careful. Is that what you're referring to?"

"Ah, you know the movie well. Your photographic memory and sense of humor never fail you. What's the other main theme?" the caller asked.

"Follow the money," Kelly replied.

"Ah, yes. Yes. You would be wise to follow that same trail. Keep up the good work."

The line went dead. Kelly had pondered his next step since his conversations yesterday. This phone call solidified his decision.

The memo calling the meeting indicated it was "High Priority," but then again the chief would like everyone to believe that all his memos deemed such stature. It was the first thing Detective Fagley saw when he opened his email, a summons to a meeting with Walsh, Lieutenant May and Lawrence Thompson, the high-profile district attorney. The meeting was set for 9:30 sharp in the chief's well-decorated office.

Fagley never particularly enjoyed these meetings. They reeked of bureaucracy and were usually called only when the chief felt there was a problem with something. Fagley didn't need to be a rocket scientist to figure out why this meeting had been called.

For nearly every Tuesday morning since they met three years ago, Kelly and the man he nicknamed Father Truth tried to meet for breakfast at the University Club at the corner of Summit Avenue and Ramsey. They almost always took a table next to the giant window in the main dining room, affording themselves a beautiful view of downtown St. Paul and the West 7th/Homecroft neighborhood on the streets below the University Club.

Their breakfast orders varied little. Two eggs over-easy with an English Muffin and black coffee for Kelly and French Toast, orange juice and coffee for Father Truth. Their conversations ran the gamut from parish gossip to Notre Dame to politics, an entertaining and learning experience for both of them. Today Kelly wasted little time with small talk.

"I'm bothered at how this funeral home case is moving," Kelly admitted.

"Why's that?"

"What do you mean why's that? Have you been following my reports?"

"Of course. How could I ever survive without feasting on and savoring your every word?"

"Did they teach you to be a smart aleck in the seminary or does that just come to you naturally?" Kelly asked.

"Oh, naturally, of course," Father Truth said smiling. "So what's bothering you?"

Kelly paused, taking a bite of his eggs and two sips of coffee before continuing.

"It's not looking good for Father Birch, and it sounds like there's much more than is being reported. What do you hear?"
This time it was Father Truth's turn to pause, gathering his thoughts and attempting to figure how much he should reveal.

"I hear he's an odd duck," he began. "There are rumors, but who knows what is true?"

"Do you think he killed those two?"

"I just don't know. I pray to God he didn't."

The two used a break in their conversation to devour more of their breakfast and enjoy the sun shining against the buildings in downtown. It was a view of which Kelly never tired. Though not a native, he considered himself a St. Paulite through and through.

"Here's what bothers me," said Kelly. "I'm struggling with what angles of this story to pursue and, if I succeed in breaking the story, how my reports will impact the Catholic church and how people view it. It's not been the best of media times for the church lately."

"That's a tough one," Father Truth acknowledged. "Have you prayed about it?"

"Sure, but I don't think God has answered me. He could just gently let me know who the real killer is, ideally not someone associated with the church, I could break it, get my Emmy and take a few weeks off."

"God doesn't always work that way."

"Really?"

"Is there some angle you haven't gone after that doesn't relate to the Catholic church or maybe you could find a positive story in what's happened to the parish after the murders. This is a tough one."

"It's not quite like covering the swimmers, bikers and runners around Lake Calhoun on a sunny day."

"No it isn't. Keep your faith, though."

Kelly stayed behind and sat in the Fireplace Room at the U Club to try to enjoy another cup or two of coffee before his next meeting. He knew the obvious and why he was bothered about potentially exposing the Catholic church yet again to a scandal, but he also had a professional responsibility. As he replayed his conversation with Father Truth, something dawned on the inquisitive reporter. He needed to talk to one individual who he realized could potentially hold everyone else's secrets.

"You all know each other, so I won't waste time with introductions," the chief said. "The word on the street is that Kelly from

Channel 6 is poking around, trying to uncover something new in the funeral home murders."

The chief obviously chose not to share with the DA the fact that the reporter had stood behind the glass the previous day during the interrogation of Father Birch. Sometimes, those facts were better left unstated when two powerful egos converge in the same room. If Chief Walsh had an unmitigated need to attempt to micro-manage his department, especially with high profile cases that attracted the media, then DA Thompson was the chief on steroids.

"So the Mayor's all over my ass yesterday wondering why Kelly's poking around. He wants to know why we haven't come close to making an arrest, and the case is more than two months old. Why don't you fill us in Detective Fagley on where things stand?"

"To be honest, we're not that much further along than we were two months ago. I would say Father Birch might be the prime suspect, but I don't think we have enough to have him charged."

"Why don't you stick to police work and let me handle the legal aspect?" sneered Thompson. "Tell me what makes you suspect him."

"He didn't have a good relationship with Phillip Grady. There are those who back that up. He owns many hunting rifles. Some would suggest he's obsessed with his guns. His alibi is weak at best, and he seemed during one interview to have some knowledge of the crime scene."

"What type of knowledge?"

"He knew that four bottles of embalming fluid were missing, and we had never made the exact number public."

"You need more," Thompson stated. "Can you bring the priest in again and pursue some different lines of questioning? Are there any other people who might have info about the priest? We're getting closer legally, but we need something more. We need a smoking gun, some hard piece of evidence."

"We'll keep working on it."

"You're damn right you will," the chief interjected. "If you two don't come up with something new soon, I'm going to have to assign someone else to the case or bring someone in from the outside for a fresh perspective. Nothing against the way you guys're handling it, but we need to arrest somebody soon, especially if that reporter starts spouting off about it on TV every night."

"And Kelly is one giant prick, if I've ever met one," stated Thompson, commenting on his relationship with the reporter which was solidified years ago.

A former star quarterback at the University of Wisconsin, Thompson attended law school at Hamline University in St. Paul. His reputation, not so much as a legal scholar but as a star athlete, landed him a clerkship on the Minnesota State Supreme Court, after which he moved to the Ramsey County Attorney's office. As an assistant prosecutor, he helped handle the case against the former St. Paul Police Chief. To this day, he felt that Fagley and Kelly compromised the case and made it harder to prosecute. Whenever the topic found its way into conversation with those involved, Fagley attempted to remain diplomatic and keep his mouth shut.

Kelly, on the other hand, was not so polite. One Friday evening years ago, while hanging with some friends at the bar at the St. Paul Grill, Kelly and Thompson ran into each other. Thompson, standing with some other members of the DA's office, struck up a conversation with Kelly about the case, even though by this time it had been three years since the Chief was exposed, in more ways than one. Still bitter, Thompson launched into a verbal tirade against irresponsible reporting and sensational journalism. Kelly simply waited, took another sip or three from his [yellow tail] the Reserve Shiraz, a well-priced Australian staple and then let loose.

"If you had half an ounce of brains, that case would have been done in a day after all the information I provided through my reports," Kelly started. "But you had to let your ego fuck it up. You turned the courtroom into a circus and completely let the defense take over, just like you did in the Rose Bowl against USC."

At that, Thompson took a swing at Kelly. But Kelly, sensing the punch might be forthcoming, had already put down his glass on the bar and deflected the punch, twisted Thompson's right arm behind his back and then mocked him even more, as the bar's patrons looked on with shock and amusement.

"Wow, what a suit! Must be 100% polyester. Let me know next time K-Mart has a Blue Light Special. Won't ya?"

The physical and verbal thrashing ended there, but gossip columnists picked up on the scuffle in the Sunday papers, much to Thompson's chagrin.

Father Fred was finishing the last of his morning coffee, catching the final few minutes of "Regis and Kelly," when the intercom on his office phone sounded. It was his secretary, informing him Archbishop Malone was on the phone. Father Fred made a quick mental count of how many days he had left until retirement, how much longer he'd have to field calls like this from the archbishop.

"Archbishop, how are you today?" asked Father Fred, masking his disgust in hearing his boss's voice yet again.

"I could be better, Father," intoned the Archbishop bluntly.

"Why's that?"

"I hear that reporter from Channel 6 is once again sniffing around the funeral home murders. You know as well as I that this could lead to problems for all of us."

"Yes, Archbishop, I'm well aware of that, but I have no power to stop a reporter from doing his job," Father Fred replied with a sigh.

"But we've discussed a plan of action, and I expect you follow through on that. Okay?"

"Very well."

"Have a nice day."

Before Father Fred could reciprocate the pleasantry, the line went dead. The relationship between Father Fred and Archbishop Malone was complicated, as was nearly every other pastor's relationship with him. He demanded a lot from his pastors, expecting them to follow his orders and requests without question. Most did so for fear the archbishop would make their lives miserable if they questioned his authority.

The coffee on Father Fred's desk had gone cold, but he sipped it anyway, a nervous reaction to the conversation that had just taken place. He knew he was losing control of the situation and, for the first time, actually felt fear as his mind played different scenarios that might occur. He knew the archbishop's stern resolve to dictate a favorable outcome to a situation like this, and he knew the lengths to which the archbishop would go to get the results he wanted. Ruthless and calculating were two words to describe his resolve.

Cindy Hughes requested that they meet somewhere outside Hudson. She was beginning to worry that people might erroneously link her to the pro-Father Birch faction or the murder investigation itself if she were spotted with a reporter. So she and Sean Kelly met at A Fine Grind coffee shop on Marshall Avenue in St. Paul. She assured him she needed to visit Macy's for some shopping, so a trip to St. Paul was no inconvenience.

Kelly had phoned Hughes the previous evening on his way home from Hudson, telling her he had some more questions that she could probably answer. There was some initial hesitation, but eventually the St. Tim's Youth Group director relented and agreed to meet. Sensing from their initial meeting and her willingness to meet again that she was a woman who could be trusted, he jumped right into his line of questioning.

"Have you ever suspected Father Birch of financial improprieties? You know, not necessarily stealing from the youth group but maybe using some of the funds in lavish ways."

"Yes, that's been a concern for the past year."

"Have you ever addressed it personally with Father Birch?"

"On a couple occasions. I had the chance to tell him, almost more as a courtesy warning, that others were concerned about his lack of detail in keeping receipts and suspected frivolous spending. He admitted he needed to do a better job of keeping records, but that he was not spending any of the group's money foolishly."

"What was your take on the situation?"

"There is certainly money unaccounted for. But because of the way the youth group operates, there are a number of people who have access to the bank account. We probably haven't overseen financial matters as closely as possible. And money is always a tricky matter. It's tough to ask someone about unaccounted funds without making it sound like you're accusing them of stealing. I don't think we have any real idea how much of the unaccounted money Father Birch actually used. It could have been someone else."

"Who else might have access to youth group money?"

"I suppose Father Fred, of course, and perhaps Phillip Grady did because of his role as financial director on the Parish Council."

"He was financial director?"

"Yeah, none of the accountants that belong to the parish really seemed to have interest in doing the job, so Phillip stepped in about a year ago, right around the same time Father Birch became the associate pastor. I guess Phillip figured his business experience at the funeral home gave him a strong enough background to oversee the church's finances in some capacity."

Kelly enjoyed his conversation with Hughes. The laid back atmosphere of A Fine Grind gave both a chance to relax and discuss matters other than the parish and anything that might be related to the funeral home murders. They finished their coffees and stood to leave. As she put on her London Fog overcoat, Hughes paused as if she was contemplating saying something.

"Have you ever talked to Tim Leeland?"

"No. Who's he?"

"He's a former parishioner. He left for St. Joe's across town in early February, just a couple weeks after the murders. He's a CPA with the St. Paul firm that did the church's audit last year. You might want to talk to him. Thanks for the coffee."

The two smiled and shook hands, but it was clear to Kelly that the conversation had ended for today. Hughes was already in the process of walking toward the door as they shook hands. It was as though she had debated whether to offer that last piece of information,

and when she finally decided to share it, she wanted no chance for any
follow up questions.

T hough he owed a phone call to his newsroom boss to apprise him of
the investigation's progress, Kelly instead quickly called Shelley
Rosen.

"I feel neglected," she informed him. "You haven't called or
asked for my services for a few days."

"You want attention? Get a dog."

"Nice as ever, aren't you?"

"I do have something, or I should say, someone I need you to
research for me. The guy's name is Tim Leeland. He's a CPA, and I
think he works for a St. Paul firm, though I don't know which one. Dig
up all you can on him, and also see if you can find a way to get directly through to him on the phone."

"Got it."

"Thanks."

"Hey, anything for you."

"I'll remember that next time I'm lonely and horny."

"That's every day, isn't it?"

"You know me too well. Now go get on the job I gave you."

I t took Shelley Rosen little time to find where Tim Leeland worked,
but getting background information on him proved more difficult.
Accountants don't find themselves in the news too often, unless they
once worked for Arthur Anderson or Enron. What she was able to cull
from news clipping services and the Internet was that Leeland had
worked for the CPA firm DeBolt and O'Brien for more than ten years,
during which time he had become a partner and occasionally received
awards from various associations. His biography on the company website indicated he had attended the University of Notre Dame. He lived
in Hudson with his wife and three kids. Property records in St. Croix

County indicated he had lived in his current house for seventeen years. Rosen conveyed all this as well as contact information when she called Kelly.

"What about his role in his parish?" Kelly wondered. "Did you find anything else there?"

"No. Still looking."

"Anything new in the newsroom?"

"Well, funny you would ask. I overheard Watson and Ashbury talking about you this morning. Seems Watson felt compelled to take a few jabs at your, as she phrased it, "alleged investigating,"and Ashbury erupted into a tirade replete with questions about why the station pays you so much."

"Those two can go fuck each other for all I care. What a bunch of stiffs. Thanks for the update, though. Good to know I haven't been completely forgotten in my absence. Stay in touch."

"Will do."

Leeland answered his direct line on the second ring, and Kelly wasted little time mentioning the two of them were both Domers, asking him what he thought of the football team's prospects this coming fall. If there's one way to bond quickly with a fellow ND grad, it was to bring up the football team. Those who had at least half a pulse could talk for hours about the football program, reliving each game from the previous season and speculating on what players would shine in the upcoming season. If a ND grad was unable to converse fluently in footballese, that served as a warning that interesting conversation on any subject would be difficult, if not impossible. Leeland passed the test, and after about three minutes of football talk, Kelly steered the conversation elsewhere.

"As much as I would love to keep talking about the Irish, I'm sure you're busy, so I'll get to the reason for my call," Kelly explained. "I'm looking into the funeral home murders in Hudson a little more, and I understand that you were formerly a parishioner at St. Tim's. Is that right?"

"Yes, but I don't understand your purpose for calling me. My family no longer belongs to that parish."

"It's convoluted, at best, but I'm looking at every possible angle, and I've learned that there were some suggestions of financial mistakes, perhaps nothing deliberate or intentional, but oversights of some sort."

"I still don't understand what this has to do with me or the murders."

"It's complicated, but I'm trying to learn as much as possible about Father Birch, specifically his role with the youth group."

"I'd love to help, but you've got the wrong person. My kids are grown and haven't been part of the youth group for years."

"But your firm did do the audit last year, right? Did you find anything alarming?"

"Listen, I appreciate your call and love talking football with you. But I'm afraid I can't help. Thanks, though."

And with that, Leeland hung up.

This was a delicate situation for Kelly. He strongly suspected that Leeland had some information helpful to the investigation. Some of that info might even be enough to implicate or exonerate Father Birch. But he also realized that if he pushed Leeland too much too soon, he'd end up with nothing except an angry CPA, which was never good, especially if that accountant has contacts at the state tax revenue office. So, instead of phoning Leeland back immediately, he typed a brief email thanking him for his time on the phone, asking him to contact him if he thought of anything that might be relevant to Kelly's investigation. He made it clear that he respected an accountant's need for confidentiality with regards to clients but asked if there were an ethical and moral way to share certain information or point Kelly in the right direction so he could find it on his own. In his final sentence, Kelly drove home the point that, as far fetched as it sounded, reputations and potentially even lives could be at stake. He respectfully signed the email "Go Irish!"

Kelly had put off the dreaded phone call long enough. He had promised his boss, Ashbury, that he'd check in with an update on the investigation. That alone was bad enough, but armed with the info Rosen had fed him, Kelly was more agitated than before.

"Ashbury here."

"Jon, Sean Kelly. Just calling to update you on the investigation."

"Let me guess, you have another Emmy-award winner."

"I just might. Rest assured that you won't sit at my table during the awards ceremony."

"How are things going?"

"I've uncovered a lot of fresh information, but I'm still trying to find the right link to tie it all together."

"Why did I think you were going to say that? You know, if you fail here, it's going to affect your next contract negotiation."

Kelly fell silent, choosing to pretend to ignore the last comment. Any response would only get him into trouble, and he knew Ashbury would try to hold it against him next time his contract was up for renewal. Plus he wanted to see how his dimwitted boss handled silence.

"Are you still there?" asked Ashbury.

"Sure."

"Did you hear I what just said?"

"Are you still there?" Kelly quipped.

"Yes, I'm here. Did you hear what I said?"

"Yes, I'm here. Did you hear what I said?" Kelly repeated.

"Okay, smartass. Enough bullshit. You either deliver some reports from your time off, or there'll be consequences."

"Anything else you want to discuss? 'Cause if there isn't, I need to get going and get to work for a change."

"Very funny. You heard what I said."

"Gotta run."

Kelly snapped shut his cell, ending the call abruptly and leaving no chance that he'd say something he might regret. Much as he hated to admit it, Ashbury did control certain aspects of Kelly's future with the station, provided there wasn't a new boss in place by the time Kelly's contract came up for renewal.

As he drove the Jag down I-94, headed once again to Hudson, Kelly shook off notions of killing his boss and every former boss, and instead focused his mental energies on how he could pursue the money angle. It had been awhile since he had last spoken with Father Fred at St. Tim's and thought today would be a good time to drop by the rectory unannounced. It was not how he usually liked to meet with people, preferring instead to have a pre-set meeting time, but he had a suspicision that Father Fred might not necessarily want to see him today. He was right.

CHAPTER TWENTY-SEVEN

Barb Fisher, the secretary at St. Tim's Rectory, was surprised to see Kelly. Most visitors wanting time with Father Fred scheduled a meeting in advance, she informed him, but she would check to see if he was available. The two emerged a few minutes later.

"To what do I owe the honor, Mr. TV Star?"

"Let's just say it must be your lucky day. Is there a place we could talk for a few minutes?"

"Normally, I'd love to chat, but I'm just on my way to another meeting."

"Can we do something later today?"

"Ah, I don't think that'll work. I'm not sure when I'll be back. Why don't you call ahead next time you're planning to be in town, and I'll see what I can arrange. Okay?"

"I guess that'll have to do. Good to see you."

"You, too."

It was always a strong indication that a reporter was getting close to information people didn't want him to have, when potential sources started refusing to talk. Kelly knew this well, and took it as a good sign that two people in the last few hours had basically refused to talk with him. That was the good news; finding the next person to interview would be the challenge.

He needed a break. His investigation had become all-consuming, offering his obsessive personality little, if any, chance to enjoy anything else life had to offer while in the midst of the investigation. After his aborted meeting with Father Fred, he drove his car to Third Street, where there were no parking meters, and then walked to the riverfront park area off Front Street and found a bench not far from the bandshell. He pulled his cell phone out, flipped it opened and scrolled through the directory until he found the name he wanted.

"What's up, you Boston College-fan wanna be?" asked a cheery Becky Lewis.

"Oh, I just figured you needed some intelligence injected into your life, and who better than I to take care of it," said Kelly, stifling a laugh.

"How's your investigation going? Still ahead of the police on everything?" she wondered.

"I suppose, but that's not saying much," Kelly admitted. "It's getting tough. So much points to the young priest, Father Nutcase, but no one can find the proverbial smoking gun, figuratively or literally."

"Have you looked into those two angles I suggested?" asked Lewis.

"I'm in the process," Kelly said. "I think at least one of them might have some meat. I'll keep you posted."

"Let me know if I can help in any other way," Lewis offered.

"Well, now that you mention it, it has been a long time since I . . ."

"Sean, you're such pig" she said.

"Ah, but at least I know I'm good at something," boasted Kelly. "Good talking to you again."

"You, too. Stay in touch."

Kelly smiled as he flipped his phone shut and stared out at the peaceful blue waters of the St. Croix River. There was something about Lewis that he really liked. More than just something. Her personality, intelligence, and a caustic wit that could rival his. Not to mention that she was smoking hot, even though she'd gone to BC. As their relationship continued to inch closer to romance, Kelly noticed that he got a funny feeling each time her number popped up on his phone.

Theirs was a unique relationship that many reporters didn't have the opportunity to enjoy. Instead of guarding all their information and theories for fear of being scooped, Kelly and Lewis talked regularly about the funeral home murders. And even though she spent just two days in January working the story in Hudson, she proceeded to follow new developments via the Internet and her conversations with Kelly. It was during the latter that she recently suggested two poignant theories, however speculative, that Kelly couldn't resist. He stood up from the bench and headed back to his Jag. He had fifteen minutes to get to his next scheduled meeting, at which he would attempt to learn if one of Lewis's theories offered any credence.

Detective Fagley sat at his desk, reviewing files from the funeral home murders. By his count, he had gone over some of the reports more than ten times each and had yet to find that one piece of evidence investigators covet, that one clue sitting between those pages that allowed them to pin the crime on one precise individual. Fagley spent the morning since the unpleasant meeting with Walsh and Thompson looking at the case with the presumption that Father Birch did not kill Grady and Illsmere. Perhaps the police were too focused on the priest and had missed an obvious clue about someone else.

Through all their interviews and examination of evidence, Fagley and company could not find a single person, other than the priest, who they felt had the motive to kill either Grady or Illsmere. By all accounts, the victims were universally liked and admired. This led Fagley to question again whether the murders were senseless random acts, committed by a deranged individual seeking money, embalming fluid, or nothing. He feared this might be the situation, and if it was, the police had absolutely no leads.

No one wanted to be publicly demoted, but Fagley realized he and May were close to facing that humiliation. Chief Walsh made it clear that he would replace them, perhaps with someone from the out-side, if they couldn't produce a prime suspect with evidence that could lead to an arrest. The thought of being embarrassed in front of the force was one thing; the thought of Thompson taking pleasure in it was even worse. Fortunately, the vibrating of his cell phone temporarily took his mind off his morose mood.

"Hey, dickhead," yelled Kelly into his phone. "I bet you're close to solving this case."

"Never been closer," said Fagley, knowing it was anything but the truth. Then he half chucked, adding, "We should have an arrest later today if you don't interfere and fuck it up for us."

"Is that you talking or Lawrence "Don't Call Me Larry Because I'm a Dildo" Thompson blowing hot air?" Kelly wondered.

"Your intuition is much too strong. What's up?"

"Got time for a smoke?"

"Right now? Sure. I'll see you in five minutes."

CHAPTER TWENTY-EIGHT

The afternoon sun was shining through the windows at the St. Croix Cigar Company, as Kelly entered. The man behind the counter nodded and smiled, recognizing Kelly. After a quick stop at the walk-in humidor, Kelly emerged with two H. Upmann Robustos, paid for them and took a seat in his normal spot.

"Here, I'm feeling generous today. You sounded like you needed cheering up," Kelly said, as he handed Fagley one of the Upmanns. "And I know nothing cheers you up like not having to pay for something."

"That may be true, but I also know that freebies make you estatic to the point that you're almost orgasmic."

"Ah, careful, I may resemble that. What's new?"

"Walsh and Thompson called a meeting this morning for an update. They're impatient, knowing that you're snooping around, and they want this case solved. It was made clear that Walsh will replace May and me if we don't produce something quickly. You got anything that might help?"

"There you go again, asking me to do your legwork. You know, in addition to getting some of your salary, I should get part of your retirement as well."

"Yeah, yeah."

Fox News was on the large flat screen TV that filled most of the width of the wall across from the three leather chairs. Kelly noticed the television coveraged focused on Paris Hilton's return to jail, after a judge overruled the sheriff's office and ordered the million-aire heiress finish serving her sentence in a private cell and not under house arrest in her luxurious Bel Air mansion. Kelly shook his head as he considered America's fascination, led by media outlets of all types. There was a time, he reasoned, when the mention of Paris conjured up images of the Eiffel Tower, sumptuous food and wine, and French haughtiness. Now Americans were more apt to be able to recite the latest goings on in Hilton's life than they were to accurately name the U.S. Secretary of Defense.

"I'm at the stage in my investigation where I can't divulge everything, but you'll be the first to know when I have something big."

"How nice. I give you information uncensored, but it's okay for you to filter it."

The agitation in Fagley's voice was plain, and Kelly knew they might reach this moment in the case. If he revealed too much, it could compromise where his investigation was leading. If he didn't reveal enough, their friendship could be jeopardized, especially if Fagley was taken off the case.

"Remember what happened when I helped you nail the chief in St. Paul?" Kelly asked.

"What does that have to do with this case?" asked Fagley.

"Well, I was up front with you during my investigation back then that I might not be able to reveal every piece of information along the way but you would look good when it was all done," Kelly reminded the detective. "Isn't that what happened? After all, I wasn't the one who got a commendation from the mayor, was I? Trust me on this one. I won't hang you out, and you'll look better for it in the end. That's provided what I have leads to anything. I'm starting to get the sense this is an extremely complicated case."

"Is there anything you can tell me, something that could help both of us?" Fagley asked.

Kelly told Fagley about the computer screen saver he saw at Dorgan's house and suggested the cops take another look at Dorgan and his computer. He also mentioned they might be served well by exploring more of the relationship Dorgan and Black had with Father Birch through the youth group. There were clues there, he suggested, that might help connect the dots. Kelly neglected to mention the financial questions; he figured his time was best spent looking at those matters while letting Fagley and his crew handle the teen connection.

"Are you going to bring Father Birch in for another round on questioning?" Kelly asked.

"Do you think we should?"

"Yeah. I'd be curious to see if he cracks under sustained pressure. I got the feeling you were getting closer when you had him in this week. I'm pretty certain he's got more to tell."

"I'd like to think so, but I just don't know. This is the most baffling case I've had in my entire career."

"Or it could be your finest moment."

"Since when did you become an optimist?"

"Always."

"Right. I gotta run. Stay in touch."

Father Birch had been around St. Tim's long enough to recognize when Father Fred was agitated. This was one of those days. The associate pastor recognized his boss's two nervous habits, excessive eating and channel surfing, both of which were displayed prominently when the pastor was upset.

Wearing his signature full-length black cassock, Father Birch took a seat next to his boss in the rectory's den. Though the two had lived together for nearly two years, they had little in common and rarely made small talk. Most conversations centered around parish duties and, when necessary, Father Fred addressing the issue of the segment of parishioners unhappy with the young priest's antics. It seemed, however, despite the lack of fluent communication, each knew some of the other's demons they sought to keep secret, and out of that knowledge developed a mutual respect, a code of silence.

"That reporter from Channel 6 stopped by unannounced today," Father Fred said, as he grabbed another handful of chips with one hand and used his other hand to click the remote to CNN. "What do you think he's up to?"

"I'm not sure," Father Birch replied, concealing his simultaneous sense of surprise and fear. "What did he say he wanted?"

"He said he just wanted to talk, probably about the murders. I told him I had a meeting and didn't have enough time."

"Did he ask about me at all?"

"No. Why would you think that?"

"Just wondering."

It was apparent to both priests, as they sat staring at Wolf Blitzer on the television screen, that pressure was mounting against both of them. They each had issues that needed to be addressed, but both were wise enough to know that if the matters at hand weren't handled delicately, they could cause ruin for both of them.

The seal of confession in the Catholic Church is something held sacred. Priests are not able to reveal any information they hear during confession, even if that information involves a life-and-death situation. The privacy that results from a confession is similar to the relationship between an attorney and client, guided by the strictest measures of confidentiality.

In recent years, lawmakers in a number of states had attempted to pass legislation to force priests to reveal information learned during confession related to child abuse. Two states actually passed similar legislation, though it was doubtful priests would acquiesce to the law, viewing Church law as a higher authority. Well-known Catholic leaders had been outspoken against such legislation. One cardinal went as far to say he'd tell his priests to ignore the law if it passed. Comments like that only sparked more criticism that the Catholic

Church wasn't doing enough to police its own priests with regard to pedophilia.

Father Birch's views on the sacrament of confession were, like so many other aspects of his life, intense. He spoke openly from the altar about the need for everyone to confess their sins frequently, once a week if possible. It was the only way, he repeated emphatically, that people should rid themselves of the dye sin cast on their souls. He wanted parishioners to believe that to be considered a true practicing Catholic in the eyes of God, one needed to confess sins to a priest regularly. With school children, he went even further, suggesting that hell awaited those who failed to participate in the sacrament of reconciliation at least once a month. He made certain he was available to hear confessions three evenings a week.

Sean Kelly convinced Shelly Rosen to use her authority as a producer to assign an intern to a little surveillance. There was a certain individual in Hudson who's routine and schedule he wanted to know. But by now, Kelly's face was too ubiquitous to allow him to walk the streets of the small river town without being noticed and causing suspicion. He knew his attempt to corner this individual was a stretch, a notion that a chance encounter and the right questions might offer the break this case needed. Det. Fagley confirmed that police still had no new leads despite revisiting early interview subjects, so Kelly figured his attempt was at least worth a try.

It took just a few days for the intern to establish a routine for the individual Kelly wanted to meet. It was a predictable routine almost down to the minute. Armed with that information, Kelly arranged to clear his schedule in the newsroom and ventured to Hudson, timing his arrival at the parking lot of the mall arcade for three o'clock. And just as the intern noted, the subject in question arrived by car at 3:15 and headed into the arcade.

Kelly followed, entered the arcade and let his eyes adjust to the darkness. The clanging of adroit sounds on the video games filled his ears, a throwback to his teen years when Ms. PacMan ruled the world. He located the individual, who took a Red Bull from the arcade's refrigerator, paid for it and made his way to his favorite game.

"Kyle," Kelly stated just loudly enough for the teen to hear him, "I'm Sean Kelly from Ch. 6, and I would like to ask you some questions."

"Why?" asked Grady, clearly startled.

"There are just some things I'm trying to piece together, and I thought you might be able to help."

"I dunno. I'm not sure I want to talk. The cops already talked to me. I got nothing to say really."

Kelly realized he had about twenty seconds to gain some semblance of trust from the teenager or the conversation would be finished.

"How's your family? Your dad doing okay? How about you?"

Again startled, not expecting this line of questioning, Grady stared at Kelly and sized him up. He'd seen him frequently on tv and knew his dad had talked favorably about him a couple times. But now meeting him in person, there was that human factor. No longer was this someone bigger than life figure talking to him through his tv. The teenager told himself he should just leave, but there was something that made him want to stay and talk with the reporter.

"We're okay, I guess," he explained. "Still kind of shocked."

"I don't blame you. What's the support at church been like? Have Father Fred and Father Birch been helpful?"

"Father Fred's okay. You know, he's Father Fred. And Father Birch, there's really not much to say about him."

"What do you mean," asked Kelly, sensing he had hit a button.

"I just don't really care for him."

"Why not? He seems to get along okay with your friends."

"Who told you that?" asked Grady, an agitated look emanating from his mouth.

Kelly didn't say anything and just waited, hoping the teen would continue. And he did.

"Father Birch is all about power, how can he get people to share his views. And look out if you don't. He'll find a way to blackmail you. Before you know, you're his hostage."

"Does he know you, Black and Dorgan deal drugs?" Kelly inquired.

"I don't have a fuckin' idea what you're talking about," Grady protested. "Where do you get off trying to play nice guy and throw that bullshit my way?"

Though angry, Grady showed no signs of an imminent departure. Instead, he took a long sip from his can of Red Bull, looked down at the video game and used his left hand to play with the joy stick. Kelly didn't know if the drug allegations were verifiably true, but the intern, much younger and street wiser than Kelly, said his observations of Grady indicated he and his buddies were dealing something.

"You know dealing drugs is not only illegal and can put you in the clink, but it's a horrible thing to do," Kelly said, cringing a little at his pontificating. "You put people's lives in danger. I've covered too many stories where the scum get away with doing a little time; it's their clients who end up dead. You're better than that, and you should know it."

The two regarded each other for a few seconds, before Kelly launched another verbal attack.

"You know, from what I've heard, you still can't account for your exact whereabouts during the time your uncle was killed. Why is that? Were you too high and can't remember? Or is that an easy alibi for something worse? Did you kill your uncle?"

Kelly waited only for a little and then handed Grady a card, asking him to call if he wanted to talk about anything. The reporter asked him once again to use better judgement and stay away from the drug business before walking out of the arcade.

The teenager was on the brink of tears, still staring at the ground and playing with the joystick. The blackout of that afternoon and other facts he'd discovered since continued to haunt him.

Detective Fagley wasted no time paying Jim Dorgan a visit. The screen saver clue that Kelly offered would probably not amount to much, Fagley figured, but it was the only new piece of information he had, and desperation was beginning to set it. He was quick and to the point, when Dorgan answered the door. Fagley asked to see his laptop, and Dorgan obliged. If the teenager had anything to hide, he wasn't making much of an attempt nor did he appear restless or agitated.

The two sat at the dining table, and Fagley asked Dorgan some questions as he puttered with the computer. He quickly reviewed some key notes from his previous interview of Dorgan, Black, and Father Birch, hoping to find a point or two that might trip up Dorgan.

"I'm still a little confused about what you did all day the day of the funeral home murders," Fagley began. "Where did you go after you bought the bullets at Wal-Mart?"

"I thought I told you already," Dorgan answered with a sneer.

"Refresh my memory."

"I came home and played PlayStation," Dorgan said cooly.

"Why didn't you tell us initially that you bought bullets?" Fagley asked.

"I guess I just overlooked it," Dorgan insisted.

"That's no minor detail, especially since we're investigating a murder."

"I forgot. Okay?"

"Did Father Birch help you buy ammunition often?" Fagley inquired.

"No," said Doran, looking at the floor. "He *never* did."

"But you said he was with you at Wal-Mart that day."

"I never said that," Dorgan stated. "He wasn't with me."

"Who was with you then?" wondered Fagley.

"It was just some stranger I ran into in the parking lot," Dorgan suggested, again looking at the floor. "I offered him ten bucks to buy the bullets for me. I can't buy them myself. They won't let me yet."

"You had no idea who this individual was or is, someone who could corroborate your story?"

"Nope."

"That's not good for you."

Fagley found the screen saver by going into the computer's control panel. It appeared just as Kelly described. An intriguing element but nothing that could be considered hard evidence. He kept asking questions, listening to Dorgan's answers while searching the computer for any other possible incriminating evidence. Technically, this could be construed as illegal without a proper search warrant, and anything he found might then be inadmissable in court. But since Dorgan had readily turned over the computer at Fagley's request, there was some ground for the search.

"Have you talked much to Father Birch lately? How's he doing?" asked Fagley.

"We talk a couple times a week," Dorgan said. "Seems like he's a little stressed these days."

"Why's that?"

"I don't know."

"Have you had your Confirmation yet?" Fagley wondered.

"Next month."

"Are you still involved in the youth group?"

"Sure, to some extent. We meet a couple times a month to finish our preparation for Confirmation."

"How's your buddy Black doing?"

"He's fine. What are you looking for on my computer anyway?"

Fagley didn't answer. A folder caught his attention. It was labeled FATHER B. When Fagley opened it, he saw a number of different files. Some where JPEG photos, others appeared to be Word documents, and within the folder was another folder labeled EMAILS. A quick scan of the emails indicated they were organized by date. Fagley clicked on one dated the same day as the murders. The time at the top of the email indicated it was sent at 3:46 p.m.

The email read:

Jim,

I suggest you keep quiet about today's matter. No one can know. I appreciate the way you've kept quiet about the incident last summer. Please do the same here no matter who tries to get you to talk. Trust that God will take care of us and protect us from any harm.

Your Friend in Christ,

Father Birch

Fagley was stunned. He had hoped to find something like this but it shocked him nonetheless. This could be the piece of evidence police needed.

"I need to take this computer to the office to have one of our specialists look at it," Fagley informed the teenager.

"Can you do that?" wondered Dorgan.

"If you don't agree, I'll take you in for questioning, and we'll still get the computer," Fagley threatened. "Which way do you prefer?"

"I guess you can take it, but I need it back," Dorgan protested. "It has all my school work on it, and I saved a lot of money to buy it. Okay?"

"I'll get it back to you in good condition. Don't worry."

Detective Fagley wasted little time getting back to the station. En route, he phone Lieutenant May, who knew computers better than the average member of the Geek Squad. The two agreed to meet at the station in ten minutes. Still in his car, Fagley phoned Chief Walsh. Normally he would not want to involve the chief unless he was certain that progress was being made. This was different, though. Fagley knew he had found valuable information on Dorgan's laptop and suspected there might be more. In addition, he felt it was time to get a search warrant for Father Birch's computer. It was certainly possible, based on the email that Fagley had already read, that both computers could contain evidence they needed to make an arrest.

The chief was immediately concerned about the manner in which Fagley had discovered the email, but he agreed that whatever information they found on Dorgan's computer could be used since the teenager willingly let the detective take a look at it and then take it with him to the station. Fortunately, Fagley had taken the extra precaution of recording the interview with Dorgan, so there was a permanent record, thus eliminating any chance of a he said/he said defense. Chief Walsh tried to contain his excitement on the phone, though it was clear he was quite pleased with the latest development. This was a case he desperately wanted solved. He agreed to call a judge, hoping to catch one in chambers before the end of the day, and get a search warrant for the rectory at St. Tim's.

Fagley and May sat together at Fagley's desk, both making sure they followed proper procedure to avoid contaminating any potential evidence, but it was May who took control. He quickly moved through the email folder, opening each one from Father Birch. The two cops remained speechless as they read one email after another.

Jim,
I know what happened during our camping outing must seem a little embarrassing to you. But rest assured, I will make sure no one gets in trouble for anything. I want you to know how much I appreciate our friendship and how far I will go to preserve it.
Your Friend In Christ,
Father Birch
Another more recent email read:

Jim,
Thank you for the continued update on your conversations with the police. I must remind you again that there is too much information that could potentially be misunderstood,

so again I recommend you keep quiet about the matters we have discussed. I am doing my best as well to make sure no one is unjustly incriminated. I continue to trust that God will take care of us, realizing the means sometimes can be justified by the end result.
Your Friend In Christ,
Father Birch

The most recent email was dated just the day before.

Jim,
I am led to believe that people are again asking more questions and making false suggestions about what we know. The police called me in for questioning again this week, and although they rattled me, I don't think I offered any information that could harm us. I again remind you it is best to keep the matters we have discussed strictly between us. Our mission, which is what God wants us to do, cannot be compromised.
Your Friend In Christ
Father Birch

Fagley and May finished reading the most recent email and looked through some other files, like the screen saver, that were in the folder labeled Father Birch. There were a few photos presumably of members of the St. Tim's Youth Group and the young priest. Other than that, there was no other data of interest in the folder. It appeared, too, that Father Birch had taken extra time to send "fresh" emails each time he communicated with Dorgan. In other words, the priest's replies contained only the text he typed, no previous emails. Quite often, people don't take the time to erase the email to which they are replying, and, therefore, allow anyone with access to the emails a chance to view the entire history of the email conversation. Father Birch left no opportunity for police to read any such information.

May opened Outlook, the program Dorgan used to send and receive email. He quickly went to the sent folder and clicked on the name strip, which alphabetized the names to which the teenager had sent emails. Most people failed to empty certain email boxes regularly, including the SENT box. It was a convenient way to keep records of emails sent, when they were sent, and what was discussed. May looked under "Birch," "Joseph," and "Father," but could not find any reference to the priest. He went back to the emails Father Birch had sent and realized he was using the sender name "Godswill." Keying back to the SENT folder, they found no evidence of emails sent to "Godswill" either. May check the deleted folder and still couldn't find any emails with that name. It was a temporary dead end, but the significance of what they had found already wasn't lost on Fagley and May, who hadn't spoken a word since they began to go through Dorgan's computer.

"Wow, this raises a whole new series of questions," Fagley remarked. "Father Birch's definitely trying to hide something, but I'm not sure we have enough yet to pin the murders on him."

"We better hope the priest's computer offers some incriminating evidence because what we have here, at least on first glance, isn't going to fly with the DA," May observed. "It simply isn't enough. It's enough to point more suspicions at the priest but not enough to arrest him. What did the chief say about a warrant for Father Birch's computer?"

"He agreed to try to get one as soon as possible. It'd be ideal if we could get that computer before Dorgan alerts anyone to the fact that we have his laptop."

"You're not kidding. Let me know what you hear from the chief."

"Will do. In the meantime, put on your conspiracy hat and see what type of scenarios you can imagine based on the emails we just read."

Chapter Twenty-Nine

The chief was able to secure the needed search warrant and sent one of his deputies to the rectory to confiscate Father Birch's computer. Father Birch answered the door when the deputy arrived. If he was shocked at the warrant, he showed little visible concern. He simply asked the deputy to follow him to his room, unplugged his laptop and handed it over. There was no attempt at small talk. The only thing Father Birch asked was when he could expect his laptop returned. He was given no specific answer. The deputy assured the priest that special care would be taken with the laptop, and that it would be returned as soon as police were finished with it. He thanked the priest for his cooperation, left the rectory and headed back to the station.

Father Fred was in the rectory's den when the police deputy arrived with the search warrant. The pressures of recent days had given him a reason to start his evening routine earlier than normal. He was already into his second glass of Kunde Estate Merlot, when the police arrived. The den's proximity to the front door gave the pastor a good view of the encounter between the police and the young priest. He also overheard the initial discussion and then watched as the deputy left with

Father Birch's laptop. The sobs that echoed from the young priest's room only increased the tension of the complicated situation the pastor faced. He pondered his options for a few minutes, taking sips of his Merlot and trying to focus on the final few minutes of "Jeopardy." He paused at the ironic dark humor the show's title presented to his current predicament and realized he could not postpone the phone call any longer.

Father Fred pulled his cell phone from his pocket and searched through the numbers, choosing the archbishop's cell. He was instructed to use this number only in cases of extreme urgency; otherwise the proper channels of calling the archbishop's office were to be followed. Father Fred knew his boss preferred his pastors to follow a strict chain of command when attempting to discuss matters with him, and he preferred that his auxilary bishops intercept and deal with any potentially volatile situations. It wasn't that the archbishop shied away from confrontation; he just felt it was best if others handled his dirty work.

"Archbishop, this is Father Fred at St. Tim's in Hudson," began the pastor. "You know I wouldn't disturb you on this line if . . ."

"Well, now you have, so tell what you think is so urgent."

"The situation we have previously discussed seems to have taken a turn for the worse. Police were here a few minutes ago, met with the young associate and left with his laptop computer."

"Did they take him as well?"

"No."

"Then what's the problem?"

"I think you know. There is a pretty good chance police will discover the topics of at least one of our conversations on that computer and possibly they'll find information related to other matters we have discussed."

"What do you want me to do about it?"

"I think under the circumstances, it would be best for you to require the transfer we discussed."

"Indeed. If you think that'll help the situation go away, then I will make sure one of my assistants notifies the individual in question and moves ahead with the transfer. You'll receive official notification tomorrow. Good night."

"Very well. You have a good night, too."

Father Fred realized the archbishop already had hung up his cell phone. He was so rattled by the conversation that he had not noticed Father Birch standing just outside the den.

"You can have me transferred, but that won't make everything disappear," Father Birch lamented.

"We all have things we don't want made public," said Father Fred. "I just think it might be best if you were moved to a different parish at this time, and I'd suggest it would be in the best interest of all of us, if you didn't say anything to raise suspicions."

"You can't just get rid of me," Father Birch responded, sounding irate. "Your problems won't go away. I love this parish, and there are many members of this parish who love me. What are we going to tell them? I was supposed to take over for you as pastor when you retire in a few months. Now you're taking it away from me? You better hope God offers me some soothing answer to this, or I might just flip."

"I trust you are not threatening me. That would not be very wise."

"What's not wise is the way you've dealt with everything. Just remember, you can confess your sins and ask for forgiveness, but that doesn't always mean you can save your soul."

With that, Father Birch stormed out of the room and out of the rectory, slamming the side door behind him. Father Fred sat stunned in the den. He hoped his request for Father Birch's transfer was the right decision and wouldn't fuel a potentially incendiary situation. As stressful as the last few months had been on the pastor, he knew things could become much worse. He flipped the channel on the TV to the Channel 6 news, took another sip of wine and then closed his eyes in prayer, at once asking God for guidance and hoping to find a way to obtain salvation.

CHAPTER THIRTY

Investigative reporters, at least those with a good sense of news judgement, often faced a major dilemma in the pursuit of a story. There often came a time in the investigation when they had ample material for an interesting story. The challenge came when the facts did not support a firm conclusion. If reporters held stories too long while seeking additional facts to achieve a reasonable conclusion, they took the risk that some other news outlet might get the scoop and run part, or all, of the story first. However, in the rush to report the story first, without a resolution, the reporter faced the possibility of losing access to control of the story and its eventual denouement.

Kelly knew he was reaching that critical stage with his investigation. He had gathered enough information over the past days to produce a couple night's worth of reports. That much was certain. But he also knew that there still wasn't the so-called "smoking gun" to pin the murders on any one suspect.

To further complicate the situation was the subject of a call that Kelly received within the past hour from Detective Fagley, who called to inform him that they had confiscated both Dorgan's and Father Birch's computers. The detective thanked Kelly for the tip about the screen saver on Dorgan's computer and offered as thanks some specific information about the emails from Father Birch. Fagley promised to call Kelly back after he and Lieutenant May sifted through the priest's computer.

If that didn't present enough confusion, Kelly's boss, Ashbury, called that afternoon to demand that Kelly find enough information for a two-part series that could air during the May sweeps in two weeks. The brash reporter merely grunted back at his boss and said he would do his best.

A melancholic pall fell over Father Birch. He was realistic enough to know his time at St. Tim's was coming to an end. That night's scheduled meeting with the youth group could very well be his last. He had to find a way to let them know how much he cared about them and many of their parents without announcing his departure prematurely. There was always the slight chance that the archbishop's office might weigh all the evidence and reconsider the transfer.

He needed to get in touch with his friend Marcus Apple, but he didn't feel comfortable discussing matters over the phone. Instead, he went to Kinkos, logged onto his Hotmail account and composed the following:

> Marcus,
>
> I write tonight in hopes that you will keep me in your prayers. My ministry at St. Tim's might very well be coming to an end. I have reason to believe that Father Fred has requested my transfer. The police today obtained a search warrant and took my laptop. Though I have been quite careful to delete certain files and emails, there is a chance they might find something. I know I have my faults and have not always been a good example, especially over the past two months, but I can't figure out why God is allowing this to happen. My sins are not as great as others. Please believe

me no matter what you might hear in the media or from fallacious gossipers.

Your Friend in Christ,

Joseph

Lieutenant May and Detective Fagley spent the better part of three hours scouring the files on the hard drive of Father Birch's laptop. They went through every email filed in Outlook Express. They searched nearly every folder on the C drive and even ran a few searches for files containing words and names like "funeral," "murder," "guns," "Dorgan," "Grady," and "Illsmere." Nothing of any value came up. There was no record of sending or receiving emails to or from Jim Dorgan. There was not one single reference to Phillip Grady. The only hint of impropriety came through searching Internet Explorer, and finding the list of recent websites the priest had visited. Clearly the young priest did have a fondness for kiddy porn.

"I can't believe this," Fagley remarked. "This guy is good. We searched this laptop and haven't found shit, except for a couple porn sites."

"There are ways to retrieve files that have been deleted, but it's going to take some time," May said. "I need to call a friend and see if he can guide me. We're getting into an area I'm not completely sure of."

"Well, don't go erasing everything. We are supposed to return this in good shape."

"Gee, thanks for the vote of confidence."

The young associate pastor sat across the table and looked into the deep penetrating brown eyes of Kyle Grady. This, the teenager knew, was his "time" with the priest, as Father Birch made it a priority to schedule one-on-one meetings with each of the sophomores preparing for Confirmation. It was the priest's way to answer any questions and impose as much as possible his rigid Catholic dogma on the young minds. This was a meeting Grady dreaded since it was scheduled two months prior to today.

"How are you, my young friend in Christ?" asked Father Birch in the manner with which he greeted so many parishioners young and old.

"How do you think?" replied Grady, disdain emanating from entire body. In the months that followed the previous summer's youth group camping trip, Grady thought about the priest regularly in ways he thought might land him a spot in hell. He avoided Father Birch whenever possible and never made eye contact with him, if possible, when their paths crossed. Grady found the two monthly Confirmation classes torturous, a penance much too strong for the wrongs he had done. He schemed for weeks how to handle this meeting with Father Birch.

"I know this is a tough time for you," the priest acknowledged. "I want you to know I'm here to help you through it."

Grady felt his body tense, his fists clenched and his lower incisors begin to chew through his lip.

"Is there anything I can do, anything that would help your situation?" the priest continued.

Grady shook his head.

"God forgives us for our sins. Yours. Mine. Everybody's. You must remember that. We all have faults. You and I know that. And sometimes, it's best if we discuss our shortcomings with only God during Confession. Telling our friends or parents about some of our sins isn't always the right thing to do. It doesn't lead to forgiveness and sometimes only makes bad situations worse. I hope you will remember that."

Grady continued to remain silent, staring down at the floor.

"You know things about me, and I know things about you that neither of us would want to get out. So let's keep it that way. Okay? God bless you."

Father Birch made the sign of the cross in front of Grady's head and bowed his own. Grady, wondering what exactly the priest knew about him, didn't utter a word, stood up from his chair, and walked out of the room.

"Hey, hotstuff, what are you doing?"

"Just wondering why you keep stalking me."

"Consider yourself lucky. What are you doing tonight? Wanna grab some Chinese take-away and come over?"

"Oh, is that an invitation for a date?"

"No, I just don't feel like forking out the cash for a 900-number tonight and figured staring at you would be cheaper."

"I'll pick up something and be over in about an hour. The usual entrée?"

"You got it. See you soon."

There was something about Shelley Rosen that Kelly loved. It was by no means a purely sexual attraction, though there was some of that. It was the fact that he could actually converse with her on a number of different topics, work-related and otherwise. What he failed to mention to her on the phone was that he wanted her opinion on his theory. He felt he finally had enough information to tie the case together and point to a prime suspect, but he needed some feedback before he took the next step.

CHAPTER THIRTY-ONE

The St. Tim's Youth Group had gathered in the school's music room for one of its monthly Confirmation preparation classes. Jim Dorgan and Frank Black sat off to one side of the room, conversing in hushed tones. Father Birch, noting their presence, ventured over to them before calling the class to order. He, too, spoke in hushed tones, first to Dorgan.

"Jim, did the police come and see you again today?"

"Yes."

"What did they want?"

"They wanted to look at my computer. They took it with them. Can you believe that? I've got a lot of homework on that computer."

"What about the emails between us. Did you erase all of them like I instructed?"

"Some of them, but I'm not sure about all of them."

"We have to stay united on this. We can't bend when the police start putting pressure on us."

Then turning to Black, Father Birch continued. "Frank, has anyone been asking you any questions lately?"

"The police came by my house again yesterday and wanted to know more about the camping trip we took last summer."

"What did you tell them?"

"I told them nothing bad had happened."

"Do you think they know anything?"

"I think they're onto us."

"Well, same thing holds true for you as for Jim. We just have to keep our mouths shut, and everything will be okay."

Father Birch spent the next hour relishing the energy he felt from the students, as they prepared for their Confirmation. He possessed an uncanny ability to block out any personal problems and focus exclusively on doing God's work, preaching His words and influencing others. His topic tonight was respect for life.

"We hear so much in today's society about people who don't respect life. There's the pro-choice group that wants to keep abortion legal. As Catholics, you must understand that there is never a circumstance when abortion is acceptable. It's wrong, it's evil, and it's sinful. Those who support a woman's right to choose are really encouraging the murder of innocent human beings. These people have no respect for life. You cannot let the liberal media brainwash you into thinking that abortion is okay. Politicians who support the pro-choice platform should be denied the sacraments at church and voted out of office. You'll soon be old enough to vote, and I hope you carry these views with you when you go to the polls.

"The same can be said about suicide, a senseless waste of life. I pray that you never face a situation in your life when you might contemplate suicide. People who say they're depressed and suicidal are weak, choosing an easy way around their problems. God has given us too much good in life to want to take our own. People who kill themselves are afraid of facing life's challenges. They have not put their faith and trust in God or else they wouldn't feel the way they do. I pray that you never face spiritual weakness."

By the time an hour had passed, Father Birch had worked himself into a frenzy, stopping at one point to compose himself after he began crying. This was nothing new to the youth group. They had seen this behavior before from the young priest, both during youth group meetings as well as during some masses. But tonight's outburst seemed more pronounced. Something about his amplified tone, his hand gestures and eventual sobbing would have led an outsider to think he was mentally unstable. The teenagers dismissed any such notion and figured it was just Father Birch being Father Birch. With the exception of three of the students, no one knew that the young priest's display of emotion was the manifestation of his recognition of premonition that something truly cruel and out of his complete control was about to occur.

Exactly one hour after they had talked, Rosen arrived at Kelly's house with Chinese take-away in hand. She was the one person who could rival him for punctuality. It was sometimes difficult to fathom that two type-A personalities could get along so well without killing each other, but both were careful not to spend too much time with one another, a mutually respected defensive mechanism to preserve their friendship.

Already on the table were two wine glasses, and a bottle of Starling Castle German Riesling in a Sterling ice bucket. Kelly poured wine into each glass, while Rosen took a seat and began to empty rice and egg foo young onto her plate. Kelly followed by dumping his extra spicy kung pao pork onto his plate and adding some Sriracha that Rosen knew to bring along in a separate container. They saved their conversation until they were ready to eat.

"So you think you've figured it out, do you?" Rosen asked.

"I'm close," Kelly replied between bites, careful not to violate a pet peeve of his and talk while chewing his food.

He spent the next fifteen minutes in a monologue, spelling out his theory. The only interruption was to eat and take an occasional sip of the semi-sweet Riesling to cleanse his palate. He outlined the case in great detail, replete with hypothesis and speculation, but somehow it all seemed to be plausible.

He suggested that Father Birch was the killer, acting out of anger, perhaps fueled by a drunken binge and trying to protect whatever existed of his reputation. Something had occurred at the youth group's camp outing the previous summer. That much was clear, and there was strong evidence from conversations about the incident involving Father Birch, Jim Dorgan, Frank Black, and possibly Kyle Grady. The incident in question, Kelly speculated, involved either alcohol or some sort of sexual abuse or a combination of the two.

Whatever the details of the incident, fallout from it seemed to fester, and Kelly reasoned that Phillip Grady had called out Father Birch and suggested that he come clean with what occurred, go to Father Fred with all the details and incur whatever punishment might face him. Father Birch refused, and when threatened by Grady, decided to silence his detractor for good, killing Illsmere in the process because the intern was a witness to the Grady murder.

Kelly continued by suggesting that Father Birch kept Dorgan and Black silent by providing them with free skeet shooting outings and alcohol. Whether he had misused or simply stole youth group money for this was unproven, though the mere suggestion of financial impropriety was more evidence that Father Birch had some troubled spots. The three seemed to have rehearsed their stories of the murder day perfectly because none of the three had yet slipped and contradicted their own testimony or that of the others.

As Kelly poured another glass of wine for Rosen and himself, he began to outline the problems the police faced. Despite everything that Kelly had outlined, they still didn't have enough evidence to arrest Father Birch. Sure, they could arrest him and the DA could charge him, but it would be a stretch. If the matter went to trial with the current amount of evidence, any defense attorney worth a nickel would pick apart the DA's case in pre-trial hearings. Even the emails to Dorgan and proof that the priest frequented child-porn sites on the Internet were not enough to pin both murders on him. To complicate matters, Fr. Birch's name appeared on the sign-in sheet at the main office of St. Tim's school, putting him inside the school building during the time of the murders, even though it was his day off. It was apparently not uncommon for Father Birch, who enjoyed his role as a parish priest and the influence he had on the school children so much that he would often spend part of Tuesdays, his normal day off, doing some type of volunteer work at the school, often helping serve lunch, which he supposedly was doing precisely at the time the murders occurred. The lunch room coordinator, with whom Kelly had spoken briefly, said she thought Father Birch helped serve lunch that day but could not be certain. Her records were not as precise as the school's sign-in sheet.

The theory kept Rosen's attention throughout their meal. She said nothing, with the exception of nodding her thanks when Kelly refilled her glass of wine, during his entire explanation. This was rare for her, who enjoyed interrupting Kelly's stories with colorful observations of her own. Finally Kelly paused and deferred to Rosen.

"So, what do you think?" he asked.

"I think you might have nailed it."

"Well, then that'll be the first thing I've nailed in a long time," noted Kelly with his predictable self-deprecating, sex-induced humor.

"What does your buddy Fagley think of the theory?"

"I haven't shared it with him yet because I wanted your thoughts on a few other things."

"And those would be?"

"Why do women find me incredibly sexy and irresistible?" Kelly asked with a sly grin.

"Only in your dreams," said Rosen, shaking her head in disbelief or disgust or perhaps a combination.

"Well, that's true. But seriously, here's the dilemma."

Kelly then entered into another nearly ten-minute monologue, during which he outlined the challenges he faced. If he told Fagley his theory, he would offer some information that the police might not have yet uncovered. That wasn't that big of a deal to Kelly because he trusted his relationship with Fagley and knew he would do the best to honor their prior agreements about sharing information and making sure Kelly was able to air the fruits of his investigation before the rest of the media got hold of something. But there was always the chance that with Kelly's theory, police might quickly arrest Father Birch, leaving no time for Kelly to report what should be an exclusive. That issue presented another dilemma.

Should he put together two reports to run during sweeps week in May, as Ashbury requested? Did he have enough information to put the whole matter into proper perspective or was he just stringing unconnected facts and using speculation to tie them together just to fill a few minutes of air time? Was he being an irresponsible journalist? The fact that he had given so much consideration to this idea impressed Rosen, who never thought ethics would get in the way of Kelly reporting a story like this.

"Then there's the biggest dilemma of all," Kelly explained and paused waiting for a reply.

"And what would that be?" she asked.

"I don't think he did it," Kelly said without pause.

"What?" Rosen uttered, shocked by what she just heard.

"I don't think Father Birch killed those two," Kelly announced again and took a sip of his wine, watching Rosen's reaction as he did.

"But you just outlined a scenario that gives clear motive and the strong probability that the priest *did* do it," she said. "And now you're saying you *don't* think he did?"

"I outlined a theory that might work with the evidence I've uncovered through conversations with people at St. Tim's and the police," Kelly began. "But I also made clear that there are holes in that theory, primarily because of a lack of evidence."

"So what do you do now?"

"That's my predicament. I can roll with the story as I outlined, perhaps stopping short of fingering the priest directly, but certainly using the evidence to suggest he's the main suspect, even if police haven't arrested him. I could get at least two parts out of the info I have regardless of whether we get all the sources to go on camera. I've got more than enough background information and enough B-Roll to keep the viewing public's interest for two straight nights. Furthermore, I'm pretty certain it'd be an exclusive that would be picked up by other media outlets. Probably wouldn't hurt my chances for a strong negotiating stance when my current contract comes up for renewal later this year.

"The flip side, though, is my contention that the priest didn't do it," Kelly continued after some more wine. "I mean I'm first to suggest this guy's a fucking nutcase. He's some kind of conservative crackpot, and possibly a homo who enjoys kiddy porn on the Internet. That gives the Catholic Church a bad name, but does it make him a killer? No, of course not.

"I also have reason to believe there's an entirely different angle to this story, that Father Birch was tied into this angle, but was not the killer."

"And what, Holmes, does that angle suggest?"

"I just don't know yet."

"Oh, that will go over well," she said mockingly.

"Yeah, I'm sure Ashbury will be quite receptive if I refuse to do a report. I think there's a different angle that I don't really know enough about to discuss."

"I'll say this," Rosen said while laughing. "There must never be a boring moment with all those voices inside your head."

"You've got that right," Kelly said grinning in agreement. "What do you think I should do?"

"I think you need to figure it out and do what you think is right."

"Thanks, Socrates, that really fucking helps."

Detective Fagley and Lieutenant May updated the chief on their latest findings or lack thereof. The chief's frustration on their not finding more on Father Birch's computer was evident in the way he grunted, shuffled papers and finally pounded his fist on the desk.

"You guys are close," Walsh proclaimed. "Now make damn sure you find a way to get some extra evidence so we can nail this nutjob. It shouldn't be that difficult. You've been working on it for over three months. Let's give the DA something his office can work with and be done with this case. Okay?"

Walsh didn't really expect an answer and wasn't offended when both Fagley and May rose from their chairs and left the office. They had been subjected to his unreasonable requests in prior cases, but this one seemed to be dragging on too long. The two investigators held out some hope that their smoking gun might be found within the next couple days. May's computer geek friend had confirmed via phone how to access files that had been deleted. He knew what would occupy his mind for the next couple days and wasted little time rebooting the priest's computer at his desk and beginning the new search process. Fagley wished him luck and asked to be called with any updates.

Sean Kelly's Jag moved slowly through the arrivals pick-up area at the Lindberg Terminal on a sunny Thursday afternoon, the main terminal at Minneapolis-St. Paul International Airport named after Minnesota-native Charles Lindberg. It took a few calls, actually more like ten or fifteen, and some gentle persuasion, but Kelly finally convinced Becky Lewis to visit for a weekend. They were clear on ground rules. She would purchase her own ticket and, despite the extra bedrooms in his house, she preferred to stay at the St. Paul Hotel in downtown. When she emerged from the terminal, he knew he made the right decision inviting her. She was more gorgeous than he recalled.

"How are you?" she said smiling as she dropped her luggage and held out her arms.

"Much better now," he said with his trademark smile as he embraced her.

"So you're going to prove to me that Minnesota has more to offer than just cold and snow. Is that right?"

"Absolutely."

"How is the funeral home story? Anything new today?"

"Not since we last spoke the other night."

"Do you think Grady's brother could have done it?" she asked.

"Oh, it's possible, but I wouldn't bet on it. I think police are starting to reconsider that angle, though. My buddy Fagley is really feeling his boss's pressure. An election year, you know."

"Only to well coming from Chicago."

Kelly told her, unless she objected, he would give her a quick tour of different areas of St. Paul. They exited Highway 5 and drove along the River Boulevard north, passing the Ford Plant and eventually winding around the University of St. Thomas. From there, he took a left on to Cretin and before she knew it, they were pulling into a parking lot behind a small, dilapidated-looking building on University Avenue.

"This is what you dragged me here to see?"

"Of course. A literal taste of St. Paul."

They entered The Dubliner Pub through the backdoor and Kelly promptly went to the bar to order two Guinness, a test of sorts to see if Lewis could handle the Irish staple. She did and a few more, as they talked about their lives, sharing a few hints of past secrets and insights into each other's personality.

Their weekend was full of enjoyment, at least Kelly thought so. Never had he crammed so much sight-seeing, restaurant dining and running into two days. He was loathe to admit to himself, but he struggled to keep up with Lewis on their runs. Only pride kept his legs moving at her pace. He also found himself more drawn to her, which strangely seemed to bother him even though that was the reason for his invitation in the first place. These were his inner contradictions that drove him crazy.

When she left on Sunday, they agreed to try to meet in Chicago before long. As he hugged and kissed her at the airport, he sensed one of those odd moments when both individuals know they want more of each other but don't know quite how to navigate. The joys of love, he reasoned, and kissed her again.

"Bless me father for I have sinned. It has been a little more than one week since my last confession, and I need to confess something I deliberately avoided last time. I was involved in the killing of two individuals. For this, I am greatly sorry and ask God's forgiveness."

PENANCE

CHAPTER THIRTY-TWO

During what would be one of his final Sunday homilies at St. Tim's, though he had no reason to know it at the time, Father Birch was at his best. He could feel God's spirit working through him as he stood at the pulpit, scanning the faces filling pews throughout the church. He found reason once again to focus on one of his favorite topics, the need for forgiveness and the Act of Reconciliation.

"There is nothing worse," the priest began, "than a soul that does not seek forgiveness. We have all sinned; we sin too often. But we all have the chance for spiritual and religious cleansing through Penance."

He continued, becoming more dramatic with each sentence, his voice towering above the any insignificant outside noise, the congregation rapt with attention. The priest paused and surveyed the faces in the pews, finding the one he was seeking.

"No matter how heinous the sin, be it theft, an illegal act, or, God forbid, the taking of a human life," Father Birch pronounced, his tone dipping for effect and his eyes focused on Kyle Grady, "no matter how venal, you can confess your sins and be forgiven."

Father Birch knew Grady, though now looking down at his hands, got the message, and then he continued.

"Even I have sinned in ways I'm ashamed," Father Birch admitted, beginning to cry and eventually sob. After a slight pause, he continued.

"I have sought God's forgiveness, and He has given it to me. I want all of you, especially those I know need it, to spend some time going to Confession this week."

The church was silent, as Father Birch made his way back to his chair on the altar. For all his faults and all his critics, this was one of his proudest moments as a priest at St. Tim's. He felt he had been honest with the congregation and could now move forward with his life.

Others sitting in the pews didn't feel the same.

Sean Kelly took his spot in the pew three rows from the back on the right side of the church that was just a few blocks from his house in St. Paul. A regular at the 8:15 Sunday mass, he preferred the rear of the church to avoid any crowding that occurred in pews closer to the front. Nothing bothered him more than when straglers, running ten or fifteen minutes late, crowded into his pew near the back of the church, forcing him to the middle of the section and to deal with his minor bouts of clausterphobia.

Kelly was quite private when it came to his religious practices. Many at the station would never guess he attended mass every Sunday, occasionally on Saturday evenings when his schedule dictated, and found time most weekday mornings to attend mass. His language and attitude toward his fellow employees would suggest he was the devil personified instead of a practicing Catholic.

Try as he did to focus on the readings and the priest's homily, his mind routinely wandered to other subjects often related to the Catholic church. As he sat through yet another reminder that the next round of capital campaign pledges were due, he thought about the funeral home murders. All logic, especially that based on religious beliefs, suggested a Catholic priest could not be capable of murder. Other transgressions, yes, but not murder. What if , Kelly wondered, the evidence and police investigation continued to suggest the priest might have had a role in the murders? How would he handle this as a reporter? He had an ethical duty, if any derivative of the word ethic could be used in the same sentence that dealt with television news, to report the facts he uncovered. But there was a gray area, the point of a story where a reporter had to make a judgement call: what was worthy of reporting and what needed more evidence before hitting the airwaves?

Kelly hated the thought that his reports might cause more harm to the Catholic Church, already the seemingly constant target of a ruthless media. He looked around the church and wondered what fellow parishioners, some of whom he considered friends, would think if his reports began to suggest a Catholic priest was a murderer. Would he be shunned? Would his pastor ask him not to attend parish masses and receive communion in the future?

He rubbed his eyes, as he rose to recite the Profession of Faith, a foundation of Catholics' beliefs. He hoped he would be guided by its principles, as he moved forward with his reporting.

The news initially came to Father Birch via phone from the archdiocese office in Superior shortly before nine o'clock in the morning. One of Archbishop Malone's henchmen called to inform the young priest that he was being transferred to St. Joe's parish in Hurley, a small Wisconsin town about an hour east of Superior. Under the circumstances, which were not outlined in the phone conversation, the move was to take place immediately; Father Birch was expected to pack up what few belongings a priest should have, load his car and be in Hurley by Friday at the latest. The pastor of St. Joe's, Father James Clausen, had been informed of the move and welcomed a young associate to help with the overload of parish duties, the caller said. Father Birch would receive a formal written notice of his transfer via fax within the hour.

Father Birch thanked the individual for the call and hung up. The transfer was not a surprise, but the young priest had held out hope and prayed continuously in between shots of Glenlivet Single Malt the previous night that somehow he would be granted a reprieve. He thought he had adequately prepared himself for the official news, but it devastated him so much he retreated to his room, shut the door and began sobbing uncontrollably for the second time in less than a day. He tried to convince himself that the move might take him out of the police's eye and that he could move on with his life. But he knew that was improbable if he remained silent about things he knew, some of which had been learned through confidential situations.

Though feeling distraught, Father Birch managed to find the strength to spend the next three hours packing his belongings, including his hunting rifles, into his gray Buick. By two o'clock he had said good-by to the rectory's housekeeper and looked for Father Fred. He was nowhere to be found, conveniently avoiding any potential confrontation, Father Birch felt. So, the young priest wrote a short note and left it on the pastor's desk.

"May God have mercy on our souls," read the note, "and may we all find the strength to live in a way that emulates Christ."

That was it. Nothing more, no signature, just a simple sentence. And with that, Father Birch, tears in his eyes, got into his car and began the drive to Hurley.

Fueled by coffee, Lieutenant May had spent the entire night at his desk, taking only a few hours to catch a nap. His exploration of Father Birch's laptop produced many deleted files; none of particular significance to the police investigation. It was difficult to determine how many deleted files existed in a form that could be retrieved. But by his best estimation, May felt he had found more than two-thirds. There was still hope.

As he so often did, Kelly used his morning run to attempt to clear his head, focusing instead on the scenery along his route and the music that filled his earbuds. This morning Kelly opted for a seven-mile run that took him down Jefferson, along Mississippi River Boulevard, across the Ford Bridge, along the river on the Minneapolis side, back across the Lake Street/Marshall Bridge, back along Mississippi River, to Cretin, then Summit, then along Cleveland and home. If he did it well, it would take him a little less than one hour.

The music of Lone Justice's "Shelter" complemented the sounds of Kelly's feet touching the blacktop. He marveled at the beauty of the morning, how the Mississippi River looked so calm and the smell of spring filled the air. He thought about the music briefly, and then realized despite attempting to use his runs as a time to clear his head, his thoughts inevitably came back to his most pressing matters. It was at that moment he realized another possible scenario, this one much more far-fetched than the theory he'd shared with Rosen the previous evening. He also realized one possible way to handle his dilemma about what, if anything, he would report when pressed into action by his boss. Not a bad start to the day. Now only if proving his new theory and placating his boss could be accomplished so easily.

Kelly got back to house his after the forty-minute run and wasted little time contacting Becky Lewis.

"Hey, it's me," he said, foregoing small talk. "You know that theory we discussed. There might be something to it. Would you call your contacts in the cardinal's office and see what you can find about Archbishop Malone?"

"No problem," she said. "I'll give you a call when I hear something."

"Thanks." Kelly shut his phone without bothering to say good-bye. By now, Lewis expected as little.

CHAPTER THIRTY-THREE

D o we have enough to charge the priest?" the chief asked
Lieutenant May shortly after noon. "You've had almost a full
day to look through that laptop. I went to great lengths for that
warrant. We better have something to show for it."

"There's not much," May responded. "But I found a
few things."

"I'm all ears."

"I've had to go deep into the computer's virtual memory to
locate files that Father Birch deleted. I just found one folder labeled
"YOUTH GROUP," which contained many photos of the priest and kids.
There were also a few word documents that appeared to be mostly
notes for the Confirmation class. Nothing damning."

"Anything else?"

"Well, yes. Let me know what you make of this. Another folder was called "PROOF," and it contained emails that had been sent to
a man named Marcus Apple, who I think edits a conservative Catholic
website. Most of the emails are pretty innocuous, commenting on various editorial content Father Birch read on the website, but listen to
this one, which was written early this week.

Marcus,

I want you to know that regardless of the rumors you hear, it's not as bad as it sounds. I'm bounded to keep certain facts confidential, which means I might have to take the fall. I appreciate any support you can offer me on your website and through your columns. My supporters at the parish continue to support me, but the police are closing in.

Please keep me in your prayers.

Your Friend In Christ,

Father Birch

"What do you make of that?" May asked.

"I think you've found it. I think you might have him."

"We can talk to the DA, but I think we need more. There's no reference in this email or the ones we found on Dorgan's computer to the murder. The priest obviously wants something kept secret, but we have no proof it's a murder."

"I think you and Fagley better call Birch in for another round of questioning. Ask him what he's hiding, why he has that fondness for kiddy porn, why he killed those two at the funeral home."

"We don't know he did that."

"I don't give a shit. Find a way to pin it on him or I'm putting someone else on the case."

"**G**oddammit!" Kelly exclaimed. "Where in the fuck did he get that?"

Kelly slammed his fist on his desk, as Shelley Rosen stood next to his cubicle, both having just watched Ch. 8's most flamboyant reporter revealing that Hudson Police had taken a renewed interest in Kyle Grady and what he might know about his uncle's murder.

"That son of a bitch Fagley," Kelly yelled as he dialed his cell. Rosen continued to stand next to him not merely out of support but to keep others away. She knew the foolish things Kelly could do and say when he was upset at being scooped.

"Before you . . . " Fagley started to say as he answered his phone.

"Where the fuck did Light Loafers get that? Is that true? What happened to our agreement?" barked Kelly.

"Slo-o-o-w down," Fagley said. "I didn't event know it."

"Bullshit," Kelly replied failing to believe his friend.

"Listen, do you want to continue in a semi-civil manner?" Fagley asked bluntly. "If not, then this discussion is over. Okay?"

"Okay. So what do you know?"

Fagley explained that the Chief and DA suggested each detective revisit a different angle individually, making use of initial interviews and focusing on people who were quickly dismissed as possible suspects. The detective told Kelly that he took the young Grady but had not even contacted him. That fact must have been leaked by someone else in the department and for some reason, which angered Fagley beyond belief, either the source chose or Ch. 8's reporter chose to mention only one name: Kyle Grady.

"Well isn't that the shits?" Kelly said.

"You're telling me. My boss is already riding my ass."

"Hey," Kelly said. "Keep me posted. My boss is headed over to my desk right now."

"Stay here," Kelly said under his breath to Rosen. "Pretend we're looking over notes for a future story."

"I thought you had all the sources in the funeral home murder case," Jon Ashbury offered in a derogatory voice that made people, Kelly first in line among them, want to smack him in the face.

"Well, even Light Loafer gets a story every now and then," Kelly said continuing to feign studying notes on his desk.

"Let's just hope this is an aberration and doesn't reflect badly on your next contract negotiation," Ashbury opined before walking back to his office.

Kelly shook his head and remained silent for a few seconds. Then he turned to Rosen. "Let's go get a drink."

Kelly and Rosen sat in silence through the first pint of Fuller's London Pride at Brit's Pub. It took Kelly all of three sips to finish and order another.

"I'm proud of you," Rosen said.

"What the hell's that supposed to mean?"

"You could have gone off on that dickhead Ashbury, but you didn't," she explained. "That's why I'm proud of you."

Despite the crowds which were predictable for early evening, they were able to snag a table in the window; most of the patrons this time of year opted for a spot along Nicollet Mall or on the Lawn on the second floor behind the pub. Rosen marveled at what she saw when she looked across the table. Though they hadn't known each other for very long, she felt she was one of a few in the newsroom and beyond who could understand the complicated reporter. Brash as he normally was on the exterior, she saw a different side, a softer persona that sought constant approval from himself and a select group of others.

She was worried about him, though. She had seen him high strung before but never quite like this. The funeral home case and its lack of success to date coupled with an irritating boss and upcoming contract talks were all taking their toll. She knew he would never admit, but his outbursts along with long moments of brooding silence suggested otherwise.

"I can't believe he scooped me," Kelly said, finishing off his second pint.

"I suspect you're busing or cabbing it home tonight, huh?"

"Unless you want to chauffeur me," Kelly suggested.

"We'll see," Rosen said. "What's really bothering you? It can't just be the story. You're too good to let one scoop get to you like this. What is it?"

"Ah, it's nothing," Kelly demurred. "Just in a bit of a funk."

She recognized his cue, and the two drank in nearly complete silence for the next few hours, he much more than she.

Chapter Thirty-Four

Television "sweeps," as they're known, were some of the most important periods networks and local stations face. Three times each year, American households are surveyed to give an accurate representation of what the public's watching. The ratings, derived primarily from these three sweeps periods in February, May, and November, helped determine what networks and stations could charge for their advertising and what companies might be interested in buying ads. At the local level, the newscasts were most important; they're what local viewers identify with most.

Sweeps offered local stations the chance to highlight extended news features that executives hoped would lure viewers and advertisers.

Against his better judgement, Kelly had agreed to come into the newsroom for a pre-sweeps meeting with Ashbury and other staffers. They wanted to know what he had found during his recent investigation, and if that material could be turned into a sweeps piece. Pre-sweeps discussions often took on such sensational components that it was difficult to understand how some people contributing to the conversation ever got a job in the news business. Their suggestions made Jerry Springer look like Walter Cronkite.

Frustrated that he had already discussed the matter over the phone with Ashbury, Kelly was terse with his recitation of what he had discovered. Then he offered his assessment.

"Let's look at this strategically," Kelly calmly stated. "First, there's a pretty good chance that other media outlets have been sniffing around a little. I haven't seen anyone, but it always concerns me. I'm pretty convinced that my sources are not the type to call other reporters to alert them to my investigation, but you never know. So, let's keep that in mind."

Kelly then spent about five minutes outlining some of the same information he had shared with Rosen the previous night. He also mentioned his concerns about running a story too soon without the prospects of an imminent arrest. When he finished, he opened up the discussion to questions.

"Why would we not run something this good?" Ashbury asked.

"Didn't you hear a fucking single word I just said or listen to what I told you on the phone?" Kelly protested.

"I think you've got something really strong here," Watson, the assignment editor added.

"Well, you still think disco is in fashion, so that doesn't speak well to your judgement."

"Give me one good reason we shouldn't include the story in next month's sweeps package," Ashbury insisted.

Kelly paused, thought for a moment, and then spoke: "I don't think the priest offed the two at the funeral home, and I don't think we're being completely responsible if we run a story that would primarily finger him as the prime suspect."

"And why don't you think he did it?" Ashbury asked.

"I just have a hunch."

"Well, fuck your hunches. You either put together a piece for sweeps, or I'll consider you insubordinate, suspend you and file a grievance with the union. Don't think that'll go over too well when we have to renegotiate your contract."

Kelly sat silently, pissed that his boss would be so gauche and unprofessional to utter his ultimatum in the presence of co-workers in the newsroom. If there was one thing Kelly cherished, it was secrecy. There were certain things he figured people just didn't need to know, and any discussion about his future employment at the station was something he figured was best kept between him, Ashbury, and the general manager.

"I'll see what I can put together," Kelly said, as he rose and left the newsroom without another word.

"You better keep me posted," yelled Ashbury before Kelly was completely out of earshot. "We're going to start putting together promos that will begin airing in two weeks."

Kelly's phone rang shortly after he maneuvered his Jag onto I-94, heading back to Hudson, and he glanced at the caller ID before answering it.

"You know what I love most about every time you call?" he asked Becky Lewis.

"And what might that be?"

"I get to hear the opening chimes of that great college fight song, 'The Victory March,' which reminds me, as if any reminder were needed, that Notre Dame not only is the greatest university in the nation but also has the best fight song."

"Ah, is that so?" Lewis said, humoring her friend.

"What did you find?" Kelly asked.

"Some interesting tidbits," she admitted.

Lewis had called her two contacts at the Chicago cardinal's office to inquire about Archbishop Malone. Bishops generally saw each other regularly at conferences and other church functions, so it was not uncommon for some in Chicago to know about an archbishop in, say, Superior, Wisconsin. The quicker one's rise through the ranks of the Catholic Church's hierarchy, the more that was known about that individual. And such was the case with Archbishop Malone.

Lewis shared with Kelly that even though the archbishop was relatively young and had only been an archbishop for three years, his name evoked immediate recognition from Lewis' two sources in Chicago. During the course of her first phone call, her contact said that

Archbishop Malone was a mover, offering to help write various documents the United States Conference of Bishops released and, in one case, actually authoring one himself on Diocesan Financial Issues, offering detailed suggestions about how to ensure the financial strength of the entire archdiocese. The document also included examples of how the archbishop had effectively used an iron fist, when needed, to guarantee that pastors at the churches in his realm delivered their share of money.

Her second call was greeted with an awkward laugh, when she explained her reason for inquiring. This source had offered valuable information, often fairly candid, in past church-related stories Lewis had reported. The response she got to her questions about Archbishop Malone puzzled her as much as it surprised her. After the initial laugh, the source launched into a verbal tirade and suggested that the archbishop in question was nothing more than a conniving power-seeking rat, focused on little that wouldn't help his own religious ascension. For some strange reason, the source continued, Archbishop Malone was viewed favorably by many of the upper ranks of the U.S. Conference of Catholic Bishops, and particularly among the more conservative cardinals, who had Rome's ear more than most.

Lewis thanked her source and prepared to end the call, when the source said there was more. The archbishop, Lewis learned, generated laughter and, at times, scorn from many of his fellow bishops for his elegant tastes. He wore shoes from Prada, ate at the finest restaurants when on the road on church business and enjoyed the most expensive wines and cigars. Fellow bishops wondered how the archbiship managed to afford such luxuries, since there was no indication of a family fortune that he might have inherited.

"Well, isn't that fucking great?" Kelly scoffed. "No wonder why these churches are always asking for money. Seriously, I once counted, and my parish asked for money related to one campaign or another during the homily portion of mass five times in a two-month period. They're as bad as public television with its pledge drives. Although I shouldn't complain about the latter. If it weren't for pledge drives, there wouldn't be any good programming on public TV."

"Are you finished with your diatribe?" Lewis asked.

"Yes, as a matter of fact I am," Kelly stated. "What are your thoughts on these calls?"

"It seems to lend some substance to what we discussed," she said. "Now I guess it's up to you to use it appropriately."

"Well, no shit. Seriously, thanks. I appreciate the help."

"Always here for you," she offered.

"I can only dream," Kelly said and hung up.

Fagley called Lieutenant May with the shocking news about Father Birch's transfer and agreed to reconvene at the police station within the hour. He then called Kelly's cell, hoping the two could combine their conspiratorial mind and make sense out of this latest development.

"Are you sitting down?" Fagley asked.

"I'm driving out to your lovely town as we speak, so I guess technically I'm sitting."

"Guess what? I just stopped by the St. Tim's rectory to ask Father Birch to come in for another round of questioning and was told he was transferred to a parish in Hurley. He packed up and left this morning."

"You gotta be fucking kidding me. What the hell is that about?"

"I don't know, but I think it warrants a quick cigar."

"It calls for a cigar and a bottle of wine."

"I'm on duty. I can't drink."

"And that's stopped you in the past?"

"Funny. Can you be at the cigar shop in twenty?"

"I'll see you then."

The unpleasant task of updating the chief on Father Birch's departure fell to Lieutenant May. Not surprisingly Walsh was less than pleased, and those who heard his colored response would argue that was stating it mildly.

"This is too much," the chief screamed. "How could you guys let him get away? This is unbelievable."

May stood silent in the chief's office, knowing that any attempt to answer the question was pointless.

"What do you suggest we do now?" demanded the chief. "How the hell am I going to explain this to the DA and the mayor? 'My guys were closing in on an arrest, but suddenly our prime suspect bolts town.' All right, keep working on the computer, but, effective immediately, I'm assigning someone else to the case. We need a new perspective. Let Fagley know."

May left the chief's office without a word, feeling more angry than upset at being taken off the case. He understood Walsh was taking the action to attempt to save face with the DA and the mayor, but it bothered May nonetheless.

"Guess what?" Fagley asked, as Kelly took a seat in one of the leather chairs at the St. Croix Cigar Company.

"Now what? The priest had second thoughts and came back to town?" Kelly remarked sarcastically as he lit a Romeo y Julieta Corona.

"May just called. The chief took the two of us off the case effective immediately."

"Oh, great. Now you're turning into the Beverly Hills Police Department. Looks good for the department's image. You might need to start drinking after all."

"You're telling me. Why do you think this guy split? Do you think he felt we were getting too close and requested a transfer?"

"Perhaps."

"Well, if not that. What else?"

"Did you ever consider he might know something someone *else* doesn't want him sharing with you?"

"And they saw to it that he was transferred?"

"A long shot, but maybe."

"You still don't think he did it, do you?"

"I have serious doubts. And the fact that I've found more evidence, however circumstantial, that indicates he didn't do it than you and your cohorts have found to pin the murders on him tells me you guys either suck at what you do or that someone else did it."

"But who?"

Kelly just shook his head and took another puff of his cigar.

Figuring he needed to decompress a little, Kelly sat on his favorite chaise lounge chair poolside at the University Club at the far corner away from as many people as possible. It's not that the other people in the pool area bothered, but instead a way for him to feel like he could survey the entire area from one vantage point. He knew he was close to breaking open the entire case, and he realized its ramifications. During breakfast that morning with Father Truth, he was reminded by his friend that priests are humans, too, not without their own faults. And some priests, Father Truth explained, have greater faults than others. But that alone, Father Truth pronounced sternly, does not make someone a killer.

Under the afternoon sun, Kelly checked his voice mail at work and, convinced that the Twin Cities were still functioning sanely without his oversight from the newsroom, went back to his book, *Windy City* by Scott Simon, an enlightening fictional tale about Chicago politics. Kelly found it difficult to concentrate, spending more time dwelling on how much he missed Becky Lewis. They kept talking about when they would next meet but couldn't quite find a mutually acceptable time. He didn't like that. Closing his book, Kelly walked over to the deep end, jumped in and began doing some laps. The cool water provided little relief from his inner turmoil.

CHAPTER THIRTY-FIVE

S ean Kelly loved Chicago. It made him feel alive. So vibrant, so diverse, so complex in different ways. He'd been coming to the city to visit for years, first while visiting relatives on his mother's side of the family who lived just across the border in Indiana and later he made many trips on the South Shore Railroad while attending Notre Dame. This visit brought added excitement and anticipation. Kelly found it difficult to concentrate on the copy of the *Sun Times* in his hands. Instead he stared out of the window of the El's Orange Line that was taking him to the Loop, where he planned to meet Becky Lewis.

Theirs was now a bona fide complicated relationship, nothing new for Kelly. They had both agreed they had feelings for each other but didn't know exactly how to proceed. Just the thought of spending time with Lewis, looking into her eyes and hearing her voice, brought out the hopeless romantic in the brash reporter, chipping away at his metalic exterior.

They spent the weekend taking in the best Chicago offers. The Billy Goat Tavern on the street below the Tribune Tower, the bike path that runs from Irving Park Road on the north all the way to Hyde Park on the south and, of course, the right field bleachers at Wrigley. On Saturday night over dinner in Wrigleyville not far from Lewis' Lake Shore Drive condo, their conversation turned contemplative.

"You're Catholic," Kelly began. "Do you think the Catholic Church gets fair treatment in the media?"

"And what in that Murphy-Goode Merlot caused you to think about that?" Lewis wondered.

"Well, naturally, it's the full fruit flavors, slight tannins and lasting finish. Seriously, what do you think?"

"I think the church gets what it deserves most the time. The funeral home story is still troubling you, isn't it?"

"What part? The part that I can't solve or the part that if I do solve it, there are a couple church goers that might not look too good."

Lewis chewed on her pot sticker, thinking about what Kelly just said and then replied.

"You can only do what you think is right. Somehow in the short period of time I've known you, I realize that you'll think this one through thoroughly before rushing to air with whatever you find. Am I right?"

"I hope so. I do."

The weekend was great, though they parted still not knowing how they wanted to proceed with their relationship. Kelly thought he knew but wasn't sure if Lewis shared the same attitudes. He did manage to get Lewis to agree to a bet on the fall's upcoming Notre Dame-Boston College game, phrasing the language of the wager in a manner that seemed to guarantee him victory, and maybe her, too, regardless of the outcome.

CHAPTER THIRTY-SIX

The next three weeks were full of stress for everyone associated with the case of the funeral home murders. Detective Fagley and Lieutenant May faced the embarrassment of being taken off the case. They went through the computers they had confiscated, eventually returning Dorgan's personally, and reviewed their notes with Detective Dick Scallen, who had been assigned the case. They shared their files and theories with Scallen, and then wished him good luck. There were no hard feelings, since it was exclusively the chief's decision to put someone new on the case.

Scallen made three trips in two weeks to Hurley to interview Father Birch and return his laptop to him as well. On all three occasions, Scallen was assisted by at least one member of the Hurley Police Department, not so much to help with questioning but to serve as an additional witness to the interviews and run the video camera used to tape the interviews. Scallen sensed that the priest was ready to confess something during each of the three interviews. On one occasion, the young priest began sobbing uncontrollably, blabbering something about how he was so misunderstood by his critics and missed his "flock" at St. Tim's. During the second interrogation, it appeared to Scallen that Father Birch was more ill at ease than during any of the prior interviews he had viewed or conducted himself. It was almost as though the priest was on some type of drugs, unable to sit still, pacing the room and talking quickly, almost incoherently at times. The third interview found a completely morose Father Birch, seeming defeated and ready to concede like a prize fighter who had been smacked against the ropes one round too many.

But try as he did, Detective Scallen was never able to elicit a confession from Father Birch. Nor was there any suggestion that he was hiding information that could lead police to the killer, as one of his emails to Marcus Apple indicated. There was a moment in the third interview when the priest sounded contrite for things that had occurred over the past two years, but when pressed for specifics, he just shook his head and said nothing.

Scallen reviewed other possible suspects and theories with Fagley and May to no avail. They just couldn't find anything that pointed to another suspect. In the weeks that followed Father Birch's transfer, Scallen interviewed Father Fred, Jim Dorgan, and Frank Black. Using past transcripts as a guide, the detective pried for anything fresh or a contradiction. He found none. Father Fred said the transfer was normal, even though it came unexpectedly to many of Father Birch's supporters. The pastor said there are sometimes needs at other churches that require a quick transfer, and this was one of those situations.

Kelly was kept updated on the investigation through regular phone calls from Fagley. Against his better judgement, he put together a two-part report for sweeps. The only on-camera interview he was able to secure came from Chief Walsh, never wanting to miss a media opportunity, even when it questioned the competence of his office. Kelly's requests to interview Father Fred, Robert Grady, Archbishop Malone, and Father Birch were all politely declined. Arguments over the scripts and focus of the two-part report were heated, as Ashbury wanted as much drama as possible. Kelly persevered through literally days of vocal dissension and put together a report that outlined the myriad of new developments in the case, including emails and suggestions of Father Birch's rift with parishioners. There was also mention of the police discovery that the priest had surfed kiddy porn on the Internet.

During the second part of the report, Kelly took liberties to offer his own assessment of the case, wrapping his opinion with facts. He was clear to point out that police had considered Father Birch the prime suspect for the last month but had not yet found strong enough evidence that indicated the priest was guilty of the murders. The report also mentioned the priest's abrupt transfer and how it raised speculation.

"Father Birch was a polarizing figure during his short stint at St. Tim's," Kelly reported, sitting on the set with the blow-combs. "His critics point to strange behavior patterns, possibly including alcohol and members of the Youth Group, as evidence that he is guilty of the funeral home killings. And while he may have occasionally frequented child pornographic sites on the Internet, no one has provided any hardcore evidence linking the priest to the murders. Emails the police discovered from Father Birch to others raised more questions than they answered, and depending on the interpretation, could suggest that Father Birch is, for whatever reason, keeping private information he might have about the real killer.

"Candice," said Kelly as he turned on-camera to his least favorite anchor sitting next to him, "the fact is everyone involved in this case wants to find the killer. But whether that killer currently resides in Hurley, Wisconsin, remains questionable, if not doubtful."

"Thanks, Sean. Great report," Candice said with pause, realizing that what Kelly had said on the set was not the same as what came across the TelePrompter. This confused her greatly.

Kelly departed the studio and made his way to his desk, where he was greeted by a boisterous voice booming across the newsroom.

"Kelly, where the fuck do you get off changing the script and editorializing like you did at the end of that report?" yelled Ashbury, showing bravado he often used to mask his insecurity. "We agreed on the script, and you changed it. What the fuck is your problem?"

Kelly, at first, did not respond and focused on picking up some items off this desk. "I think it was a pretty fair summation, and I know

I can sleep tonight," Kelly calmly replied in stride, as he made his way out of the newsroom. Ashbury's continued yammerings followed, but Kelly paid no attention.

The ratings for Thursday and Friday, the nights Kelly's reports aired, were the highest the station had enjoyed in more than a decade, easily placing Channel 6 back in first place not just for the ten o'clock news but for its early newscasts as well, which utilized time to shamelessly promote and review some of what Kelly reported.

CHAPTER THIRTY-SEVEN

The body of Father Joseph Birch was found hanging inside the gym locker room at St. Joe's school in Hurley, Wisconsin, shortly before 7:30 on Friday morning, October 21. Fortunately, it was a school janitor and not a student who found the priest. His body was cold and his face blue. On the ground beneath his body was an envelope.

The janitor recovered quickly from the shock of finding a body hanging, grabbed a chair and carefully undid the belt looped around the priest's neck. He gradually lowered the priest's body to the ground and checked for a pulse. Not surprisingly, there was none. The janitor then pulled his cell phone from his pocket and dialed 911.

"Nine one one Emergency, how can I help you?" asked a lady at the other end of the phone.

"I'm calling from the gym at St. Joe's grade school," explained the janitor with a slight tremor in his voice. "There's a dead body in the boy's locker room. Please send someone immediately."

The police arrived within eight minutes of the janitor's phone call and began casing the scene. One officer took the janitor into the gym, where he peppered him with questions.

"When did you find the body?" the officer asked.

"I think it was just before 7:30," answered the janitor, his voice still wavering. "That's when I usually make my rounds through the locker rooms to make sure they're clean for the day ahead."

"Can you describe how you found the body, what position it was in?"

"Sure," the janitor began. "It was hanging from the big pipe that runs across the ceiling of the lockerroom, right above the benches. He looked dead. His face was blue, and when I touched his arm, it was pretty cool, maybe even cold."

"Did you call 911 immediately or yell for assistance?" the officer inquired.

"No," the janitor admitted. "I still wasn't completely sure he was dead, so I hopped onto the bench and carefully undid his belt from around his neck and lowered him to the ground. There was no pulse, so then I called 911."

"Did you see anyone unusual around the school this morning?"

"Not that I can remember."

"Did you touch anything else other than the body?"

"Not deliberately, but I might have," admitted the janitor.

The officer thought the janitor appeared uncomfortable answering the questions. He understood why, but knew there were standard procedures to cover. The officer paused, looked around the gym and attempted to gather his thoughts. After a quick glance at his notepad, he resumed questioning, hoping he didn't forget to ask any important questions. It was, after all, the first murder case this young officer had ever worked, and he didn't want to botch anything.

"Was there anything else out of the ordinary? Did you scan the room?"

"I can't recall anything unusual."

"What about a note?" the officer asked.

"I just found this envelope, but I haven't opened it," the janitor explained.

"Okay. Do you mind waiting here for a few minutes in case anyone else has other questions?"

"No problem."

Sam Davidson, the Hurley Police Chief arrived at the school around 7:50. This was a small town, and it wasn't every day a body was found hanging in a Catholic school gym locker room. Consequently, the chief was notified immediately, and he instructed his officers—there were only two others on duty—to make sure they wore gloves and didn't disturb any evidence. He also asked them to call the state police and sheriff's department right away. Some of Davidson's counterparts might have found this method excessive for what appeared to be a suicide. But unlike other police chiefs who sometimes let their egos muddy a crime investigation, Davidson took a pragmatic approach in a different direction. He felt the best way to avoid making any big mistakes in a potentially volatile situation was to bring in outside assistance from the start. Then if things got messed up, more than just his department would have to answer critics. If things went well, the chief and his department could relish in the credit.

By the time the chief arrived on scene, one of his assistants, Officer Jenny Brandt, had already begun to photograph the scene and made a tentative identification of the victim. She was a St. Joe's parishioner and regular Sunday church goer. She recognized the dead male, who was wearing traditional black cleric's garb, as Father Birch, the young associate pastor who had joined the parish around May. She found the morning's discovery particularly disturbing, since she was part of a group of parishioners that had been fond of the young priest.

Not until representatives from all departments arrived and surveyed the scene did the chief suggest they inspect the envelope, presumably thought to be a suicide note. While the county medical examiner took additional photos and inspected the body for any signs of struggle or attack, talking into a small digital voice recorder as he did so. Then the body was lifted onto a gurney, the chief saw the envelope beneath it, scooped it up and walked outside the locker room into the gym. There, with other law enforcement officers surrounding him, he opened the envelope, pulled out the piece of paper inside, held it in

front of him so others could see it as well and began reading the letter
to himself.

> My Dearest Friends,
> I am deeply saddened to be writing this letter today, but the
> events of the past year have left me with no other option. It
> is no secret that I have been a prime suspect in the funeral
> home murders and hounded by police for months.
> Throughout that time, I have struggled with alcohol abuse,
> forms of depression and other inner demons. The battle to
> overcome these has become too much for me to handle. I
> cannot continue. Please forgive me and, when you think of
> me, don't feel sad but instead carry on the great words and
> deeds of Christ that we have shared together.
> With You In Christ,
> Father Joseph Birch

"Seems pretty straight forward," the chief said. "A simple suicide note. What do the rest of you think?"

By then the medical examiner had joined the group in the
gym. He was the first to speak. "On cursory exam, I see no visible
signs of struggle, at least nothing to indicate he was murdered," he
explained. "So, at least initially, I would agree with you, Chief."

The others in the group concurred, and the chief said he'd
contact the police in Hudson.

Suicide was never a cause for celebration. But that day, there was joy
on the faces of the members of the Hudson Police Department, a sense
of relief. Father Birch's suicide note had validated the laborious, and
often frustrating months of investigation. People like Detective Fagley
and Lieutenant May knew they had failed to produce enough evidence
to arrest the priest, but they felt his suicide and note gave credence to
their focus on him as a prime suspect, thus exonerating them and the

entire department from public criticism concerning how they had handled the investigation.

Chief Walsh spent more than an hour on the phone with his counterpart in Hurley, going over details of the scene the school janitor first discovered that morning. The two men both wanted to insure that this matter was put to rest with the young priest's death. They didn't want to leave a shred of doubt that Father Birch did indeed kill Phillip Grady and Charles Illsmere at the funeral home on that cold January day. They didn't want their respective departments subjected to an endless questions from would-be conspiracy thrill seekers

At 8:37 that morning, Kelly phoned the Channel 6 newsroom with details of Father Birch's suicide. True to his word, Detective Fagley had phoned Kelly at home as news of the priest's demise was still spreading through the Hudson police station. The reporter dictated a three-line story the newsroom could put as a scroll on the bottom of the screen during the "CBS Morning News" and update its website. He then quickly coordinated getting his favorite photographer, Cindy Benson, and took off for Wisconsin, spending the better part of the morning and early afternoon in Hurley, using Shelley Rosen and another photographer as reenforcement to get reaction from the citizens of Hudson and parishioners at St. Tim's.

Word of Father Birch's suicide fell like a brick on the already-divided St. Tim's parish. Those who loved and were inspired by the young priest during his short stay at the church were visibly devastated, stopping by the church to pray in groups throughout the day. The extemporaneous vigils represented an outpouring of grief that far surpassed what had occurred months earlier for Phillip Grady. Meantime, for the families of the funeral home victims, there was a sense of closure to the case that had wrecked havoc on their lives, a chance to finally move on with rebuilding their families with the knowledge of the killer's identity.

At St. Tim's rectory, Father Fred, whose retirement had been postponed after Father Birch's abrupt transfer, sat at his desk in his office when his cell phone rang. Picking up the phone off the desk, Father Fred looked at the incoming number and answered.

"Hello?"

"It seems like this situation is finally over," Archbishop Malone pronounced sternly. "We can all go on with our regular lives and not worry any more about any of his skeletons going public."

"I suppose we can," suggested Father Fred.

"I appreciate all your cooperation during these difficult past few months," the archbishop acknowledged, both knowing full well how the archbishop's reputation remained intact.

Realizing the caller had already hung up at the other end, Father Fred gently flipped shut his phone and placed it on his desk. It had been a tumultuous year, but now everything seemed to be resolved. It was time for the parish and its pastor to move forward and put this situation behind them.

CHAPTER THIRTY-EIGHT

The sun shone through the beautiful stained glass windows on the eastern side of the church, as Sean Kelly sat for the first reading. His regular Sunday custom - awake around seven, listen to WCCO-Radio news, brew some coffee, skim the Sunday papers, shower and head to church - landed him in his favorite pew, three rows from the back. He long hoped to get a chance to play his trumpet at the 8:15 mass someday, but had yet to convince any of the parish's musical geniuses to give him a try-out.

Kelly looked at the colorful artwork displayed in the windows, much of which depicted Jesus Christ. The reporter wondered how the media would treat Christ if he were alive today in an age of electronic newsgathering devoid of any form of human compassion. Not too well, Kelly thought.

He often thought the Catholic church was treated unfairly by the media both locally and nationally. To be fair, the issue of sexual abuse by priests, when it finally came to light, was too important a story to ignore. But that seemed to be almost the only aspect of the Catholic church that received any media attention. It bothered Kelly that rarely, if ever, were the social issues that Church supported and the charity it provided the poor in the news.

He was appalled recently when the media appeared to rally against Mary Jo Copeland, the founder and leader of Sharing and

Caring Hands, a Minneapolis shelter for the homeless. A modern day saint in the eyes of many, including Kelly, Copeland often was greeted with scorn from the media and other members of society when she wanted to expand her shelter or create an orphanage in, god forbid, the suburbs. Imagine how that upset the NIMBY (Not In My Backyard) types. When Ch. 6 and other outlets reported that Copeland's shelter was a haven for drug dealers, Kelly protested to his boss and other producers, saying the reporter on the story was not telling the full story. How convenient, Kelly suggested, that the critics of Copeland spoke out loudly as Opening Day for the Twins' 2010 season neared. It just so happens that the new stadium is located across the street from the shelter.

Yet here was Kelly, engrossed in potentially the biggest story of his career, and he was unsure how to balance his competitive journalistic nature with his Catholic faith and personal desire that the church get a fairer shake in the media.

The associate pastor took a break from financial matters and discussed the need for love and forgiveness. Father Truth, as Kelly nicknamed his friend as a pun on his real name and for his penchant to speak uncensored opinions however upsettting, stressed the need to overlook people's flaws and instead focus on what they do well. At that point only, Father Truth stated, can we begin to lead better Christian lives following in the footsteps of Christ.

Three days after word of Father Birch's suicide circulated throughout Hudson, envelopes with no return address arrived in three different mail boxes in Hudson, those belonging to the families of Kyle Grady, Jim Dorgan and Frank Black. The postmark read Superior, because Father Birch ensured he mailed one envelope containing the letters all with correct postage to the postmaster in Superior along with a short note asking the postmaster stick the envelopes into the mail system.

Dear Boys,

My friends in Christ. I'm fairly certain that by the time
you read this letter, I will no longer be with you in the flesh
but will always be with you in spirit. The last year has been
trying and stressful for all of us. It's at these times we need
the Lord's guidance and support more than ever.

We all know what happened on different occasions over
the past year. We all have our reasons for what route we
chose. We have all made mistakes. But the Lord Jesus
Christ forgives. I ask for your forgiveness and ask that you
each seek God's forgiveness for what you've done. Let us
pray that nobody ever uncovers the real truth.

Your Friend in Christ,
Father Birch

The fact that the letter began by only saying "Dear Boys" worried
Grady. He didn't know who else received a copy. He figured Dorgan and
Black received a copy but wasn't even certain of that. The post-high para-
noia encompassed the teenager. What if someone other than the three
boys received this letter? How might it implicate him and the others?
What could he do to quash any potential problem? He just didn't know.

"Is this Sean Kelly from Ch. 6?" the caller asked.

"Yes," Kelly said, habitually grabbing a pen and legal pad on
his desk to take notes.

"Do you know who this is?"

"I think I have a pretty good idea."

"Well, you said I could call if I ever wanted to talk. So here I
am, I guess."

"What's on your mind?" Kelly asked.

"I think Father Birch got a bad rap. I don't think he did it. He wasn't perfect, but I don't think he did it."

Kelly listened and took notes, doing his best to make sure his handwriting was somewhat legible.

"I know everyone wants to blame him and thinks he did it," the caller continued. "But there's so much more to the story. I'm not even certain of everything."

"What else do you know?" Kelly wondered.

"There were people at St. Tim's who didn't like Father Birch, and they would do anything to get rid of him. When people started talking about the Youth Group camping outing, what might have happened with him and us, that gave them a way to start putting pressure on him. And then there was something about money."

"How do you know anything about the money issue?"

"I heard people talk. Nothing concrete. Just rumor. They said he took some from the Youth Group and used it on himself. I don't know if it's true."

"What made you decide to call today?"

"It's just too much. There's so much happening I can't keep it all straight. Don't know who to believe, who to trust. Do you think he was the killer? Maybe I shouldn't be bothered at all."

Kelly considered the question, taken back by the caller's state of mind.

"I'm not sure what to think," Kelly answered, trying to be as diplomatic as possible.

"I think there are still a couple people who need to answer where they were the day of the killings."

"Like who?"

"I gotta go."

Before Kelly could get out another question, the line went dead. The conversation, if believable, raised new suspicions. Like his arcade conversation with Kyle Grady, the information was tenuous and not something Kelly would use in a story without corroboration. It did, however, rekindle a theory he'd held for the past few weeks, and he knew right where to go to try to confirm it.

Forty miles east in Hudson, Jim Dorgan sat by himself wringing his hands and pacing through his house. He wrestled with his decision for more than a week, ever since the letter from Father Birch arrived. Today, he acted on his plan and called the reporter from Ch. 6. He hoped he had made the right decision.

"Bless me Father for I have sinned. It's been a little more than a week since my last confession. Here are my sins. At times, I am selfish and manipulative, using people to get what I want. I have not always dealt well with challenging moments in the past week, sometimes resorting to unkind words and actions but they were always well intentioned for the betterment of everyone. For these and all my sins, I am truly sorry.

CHAPTER THIRTY-NINE

Kelly sat with Shelley Rosen at an outdoor table at Fat Lorenzo's, a popular neighborhood pizza and pasta restaurant in south Minneapolis. They enjoyed the beautiful sunny autumnal afternoon, perhaps one of the last ones before winter, along with a bottle of Louis Jadot Mercury, an excellent red Burgundy. Kelly insisted they both take cabs, so they could drink as much as they wanted and sort through any final theories surrounding the funeral home murders. A so-called John Doe hearing was scheduled to begin in St. Croix County Court the following week, during which a judge would hear evidence supporting the thesis that Father Birch was the killer. After all the evidence was presented, the judge would offer his opinion and presumably the case would finally be closed less than a year after it began.

"You still don't believe the priest did it, do you?" Rosen asked in between bites of her pepperoni pizza.

"Perhaps, but the few angles I had left to pursue are drying up real quickly," said Kelly, sounding disappointed that he was unable to prove his theories and was now nearly content to accept that Father Birch had been the killer all along.

"Like your love life, huh?" Rosen said, smirking.

"Hey, listen, bitch, you've obviously been around me too much. My wonderful jaded sense of humor is rubbing off on you,"

Kelly said, struggling to contain his laughter. "Which is fine; just don't use it on me."

"Oh, poor baby. Have another sip of wine, and you'll feel better."

The two were interrupted momentarily by the noise of a Northwest Airlines 737 coming in for landing at the airport, which was only a few miles away.

"You know, I'm easily fascinated. How do they get those birds to stay in the air?" Kelly said.

"I don't know, Mr. Boeing, how do they?" Rosen wondered.

"What do you think? I shared my theories with you on this case. You think there's anything left?" asked Kelly.

"Normally, I respect your logic, your inimitable intuition and your ability to pursue stories most other people don't even realize exist," admitted Rosen. "But I have to say in all honesty, this time I think you're high, been smoking too much doob or something."

"Don't I wish."

"Seriously, this hearing next week is going to show a preponderance of evidence against Father Birch. It's a going to be a blow-out, kind of like the last five USC wins over your beloved Irish."

"See, there you go again," Kelly stated with sarcasm. "You never would have had the *chutzpah* to address me like that when you arrived at the station last year as a young grad looking for a master's footsteps to emulate. Now you're just another smartass with hot tits. Next thing you know, you'll be getting paid hundreds of thousands to read the news and smile."

Three bottles of wine later, the two friends wobbled to their respective taxis and headed home.

The phone was ringing when Kelly walked into his house. He grabbed the remote, flipped on the TV and picked up the phone, realizing as he did that he was not in the best shape to carry out any semblance of a coherent conversation, which, of course, would not be a first for a man who once made drinking and dialing a late night sport.

"Hello," Kelly said.

"It's been awhile, so I thought I'd give you a call."

It had been some time since the caller last phoned, but Kelly recognized the female voice immediately.

"How have you been?" asked the caller.

"Not bad. And you?" Kelly replied.

"I'm good, but I'm anxious to see how much information is revealed in the John Doe hearing next week," she replied.

"Do you expect any surprises?" the reporter asked.

"No, not from the hearing."

"What do you mean by that?" he inquired

"You never did report much on the money trail, did you?" the caller asked, reminding Kelly of some of her earlier tips.

"No, I suppose not," he admitted. "Was I at least on the right track from what you could gather from my reports?"

"Nope, not at all," she replied firmly.

"Then where should I look and what am I going to find there anyway?"

"I think you've been on the right path before, you just didn't find the answers," she advised.

"The answers to what?" he asked.

"It's complicated."

"No shit."

"Oh, a little touchy this afternoon, eh?" she said, chiding Kelly.

"Tell me this. Did Father Birch kill those two people?" Kelly asked in a voice that almost demanded a straight-forward answer.

"I couldn't say for sure," she admitted.

"Do you think he did?"

"What do you think?"

"I think you're either certifiably crazy or you know something you want me to find and make public."

Kelly began taking notes on the conversation, something he normally didn't do when his secret source called. But today, with all the wine he'd consumed, he was still coherent enough to realize he should write down some notes lest his alcohol-sodden brain play memory tricks on him, as it had been known to do during past benders.

"You got your money's worth out of the Notre Dame education. I will say that."

"Well, I got my parent's money's worth," he admitted and then ventured back to the main topic. "If, hypothetically, you know something that's so important to this case, why did you wait so long to call again?"

"Oh, I really didn't figure it would play out like it did over the last month," she assured him. "And with the John Doe hearing next week, I figure certain people might feel a little more relaxed knowing the hearing will pretty much convince the public the young priest did it."

"And?"

"Come on, Wood-stein, you're smarter than that. You'll figure it out."

With that, the caller hung up. Kelly felt his source sounded disappointed that he hadn't done a better job researching her tips. Then he shook his head and wondered if she was just some psycho having fun at his expense. Whichever the case, her call was once again enough to renew his interest in the case, just when he thought his obsessions were finished.

CHAPTER FORTY

The John Doe hearing began as scheduled on October 10, and took just four days. St. Croix County District Attorney Lawrence Thompson reveled in the spotlight of the media, finally getting his chance bring this case to court, or at least the next closest thing to it.

The hearing, included testimony from Detective Fagley and Lieutenant May, who talked at length about their interviews with Father Birch and the subsequent search of his computer, offered the introduction of two substantial pieces of evidence. They also questioned his whereabouts on the day of the murder and why he was able to provide the precise number of bottles of embalming fluid that were missing, which police said pointed to specific knowledge of the crime scene that had not been made public.

Police discussed the fact that the funeral home secretary Shirley Hennan remembered seeing a car that resembled Father Birch's gray Buick, as she returned to work after lunch on the day she discovered the bodies. Police said this fit the classic description of a killer, who often likes to revisit the scene of the crime to witness the reaction.

Luther Carson, the deacon at St. Joe's in Hurley, testified that on the days leading up to his death, Father Birch talked extensively about the past year, sometimes appearing distraught if not intoxicated, and at one point told the deacon, "They know what I did. They're going to get me." This was taken to be an admission of guilt to killing Grady and Illsmore, though the deacon noted that Father Birch never mentioned the words "killing," "murder," or any specific names.

St. Tim's parishioners testified that Father Birch, on more than one occasion was accused of supplying alcohol to minors and attempting to sexually abuse them. This occurred, according to testimony, on more than one occasion and with different individuals. Those testifying said they brought the matter to Father Fred's attention but heard nothing beyond that, so it was unclear whether any investigation took place after the initial reports. Father Fred was not called to testify at the John Doe hearing.

In the end, the judge acknowledged that the evidence presented was largely circumstantial. But on a scale of one to ten with ten being the strongest, it was his opinion that Father Birch's guilt in the killings was a ten, one that left no reasonable doubt after the confluence of testimony.

With the ruling, Hudson Police considered the case closed.

Chapter Forty-One

St. Paul's Rice Park basked in the noon sunshine, offering the illusion that it was a pleasant enough day to spend some time outdoors, and many St. Paul workers took a moment to enjoy what was perhaps the last tinge of autumn. Rice Park, a signature of downtown St. Paul, was surrounded by history. On the north side stood the Landmark Center, a former court building used for office space and private gatherings. It was also depicted in the Disney movie *Mighty Ducks*. On the west side of the park sat the Ordway Performing Arts Center, named after one of 3M's founders and home to the St. Paul Chamber Orchestra as well as many broadway musicals. The park's east side bordered the St. Paul Hotel and its restaurant, the St. Paul Grill, one of the best places to eat in downtown St. Paul. And on the south side of the park stood St. Paul's main public library, recently restored and as grand as ever. Rice Park also included a statue of St. Paul-native F. Scott Fitzgerald on one end, and just across Minnesota Street at the other end of the park, a statue of Herb Brooks, the coach who led the 1980 Olympic Hockey Team to its Miracle on Ice.

Kelly felt electric whenever he walked through the tiny park, but this day he was more enthused in anticipation of what faced him. The person he expected to meet, someone he had never seen before in person, phoned him early that morning, sounding somewhat harried, and requested a meeting. It was the caller's suggestion that they meet in Rice Park, hoping to blend into the noontime crowd. As instructed, Kelly walked diagonally through the park starting in the northeast corner. His stride, as usual, was one of purpose, his black shoes clicking against the cement sidewalk, and the double vents of his Savile Row blue pinstripe suit coat flapping in the slight breeze. As he neared the other side of the park, Kelly recognized the Notre Dame baseball cap the caller said he would be wearing and took a seat next to him on the bench.

"Thanks for coming," Tim Leeland said, eyes darting back and forth to see if anyone recognized them.

"No problem," said Kelly. "What can I do for you?"

"If I seemed rude the first time we spoke on the phone, I apologize," noted the accountant.

"No worries."

"I was caught off guard when you started asking questions about St. Tim's and just didn't feel comfortable talking about anything related to the church," Leeland explained, continuing to survey the park to see if he recognized anyone who might potentially recognize him. "I meant it when I said that was part of my past; I belong to a different parish now."

"I understand," Kelly said, nodding and observing Leeland's nervous body language, behaviors that Kelly often saw in sources just before they were ready to offer some prime info.

"So, you're probably wondering why I asked you to meet," Leeland said. Leeland's voice was measured, his sentences halting as if he was still not certain whether this meeting was a good idea. He continued to fiddle with his wedding ring, as he scoured the park one more time. Convinced no one was paying attention to them, he picked up the conversation. "I can't comment on specifics dealing with our clients," he said clearly, making sure Kelly knew he was not about to commit any ethical violations. "You understand that, don't you?"

"Certainly, and I respect that."

"Did you ever see the movie *Class Action* with Gene Hackman?" the accountant asked.

"One of my favorites," said Kelly with a smile.

"You remember the scene in which his daughter, who's opposing counsel, realizes something was deliberately kept from Hackman and finds a way not only to alert him to the missing evidence but also helps him find a different witness?"

"Sure."

"Well, let's just say this conversation might follow that MO, at least vaguely," Leeland said.

"Okay, I'm still listening."

Leeland explained that he really had no intention of sharing the information he was about to divulge, but he was wrought with guilt following Father Birch's apparent suicide. He wasn't particularly fond of the priest, he admitted, but felt sorry for him, speculating that he was more a victim of certain circumstances.

"You've covered your fair share of murders, I assume," Leeland continued. "What do you think leads someone to pull the trigger?"

"I suppose robbery, retribution, money," Kelly surmised.

"Or silencing a potential enemy?"

"That's basically what the judge in the John Doe hearing ruled."

"That's right," Leeland said and then continued. "What do you know about accounting practices?"

"A little and not enough," Kelly admitted. "My dad was a CPA, but I had to drop Intro to Accounting my sophomore year at ND because I was flunking. Apparently keeping inventory of my beer supply was not enough for a passing grade."

"Well, then, you may or may not know that audits are performed to make sure there's an accounting for all the money that goes into and out of a business. When there's a discrepancy of less than, shall we say one percent of the total amount, it's usually written off as no big deal. But when there's a difference that exceeds one percent, the auditors tend to get concerned. But you must remember, that the auditors can only present the facts and make recommendations on how to fix any discernable problems; we cannot make any final decisions, and it's not our job to make public our findings, which can present a moral quandary. Following me?"

"Sure."

"So if an audit turns up a so-called red flag, the auditor will then present the total report and highlight what's wrong. Generally more than one person sits in on the presentation, but the owner or CEO is almost always present and aware of the audit's outcome. The responsibility to correct any problem then falls on the CEO or whomever else might be part of the presentation, usually a CFO or finance chair or someone in a similar capacity."

Kelly's mind was racing with questions and conspiracy theories, but he was afraid to ask for fear it would silence Leeland. Instead, he just looked at the person sitting next to him on the bench and nodded his head every so often.

"I don't know for certain who murdered Phillip Grady and his intern," Leeland stated bluntly and then paused again, wondering how he should phrase what he wanted to say. "But I can tell you this: there were two people from St. Tim's in the room when we presented the results of the 2006 audit, and Father Birch was not one of them."

Kelly nodded and started to ask a question, when Leeland stood, put a finger to his mouth to indicate quiet and smiled. "What do you make of ND's chance this weekend against USC?" Leeland wondered.

"You'd like to think it's our year, but the Trojans are loaded," said Kelly.

"Go Irish!!" said Leeland, as he walked away.

"Yeah, Go Irish!" Kelly mumbled, fully aware that he was just given some very intriguing information that still left open a myriad of holes in his investigation.

Kelly's feet felt like they were floating slightly above the ground, as he ran on the grassy boulevard that divides the east and west lanes of

Summit Avenue. The trees on the boulevard shaded some of the noon-time sun, a welcome sight after a number of cloudy days. It was a rare moment of inner peace.

Kelly's mind shifted, as it normally did while running, to the funeral home murders and the Grady family. How were they dealing with the aftermath of the tragic killings and the police's inability to find enough evidence to charge a suspect? He wondered, too, if his reports, keeping the murders in the public's mind, were having a detrimental effect on the family's ability to heal their grief.

As he waited for the light to turn green at Snelling, Kelly thought about Kyle Grady, the victim's nephew. Something wasn't right with him. Kelly knew police had interviewed the entire family, including Kyle, on at least two different occasions, more for some family members. But according to Fagley, police found nothing to indicate any family member knew anything about a potential suspect. Still something bothered the reporter about Grady. Kelly knew from his meeting with Grady that there was reason to suspect he had some more information to offer. The fact that Dorgan and Black essentially worked for him as drug runners added to that suspicion. It was quite possible, Kelly felt, that Kyle knew something about the killer but was being blackmailed, so to speak, into silence. Who would have such powerful information to silence a young kid when his uncle's killer was still on the loose?

Kelly wound his way down Cleveland and then up a side street to his house. He unlocked his front door and peaked inside for a glimpse at the clock on his cuiro cabinet. Despite feeling good throughout the run, he was three minutes over his targeted time. And just like that, his mood reverted to a pallor of inner gloom in which nothing is ever quite up to his strict standards.

Archbishop Malone was not unlike his counterparts across the country. He enjoyed the status and power his position offered, and not unlike anyone with so much at his disposal, the archbishop went to great lengths to insure nothing disrupted his life. He demanded absolute loyalty from his pastors, imposing demands upon them that many other bishops nationwide would consider atrocious. But he got what he wanted, using past examples to strike fear into would-be critics. It was widely known throughout the archdiocese that the archbishop could make a pastor's life miserable if he did not fulfill all of the archbishop's requests or chose to question those edicts. It wasn't uncommon for the archbishop to threaten, some would even say blackmail, priests he felt weren't performing their duties to his expectations. Two pastors had actually lost their parishes and were relegated to lowly assignments within the archdiocese for purportedly having the audacity to question their boss's authority.

When it came to St. Tim's and the Father Birch "situation," as the archbishop referred to it, he was even more vehement in his desire to make sure certain facts stayed "in the church." Following the priest's suicide, the archdiocese took a proactive approach to addressing the situation as thoroughly as possible, issuing its own question-and-answer doctrine, which appeared in the diocesan newspaper and on its website before being picked up by other media outlets.

The statement addressed concerns over whether Father Birch was required to submit to a psychological evaluation (yes, and it was determined that he was "problem free" and "appeared healthy"), whether the seminary required evaluations of Father Birch (yes, and it concluded he was a proper candidate), when allegations of Father Birch's sexual misconduct were first brought to the attention of the archdiocese (2005, shortly after his arrival at St. Tim's), whether there was contact between the archdiocese and alleged victim (archdiocese claimed the St. Croix DA never responded to requests for the youth's identity). The Q&A also discussed if the archdiocese ever thought Father Birch could be capable of killing someone (no, there was no indication), if it held back any information (no, the entire diocesan file on Father Birch was turned over to the DA prior to the John Doe hearing) and the archbishop's reaction (appalled and apologetic, taking all responsibility).

Though intended to quell any existing and potential future criticism, the Q&A disturbed, in one way or another, almost anyone who followed the case or had some connection to St. Tim's. The anti-Father Birch faction at St. Tim's again voiced its concern to Father Fred and the media that more should have been made public about the sexual allegations and that a priest with a record like Father Birch's should never have been allowed to serve in a parish. Others felt the archbishop was merely trying to save face. They were infuriated by the archbishop's response, going public with a statement after everything had occurred, appearing to feign ignorance of the entire "situation" while it was taking place and then asking people to forgive in much the same way the archbishop said the Lord would forgive.

Since the release of the statement, Kelly had read it at least ten times, each time trying to find a different motive to dissect. He didn't care for Archbishop Malone, who appeared too smooth, almost slick, for Kelly's liking. There was something suspect in the way the archbishop seemed to conveniently ignore Father Birch's alleged sexual misconduct. Or there was the possibility that the archbishop was using the information to further a different cause.

One person Kelly had not yet interviewed was Marcus Apple, Father Birch's friend who wrote about the fallen priest frequently on his website. Recent postings were filled with comments from Father Birch's supporters, using the Internet as a public forum to share their grief and express their condolences to the priest's other followers. Some even used the site to lob harsh accusations at the anti-Father Birch camp, blaming them for creating pressures that led to his suicide. Kelly read the postings daily, hoping for the rare chance that he might find something substantive.

Apple didn't list a phone number on his site, a practice that was quite common in today's cyberspace-dominated world. Many people found the Internet a convenient excuse never to talk to people. If it weren't for cell phones, voice-to-voice communication might be lost forever. Rarely would Kelly email someone he didn't know, but he could not seem to track down any other contact information, so he fired off a simple email to Apple, asking if the two could meet for coffee to discuss Father Birch, tie up some loose ends.

The reply was prompt and terse. Apple said he didn't meet with other reporters to talk about his friend. Period.

Staring at his computer screen, wondering whether pursuing a meeting with Apple was even worth the effort, Kelly shot back one more salvo, promising himself it would be the last.

Marcus,

I understand your reluctance to discuss Father Birch with anyone other than your close friends and those who visit your website. But I've received information recently that suggests Father Birch might not have been the killer after all. I'm going to follow up on this, and it would be helpful to be able to speak with you. Without assistance from someone like you, there's no chance Father Birch's name will ever be cleared, if, in fact, it should be.

Please let me know what might fit your schedule for a short meeting.

Regards,

Sean Kelly

The "Victory March" ring tones chimed almost immediately after Kelly sent the email. The caller's number was blocked.

"Hello," Kelly said.

"Is this Sean Kelly?" asked a male voice.

"Yes, who's this?" the reporter asked.

"I think you know," said the caller with anger welling in his voice. "What makes you think you can keep probing into Father Birch's life? Hasn't he been through enough? What sort of new information do you have and what makes you think I have anything to add?"

"Okay, slow down," Kelly said calmly and then asked: "Am I right to infer this is Marcus Apple?"

"Yes," Apple admited.

"I'd just like to sit down and talk with you a little about Father Birch, some of the things he might have discussed with you and compare notes with what I've found."

Kelly, who's personality could be so brash with most, could somehow gently persuade people to talk with him, even if they were previously predisposed to telling him where he could go. Apple agreed to meet the following morning at Dunn Brothers Coffee on Grand Avenue in St. Paul.

Marcus Apple looked just like his photo on his website. Clean cut, black hair, a dark complexion, and slightly chubby. Kelly waved to him from one of the tables that was slightly elevated on what amounted to a large window ledge. Apple got himself a skim latte and sat down.

"Thanks for taking time to meet," Kelly said respectfully. "Did Father Birch ever mention anything to you about financial problems?"

"What do you mean?" Apple asked, obviously surprised either by the lack of small talk or the frankness of the questioning.

"Did he ever complain about not having enough money to enjoy himself as a priest, support his hobbies?" Kelly wondered.

"No."

"Did he ever speak of financial problems within the parish? Did he think it was run well? It is a business, after all."

"Why do you ask that?" Apple inquired, now visibly surprised by the subject of questioning Kelly had prompted.

"I'm just curious."

"Now that you mention it, I remember he said something late last year or in early January, something about someone wanting to blame him for missing money," Apple recalled in between sips of his latte. "Let me think. He said he knew who took the money but couldn't say anything because he was afraid he'd then get reprimanded for something else he'd done."

"Was he more specific, or do you know what he was referring to?" Kelly asked.

"Now that you mention the issue of missing money, I remember exactly what he said. He said, 'If I blow the whistle on the person taking the money, they're going to nail me. They've already threatened me.'"

"Did he say who 'they' was?"

"No."

"If you think of anything else that might be helpful, please give me a call or drop me an email. Thanks for your help."

"No problem."

Taking their normal spot in the oak-paneled main dining room of the University Club, the eastern sun shining through the windows on what promised to be another beautful fall day, Sean Kelly and the man he affectionately referred to as Father Truth sat in momentary silence. The priest knew his friend was wired more tightly than normal with big decisions facing him.

"What's bothering you?" the priest inquired.

"Where do you want me to start?" asked Kelly, pausing only to take a gulp of his black coffee before continuing. "The John Doe findings would make it easy to walk away from this case. My boss wants me to, figuring I have nothing more to report and am just wasting company time."

"So why don't you?"

"Come on, you don't take the John Doe judgement at face value, do you?"

"Sometimes," Father Truth began in a deliberate tone, "it's best if we have faith in what cannot be logically or irrefutably explained. It's faith after all."

"So you're saying I should walk away. Enough harm has been done already."

"You just said that, not I."

Kelly surveyed the room, ostensibly looking at the other tables, where businessmen were gathered presumably working through the initial concepts or details of the next big deal. However his mind was really where it had been for months, on the case and how his reporting might affect people and the church he loved.

"If there's a cover-up of some type, it needs to be exposed," Kelly opined.

"But you must make sure you have all the facts straight before you make any allegations," Father Truth cautioned.

"Here's what troubles me," Kelly continued. "Father Birch seems to represent, if even a fraction of what's been alleged is true, some of the gravest contradictions within the church."

Father Truth considered Kelly for a moment and took a sip of his orange juice.

"On one hand, he most likely was gay or acted occasionally on homosexual tendencies, the latter of which is clearly against church teaching, and that fact that it might have involved teenagers is deplorable. And there seems to be enough evidence that it was covered up by church officials on more than one occasion, something I think as despicable as the offensive action itself."

Father Truth just started at the reporter, wondering where he was headed next.

"Then, on the other hand, this same priest was a neo-conservative, scary to a point, wanting, among other things, to deny holy communion to politicians where were publicly pro-choice. I think the church is headed backwards here. You're pro-life. Would you deny communion to an elected official who's pro-choice?"

"No," said Father Truth. "How am I to know they didn't change their view and go to confession right before mass?"

"And look at the recent outrage against the diocese when it cracked down on gay pride celebrations at St. Joan of Arc in Minneapolis. I know the archbishop can't condone certain groups and actions, but these are loving individuals who want to practice the Catholic faith and be part of the church. Shouldn't they be embraced like everyone else? Lord knows we all have our own sins."

"I think you need to cut back on the caffeine," Father Truth said with a big smile on his face, though it was clear to Kelly his spiritual mentor was less-than-pleased with the diatribe. "I think you need to pray some more and give serious thought to what impact any future reports on this matter might have on everyone involved. That's my advice."

The two finished their breakfast in near silence, a rarity, and as he departed the U Club, Kelly felt his prayers for guidance had just been answered.

CHAPTER FORTY-TWO

T wo weeks later, as he sat at Chicago's Midway Airport on the Sunday following the Notre Dame-Boston College game, Kelly thumbed through the Chicago *Sun Times*. He preferred the tabloid format and edgy editorial of the *Sun Times* to its more polished rival the Chicago *Tribune*, which was less a city publication than a worldly daily. He read and reread the game stories and analysis that summarized Notre Dame's 55 to 10 victory over a team from the school that seemingly owned the Irish for more than ten years. It still pained Notre Dame fans to think of the 1993 BC upset, which cost the Irish the national title. The program had not been the same since. Domers could take solace in knowing that Boston College was full of students who had been turned down by Notre Dame. In fact, one of Kelly's close friends once remarked to someone at a tailgater in the parking lot prior to a BC-ND game in Boston that BC English students' first assignment was to explain in 100 or fewer words how they dealt with not getting into Notre Dame.

He had called Lewis immediately after the game on Saturday to make sure she shared his excitement. A terse reply and a click indicated she was not in a festive mood and didn't care to talk.

After boarding the flight and looking for any distraught BC fans he could torment with his ugly green blazer replete with an ND crest patch on the front pocket, Kelly took his seat and sifted through the rest of the paper, reading first Robert Feder's media column and moving back toward the front of the paper from there. A story on page fourteen caught his eye. It reported that a priest in a northern Chicago suburb, a much-loved pastor for more than ten years, was forced to resign after allegations of swindling money from the parish were proven. The priest, court documents indicated, had absconded with more than $15,000 a year for a ten-year period. Parishioners, it was reported, became suspicious when someone questioned the pastor's lavish life-style that included first-class trips to Europe, a luxury car, expensive and innumerable trips to the local salon for pedicures and manicures, not something often associated with a parish pastor. All of these perks could not have been possible on a priest's salary or without an inheritance, which the pastor did not have, without the support of the parish coffers, though court records indicated the pastor was shrewd enough to avoid keeping records of such splurges.

The Northwest Airlines 737 took off shortly after nine, heading first east over White Sox Park, otherwise known as The Cell, and then turned north to fly along Chicago's shoreline. Kelly marveled at what a fascinating city lay below, made even more beautiful by the sun gleaning off the sky scrapers and the waters of Lake Michigan. He couldn't stop thinking about the story he just read. How could someone get away with stealing money in that amount for so long? Then it hit him. However far-fetched, he had found the missing link that nearly completed the theory he first formulated while running along Mississippi River Boulevard shortly before his two-part sweeps story aired. Now he just needed proof.

The congregation at St. Tim's received a special guest that Sunday in the form of Archbishop Malone. He felt the timing would be good, since the diocese just released its statement on the Father Birch situation recently. He was wise enough to know that the parish needed healing, since it was still not only a parish divided but also in the healing process. The archbishop intuitively realized that proper attention could go a long way in healing the wounds that still prominently existed. The sooner the parish mended, he reasoned, the less chance he would have to address any more unpleasant history.

He addressed the parish during the homily portion of each mass, attempting to appear as solemn as possible. The truth was he couldn't wait until his morning ended and he could be back on the road to Superior. The parish and its troubles had produced enough stress to last a lifetime. He figured now it was time for damage control to ensure nothing and no one at St. Tim's could stand in the way of any future promotion. He figured it would be simple enough to get through his homily, a malaise of feel-good banter coupled with some excerpts from the Bible on forgiveness. He didn't anticipate the hostility he later faced while greeting the congregation at the rear of the church after mass. The two early masses produced little dissent, but the ten o'clock mass, the one which Father Birch normally said, was packed with people, all of whom seemed to have words they wanted to share with the archbishop. Father Fred, who concelebrated each mass and introduced the archbishop, stood off to the side and watched as pro-Father Birch forces and anti-Birch factions alternated their comments as they exited the church.

"How could you say publicly that Father Birch was a murderer, when you know nothing of the situation?" asked one lady.

"You let a child molester continue to work with children in this parish. You should be ashamed of yourself," said another.

"I'm writing the Vatican about you. You'll never get another promotion after they read the real truth," threatened a third.

"How would you ever let Father Birch serve in this parish knowing about what happened to him at the seminary? And then you try to wash your hands clean of it?" proclaimed a fourth, and that was just the start of the onslaught.

The archbishop did all he could to keep his phony smile going, as he shook hands and nodded, as if agreeing with everything his critics said. He had no intention of responding, finding most of the verbal assaults somewhat innocuous, if not just plan bothersome. But one comment gave him pause and momentarily wiped the perma-grin off his face.

"Judas was sullied by his greed for money. Archbishop, I know that this church is no different."

When he and Father Fred finally made their way back to the sacristy to take off their robes, the archbishop cornered Father Fred, taking care to make sure no one could hear what he was about to say. "I thought you told me everything was under control," he said, clearly looking for someone to blame.

"It is to the best of my knowledge," Father Fred replied tersely, not appearing as he wanted to play any of the archbishop's games.

"Then why such rancor outside the church today? Are you not capable of calming your own parishioners?" asked the archbishop.

"If you hadn't noticed, they've been through a lot and are still quite emotional about it."

"Well, that's what concerns me," the archbishop said with a cold tone to his voice. "Emotional people sometimes do irrational things. Don't let that happen. We've worked hard to take care of everything, and I want it to stay that way."

Father Fred didn't bother replying. The mere presence of the archbishop made him uncomfortable, and he took some solace in the fact that for once someone else had to field the anger of his parishioners. He knew he had followed the archbishop's orders, and in doing so, he, too, had thought the situation would turn out better.

Sunday's eleven o'clock mass was packed, just one of many reasons Kelly tried to avoid it. His travel schedule this weekend, however, offered few alternatives. He took a seat in the back of the church behind the opaque plexiglass that theoretically serves as a sound barrier for crying babies. From this vantage point, Kelly could not get a clear view of the altar. Symbolic, Kelly thought, of the current state of his own life, one lacking clarity.

He sensed a denoument to the funeral home murder case was nearing, and he had a strong feeling at least one of his theories would come to fruition, putting him again in a delicate situation. From a professional standpoint, this story had Emmy written all over it. There would be a price, though. Kelly knew if any of this theories played out, his reports could have a devastating impact on a few individuals.

Was it worth it? Did he have a choice on what and how to report? This was a dilemma he had never faced in his career, and he felt the stress taking its toll. His co-workers found him slightly edgier than usual but thought little of it, writing it off to his normal disposition.

BENEDICTION

Chapter Forty-Three

Putting together the final pieces in an investigative report could become the most exhausting process. There were the facts, but there was also a good amount of speculation, which somehow had to be confirmed. If a reporter asked the wrong question of the wrong person, any logical resolution to the report could end quickly. Kelly had the benefit of experience, and as he liked to phrase it, the ability to learn from previous alleged mistakes. He had spent the entire flight from Chicago formulating how he was going to attempt to find the last shreds of information he needed and in what order he was going to talk to people he felt could confirm his suspicions.

His first call went to Marcus Apple, who he still believed had some valuable information he had not shared at the coffee shop. Apple sounded surprised to hear from the reporter on a Sunday but agreed to meet within the hour at the same Dunn Brothers.

With no time to waste, Kelly jumped right to his point when Apple sat down with his latte.

"I don't think Father Birch killed those two people, but I need your help proving it," Kelly said. "You've had a few days to think about our conversation, which I presume you did, and I'd like to know if you thought of anything that might be useful."

Kelly had been right. Apple spent the better part of three days since they're last meeting contemplating whether sharing some of Father Birch's intimate emails would be a violation of their friendship and whether Kelly would treat the information well.

"Father Birch was pretty distraught during the final weeks of his life," Apple began, speaking softly with a deliberate and measured manner. "There were times his phone calls to me were filled with emotional pain. Usually the calls came late at night, and he sounded as if he'd been drinking. He said he didn't know what he should do, who he could talk to. There was one call, in particular, that stands out. In it, he talked about the sacrament of Reconciliation, how he found it so ironic that he would preach the need for people to attend penance but it was through the sacrament that he learned the killer's identity."

Apple stopped talking, and he seemd unsure if he should proceed.

"Let me get this straight," Kelly interjected. "He told you who the killer was."

"Not exactly," Apple admitted. "He said it was not a face-to-face confession, but he recognized the person's voice."

Now it was Kelly's turn to take a sip of his coffee, a decaf because it was past noon, and process what he just heard. If true, it confirmed his long-held positions. But also felt this group of religious fanatics, and Apple was one of their leaders, wouldn't hesitate to convince themselves of some facts that could exonerate Father Birch.

"And he confessed to the murders?" Kelly persisted.

"Yes, apparently."

"Did he name the person?" the reporter wondered.

"No."

"Did he offer any clues to whom the killer might be?"

"Not really."

"Do you believe him . . . because there's plenty of evidence that suggests he was the killer?" Kelly asked, trying to cast doubt on the entire tale.

"I don't know," Apple admitted. "He was a good friend, and friends usually don't lie to each other. But, like I said, he was an emotional wreck those final days of his life, and that's when he finally told me."

Apple took another sip of his latte and then explained that Father Birch wrestled with how to handle the information. He knew the Seal of Confession technically barred him from taking that information to anyone, but he also knew that the police were intent on blaming him for the murders.

"You mentioned last time we met that Father Birch told you someone had threatened him," Kelly said. "And he said that kept him from mentioning anything about the missing money. It was blackmail of sorts. Do you recall anything else related to this?"

Apple sat silent for some time, debating what he should say. Then he said, "This is a tough one because again I'm not sure how much was said or written while he was under the influence of alcohol. He once said he felt sorry for his friends in the Youth Group. He didn't mention names, but I suspect he was referring to the kids. He once said he felt guilty about getting them involved in the whole complicated mess and wished the camping trip never happened."

The Packers game on Fox was just coming back from the two-minute warning when Detective Fagley's phone rang. He took one look at the phone number and shook his head in dismay before answering it.

"Are you aware the Packers are down by three and driving with two minutes left?" Fagley asked the caller. "And you have the nerve to call me right now?"

"Trust me," Kelly said, "if I gave a shit about you or the Packers I wouldn't be calling. You can watch the game while we talk. I think even you are capable of doing two things at once, as difficult as you might find it."

"You're such an ass. What's up?" Fagley asked.

"I've got some new leads on the funeral home murder case," Kelly informed the detective.

"Have you been drinking heavily again?"

"Listen, asshole, I'm serious."

Kelly spent the next five minutes outlining his case to Fagley and suggesting how he wanted to proceed. Since there were potential legal issues involved, he wanted to make sure the detective was apprised and got his feedback on how best to proceed. The discussion was momentarily interrupted by Fagley's loud outburst.

"Oh, shit! You piece of shit, Favre. Why didn't you quit last year when you should've?"

"Another interception? There's a shock," Kelly said mockingly.

"Fuck you."

The two agreed that it was best that Kelly proceed however he saw fit, and if he turned up any new information, then he would pass it along to the police.

CHAPTER FORTY-FOUR

Knowing she would enjoy being part of the action, Kelly phoned Rosen early Monday morning to update her on his latest theories and how he was going to try to get some people to talk on camera today. Did she want to come along? Sure, she said. Normally he preferred to operate alone, but he figured Rosen might add a calming effect to the interview requests. The reality, Kelly realized, was that he had little more than conjecture for his theory. To confirm his speculation, he needed at least one and probably two individuals to speak with him. If they did it on camera, that would be even better.

This was one part of his job Kelly really despised. He knew the tactics he had to employ to confront these two individuals, and he understood the high likelihood neither would be willing to talk openly with him. He spent the better part of his morning run trying to devise just the right questions and wording to provoke the needed responses. The reality is that the style of reporting, shock journalism as he sometimes called it, was dirty, something one might expect to see from Geraldo Rivera. Yet the end results often reaped some common good.

Kelly strutted through the newsroom with purpose and anticipation
of the exhilarating day that lay ahead. Always aware of potential gold-
en moments on camera and that today's reporting might bring some of
those, he had chosen one of his favorite gray pinstripe suits, loud
enough to convey a distinct sense of style with the right amount of
class. A light blue checkered shirt with French cuffs and a loud pink
tie with light blue stripes completed the fashion statement.

"Hey, Watson," Kelly barked across the newsroom to the
assignment editor. "I need Benson all day, and I need her now."

"Sorry, but I don't recall assigning anything to you," Watson
replied sarcastically.

"Listen. I'm on to something big, so don't fuck it up by pulling
this power bitch act on me. I don't have the time or patience for it."

"I'm not just going to assign a photog to you and let the two of
you go joyriding," Watson said. "You have to at least tell me what
you're up to."

"First, let me remind you of your short memory that last time
you and Ashnuts accused me of taking time off. I produced the best
reports and highest ratings this station has seen in years," Kelly stated. "So just get me Benson, and I'll be on my way."

"Tell me what you're up to," Watson demanded.

"I'm up to about ten on my pissed-off scale."

The bickering continued unabated for a few more minutes
before Watson, against her better judgement, summoned Benson and
told her of the assignment. Kelly promised to keep Watson informed
of his progress. He had yet to tell her what he was up to.

Benson, Kelly, and Rosen sat in silence for the first fifteen minutes
of the car ride to Hudson before Kelly finally spoke. He reviewed their
agenda for the day and how they would pursue the interview subjects.
The first round of interviews was prearranged. Kelly had already
placed a call early that morning and scheduled the meeting, making

clear his intentions to film the interviews. That would be the easiest part of the day.

It was just after 9:30, when the news van pulled into the parking lot at the Grady Funeral Home. Robert Grady was initially reluctant to meet and even more apprehensive about doing an on-camera interview. He considered the issue of the murders settled and, like the rest of his family, was attempting to put the bad memories behind them and move on with their lives as best as possible. He told Kelly that doing an on-camera interview could be bad for the entire family. But when Kelly explained the reason for the interview request, Grady was persuaded.

Benson quickly set up her equipment in Grady's office, fit both him and Kelly with wireless microphones, did a test run and nodded that she was ready whenever they were. The interview covered different topics related to Grady's deceased brother, including the contentious relationship he had with Father Birch.

"You mentioned once when we spoke that your brother had a heated discussion with someone on the day prior to his death and that he threatened to go the archdiocese with information," Kelly began. "Do you know who he was talking to?"

"It was Father Birch."

"Do you know this for sure?" Kelly asked. "I mean did you ever hear him address the caller by name or make mention of it afterward."

"Now that you mention it, I guess I never did hear a name mentioned though he did say 'Father' at least once, and Phillip didn't discuss the phone call afterward," Grady admitted.

"So presumably it could have been a priest other than Father Birch on the phone?"

"I suppose you're right."

Benson got some cutaway shots of Kelly nodding his head after the conversation concluded and then moved her equipment to a conference room, where Shirley Hennan had agreed to be interviewed. She talked about what she saw the day of the murders, including the gray Buick she noticed parked down the block from the funeral home when she returned from lunch.

"Did you find anything unique about the Buick?" Kelly asked.

"Well, for one, cars don't usually park on that part of the street, so it caught my eye," Hennan explained, appearing calm as the questioning began. "And the person in the driver's seat appeared to be wearing a priest's collar."

"Did you see anyone else in the car?" Kelly asked.

"Yes, there was a young man, who looked like a high school student, in the passenger seat."

The next four hours were sheer torture for Kelly and the two women with him. Never one known for his patience, he clicked his pen incessantly, paced outside the van and occasionally sang, much to the dismay of Benson and Rosen. Their next interview wasn't scheduled until three. In reality, it wasn't even scheduled but instead was going to be an interview on the fly with the element of surprise worked in for good measure. The crew discussed exactly how they would handle it. They decided that Kelly would hold a boom mic, Benson would use her main camera to shoot the interview, and Rosen would make sure no one got tangled in the mic's cord.

To pass the time, Kelly placed a call to Lewis in Chicago. After promising not to gloat too much about Notre Dame's win over her alma mater, he offered a little insight into what he was doing, telling her he would call if anything broke. She wished him luck.

Kelly felt a sense of foreboding during the four-hour wait. If the next interview and the one that followed produced the material he thought it would, his story would be sensational. But he knew it would come at a price. When he did other investigative reports, the subjects exposed, quite literally in the case of St. Paul's police chief, generally were scumbags and deserved their fate. The people involved in this case were different.

At just a little after 2:30, Kelly placed a call to Detective Fagley. An early morning phone call to Marcus Apple confirmed what Kelly suspected, and, as a result, he suggested Fagley meet them at the site of their next interview. That way if something that carried any legal substance were discussed, the detective could act on it immediately.

The news van pulled into Jim Dorgan's driveway shortly after three o'clock, hoping the teenager had already returned from school. The beat- up Ford F150 in front of the garage indicated their instincts were correct. Fagley's Malibu pulled in behind the news van. There were no pleasantries exchanged, just the nodding of heads. Within minutes, Benson assembled what she needed and handed the boom mic with a long cord to Kelly. The four then made their way to the front door. Dorgan opened the door and greeted them almost immediately.

"What's going on?" the teenager asked.

"We want to talk to you about a couple things," Kelly replied, holding the mic a few inches from his face as he spoke and then pointing it back at Dorgan.

"About what?"

"There are a few missing pieces to the funeral home murders that I'm trying to tie together, and I think you can help me," Kelly said

"That case is closed."

"Let me rephrase what I just said," Kelly stated. "There are a few missing pieces, and I thought it would be in the best interest of your future to talk with me."

After a short pause, giving Dorgan time for consideration and making sure he realized Detective Fagley was present as well, Kelly continued with the camera rolling.

"It won't take long, so we can just stand out here and talk," Kelly said, realizing that the light was best outside and wanting to give

Dorgan the impression the interview would be simple and sweet, though it was just the opposite. Dorgan stepped outside, showing only the slightest concern, a facial expression that conveyed more a feeling of annoyance than fear.

"Do you know that most people convicted of murder spend the rest of their lives in prison?" Kelly asked. Not waiting for an answer he continued. "But you're only a teenager, and I suspect an attorney could prove there were extenuating circumstances that led you to commit such an horrific act. Why did you do it?"

"What are you talking about?" Dorgan demanded, starting to show signs of panic.

"You shot Phillip Grady and Charles Illsmere in January. What I can't figure out is why. Why did you do it and then let your friend Father Birch suffer all that anguish being considered the prime suspect?"

"That's ridiculous," said Dorgan, nervously shifting his weight from one leg to the other as he did.

"I think so, too," Kelly agreed somewhat facetiously. "I would never treat my friends that way, unless they deserved it. In that case, they wouldn't really be my friends."

The tension from the interview was palpable for all five individuals standing outside the Dorgan home. The few words the teenager spoke now had a tone of fear, and his eyes darted from one person to the next, not focusing on any one individual for more than a few seconds.

"You've got it all wrong," Dorgan insisted.

"And how's that?"

"You don't understand. It's all so complicated."

"You, Frank Black, and Father Birch all had your stories in order. None of you ever contradicted what the others told me or police. That was pretty good. Then I figured it out, however outlandish it first seemed. Father Birch gave you booze during the Youth Group's camping trip and then sexually molested you and your friend Frank. That put you in a compromising situation, so to speak. I'm guessing you should have reported it to the Youth Group director, Father Fred, or even the police. But what teenage boy wants his friends to think he's a faggot, some type of perverted queer. So instead of saying anything, you and Frank remained silent. Am I right so far?"

Dorgan just nodded his head.

"But I learned that the incident was brought to the attention of Father Fred and wondered what he did about the situation, why it seemed Father Birch was never reprimanded for his behavior. This was more than one little sexual encounter, though. Father Fred used the incident as blackmail. He wanted Father Birch's silence on a different church matter, and fearing he'd be publicly humiliated and punished if not thrown out of the priesthood he loved, the young priest kept quiet. Even when you confessed to Father Birch that you killed those two at the funeral home, he respected the Seal of Confession and didn't make anything public."

"Wait, then how do you know I confessed the murders?" the young teenager shouted.

Heads turned. This was more than a question. The tone of Dorgan's voice admitted guilt. He *had* confessed the murders to Father Birch.

"Father Birch emailed a friend of his often in the days preceding his suicide, and in one of the emails, he said he knew the killer's identity from confession but couldn't do anything about it. I asked his friend if he ever shared the name of the killer, and his friend said no. But when I called the friend this morning with one simple question, he confirmed it was probably you. I asked him if Father Birch ever indicated the age of the confessor. That was enough to jog his friend's memory, and he recalled one reference in the email in which Father Birch said it was a shame that a young teenager could commit such an act."

Kelly paused to gather his thoughts and let Dorgan respond if he wanted. The teenager remained silent, stunned by the accuracy of what he just heard.

"While I followed this case and talked with many people, I struggled to find your motive," Kelly continued. "Initially I thought you wanted the embalming fluid, some of which you took from the crime scene, presumably as payback for your lurid deed. You could mix it with the marijuana the Cropdusters are selling. But there had to be more. It wasn't just a simple robbery gone bad. When you bought the ammunition at Wal-Mart that wasn't a random person who agreed to purchase the bullets for you, and it wasn't Father Birch, was it?"

Dorgan shook his head, confirming Kelly's question. The tape kept rolling.

"It was Father Fred," Kelly stated firmly, dropping a bombshell that no one else, including Rosen and Fagley as much as they knew, expected. "He picked you up here, drove you to Wal-Mart and then took you to within a block from the funeral home. You then walked to the funeral home, did what you were instructed to do, took the four cans of embalming fluid and walked back to the car, where Father Fred was waiting for you. I have my suspicions why he wanted Phillip Grady silenced, but I really struggled to put my finger on why you agreed to do the dirty deed. It was blackmail, wasn't it? Father Fred told you he'd turn you in to the police for underage drinking if you didn't go along with his demand, and that would have resulted in major problems for you. Isn't that right? That's why you called me the other day. A cheap ruse to try to put the blame on someone else."

Dorgan nodded his head in agreement. Then, for the first time since January, he cracked. "I didn't want to do it," Dorgan said as he began to cry. "But Father Fred scared me. It was the underage drinking. It was the sexual abuse. It was all too much. I was scared. I was already in trouble at school, could've been headed to jail, and I didn't need any more problems. It was just crazy. I'm so sorry. Please believe me."

Dorgan began sobbing, as Fagley stepped forward to cuff him and read him his rights. Benson continued to film.

Fagley made a quick phone call from outside Dorgan's house. It was determined earlier in the day that if Dorgan gave himself up, a squad would be sent to transport him to the station, where he would be booked and held. It took less than five minutes for the squad to arrive, about the same amount of time it took Benson to dissemble her gear and load it into the van. Fagley agreed to follow the van to the next interview.

CHAPTER FORTY-FIVE

ather Fred had just opened a bottle of Chianti when the doorbell rang. In disgust, he rose from his favorite chair and went to answer the door. What greeted him made him wish he had already consumed the full bottle before he opened the door.

"Ah . . . Mr. Kelly, to what do I owe the pleasure?" Father Fred asked, realizing the reporter was not alone and the photographer was rolling tape.

"I don't like having to do this," Kelly explained. "I really don't. Jim Dorgan just confessed to us that he killed the two at the funeral home."

Father Fred stood speechless. He was wise enough to know this could be a bluff and kept his mouth shut.

"You blackmailed that kid into doing your dirty work," Kelly continued with an accusatory tone. "You bought the bullets, you drove him to the funeral home, and then you set it up so everyone would think Father Birch did it. That's disgusting. For all his demons, Father Birch deserved better."

Father Fred still had not moved from the entry way to the rectory. He merely stared at the parking lot, measuring his options.

"Phillip Grady was your friend. You said his funeral mass. But you had him killed so he wouldn't talk. You had him killed because he knew it was you, not Father Birch, who was stealing money from the Youth Group."

"You have no proof of that," Father Fred replied defiantly.

"Well, no and yes," Kelly admitted. "I don't hold any hardcore evidence. I'll admit that much. But let me tell you what I do know. I know you kept Father Birch quiet by threatening to take his sexual past public. I know you probably didn't use the money you stole on yourself. I know that a DA can subpoena Tim Leeland, and he most likely would reveal the discrepancy from last year's audit. Furthermore, thanks to the excellent reporting by Shelley Rosen here and some sources I have in Chicago, I know all about the archbishop."

It had taken some digging, but Rosen had discovered that Archbishop Malone enjoyed a lavish lifestyle, more than anyone suspected, much like the priest in the northern Chicago suburb. There were first-class trips, expensive meals at the finest restaurants when he traveled, a nice car, and so much more. Upon further inquiry, Rosen found the names of priests that had incurred the archbishop's wrath and contacted them. Most were reluctant to say anything, but one did admit that he was demoted and sent to another diocese because he refused to acquiesce to the archbishop's demand that amounted to extortion. Somewhat confused and stunned, Rosen dug deeper and learned from this priest that the archbishop required each pastor to pay him a percentage of what the church took in each year. He didn't care where the money came from; he just wanted to make sure it was paid to him. It afforded him the needed means to sustain his lifestyle. In the case of St. Tim's, it amounted to a payment of $4,500 a year.

"Phillip Grady was going to blow the whistle on you," Kelly continued. "He threatened you on the phone the day before he was killed and said he was going to take the matter to the archdiocese. Sad thing is, his allegation would have fallen on deaf ears there. What happened? Did you get scared that he would reveal his knowledge to other members of the parish if the archdiocese did nothing?"

Father Fred remained silent, almost in a daze, realizing his worst nightmare was coming true. Fagley stepped in and cuffed the pastor, reading him his rights. A squad with two officers was waiting in the parking lot to take Father Fred to the station.

It was shortly after five when Father Fred was led away from St. Tim's rectory. Kelly wasted no time.

CHAPTER FORTY-SIX

Assignment desk, Watson."

"It's Kelly. Shut up and listen. Here's what I've got. Hudson police have arrested two people in conjunction with the funeral home murders. They're being held and will most likely be charged tomorrow. One is a teenager, one of the original suspects, and the other is Father Fred, the pastor at St. Tim's. There's much more to this story for a follow-up piece, but I want to get this on tonight. I hesitate to wait until ten, in case news leaks, but I think that might be best. We can't do a live shot from here. So I could feed you the story for six, but that alerts all the other stations. I think you should clear four to five minutes for me at ten. Talk to the producer."

"You've got to be kidding. Four to five minutes?" Watson asked.

"We've got dramatic video, and it's because of me that these arrests were made. *Capiche?*"

"You are so full of yourself."

"And you are so full of shit that you don't recognize the story of the year when it hits you on your fat ass. Get me that time. We're headed back to the station."

All day long, Kelly had thought through how the newsroom could best handle the situation with the timing considerations. He discussed it with Benson and Rosen, conceptually at least, on the way to

Hudson that morning and again after the Father Fred interview. They all agreed it was worth the risk to wait until ten to break the story. The station could start promoting it during *CSI: Miami* at nine o'clock. How fitting.

Back at the station, Kelly was in the zone, not harried by any of the deadline pressures as he and Benson sat in the editing suite sifting through video. The tension was made greater by the fact they had to blur the face of Dorgan, since he was still a teenager. Benson had seen it before on occasion and marveled at his ability to block out any distractions and condense large amounts of information in a short period of time, making an otherwise complex story short and understandable.

By 9:45, the story was ready for broadcast. Kelly wrote a short lead-in for the dim-witted blow-comb, taking great care to use words simple enough for her to read. He then wrote his lead and conclusion, which he would report from the set. A quick stop in make-up, and he was ready for air.

"Shocking developments tonight in the Hudson funeral home murder case," the anchor read in her lead. And it was our own Sean Kelly who broke the case. He joins us now. Sean, your investigation tipped police to those involved."

"Yes, Candice. Despite suspicions, accusations and even a John Doe hearing that suggested otherwise, what we're about to show you tonight vindicates Father Joseph Birch in the January murders of Phillip Grady and Charles Illsmere."

He succeeded in getting a full five minutes for his report, almost unheard of in commercial television news. But even his boss, Ashbury, for all his mental shortcomings and lack of news judgement, realized a winner when he was hit over the head with it. The two spent almost twenty minutes debating, arguing viciously over how much time the story deserved. In the end, Kelly won.

The response was immediate and intense. Every other media outlet had to credit Kelly and Channel 6 with not only breaking the story but breaking the investigation for police. Even the daily newspapers, the *Star Tribune* and *St. Paul Pioneer Press*, whose reporters usually took a scornful attitude toward television reporters who they feel got paid much more for much less work, wanted to interview Kelly. He enjoyed spouting off during the interviews, reminding the print reporters that he was the one with the guts and intuition, not to mention raw ability, as he remarked, to solve the murder investigation in a way no one else considered.

Father Fred and Jim Dorgan were formally charged the following day. DA Lawrence Thompson savored his time in the spotlight, until someone asked him during a news conference why his office and the police had completely whiffed. As he did under pressure years before in the Rose Bowl, Thompson folded and uttered something unintelligible, offering no credit at all to Kelly.

Kelly was not at the Thompson news conference, opting instead to make a trip to Superior, where the second part of the story provided another bombshell for viewers and the entire Catholic community. Detective Fagley passed along information about the archbishop's extortion to one of his friend's in the Superior Police Department with the provision that Kelly and his camera crew be allowed to follow police when they went to arrest the archbishop.

The archbishop's arrest was another scoop and ratings winner for Channel 6. With the manner in which it was covered by other media outlets, it amounted to free promotion for the station leading up to sweeps. Ironic that management would reap the benefits of the performance of its biggest nemesis and pain in the ass. For his part, Kelly, who had been working without a new contract for the past few months, decided it was a good time to renegotiate an extension. As usual, he was right.

EPILOGUE

Most reporters would have enjoyed the days and weeks that followed the reports on the funeral home murders; Sean Kelly did not. His story was the talk of not only the Twin Cities media, but national outlets, including all the major networks, which picked up the story and featured countless interviews with Kelly. Award nominations followed. He was given the credit he deserved and rewarded nicely with a new contract, much to the dismay of his boss. Still there were too many inner demons plaguing him, which he discussed openly during many phone conversations with Becky Lewis and breakfasts with Father Truth. It was during one such breakfast at the University Club shortly before Christmas that Kelly finally found some answers.

"Why do you keep beating yourself up about the reports?" Father Truth asked.

"Well," Kelly began slowly while looking out the window at the frosted trees glistening in the early morning sun. "I keep wondering whether the church would have taken care of its own problems and been better without my reports exposing them."

"And do you really think that would have happened?"

"No, probably not."

"Did you report anything that wasn't true or do anything ethically dubious during your investigation?"

"No, of course not."

"Listen, Sean," Father Truth said, taking on a very serious tone. "I know how much you beat yourself up about the reports during the time they aired and since then. But you did what you thought was right. You used good judgement, and I'm convinced your Catholic faith guided you. And we must remember that even the Catholic Church has a bad apple or two on occasion. That archdiocese, St. Tim's, and the entire Catholic Church are much better now because of your reporting. You'll probably never get a 'Thank You' note from the Vatican, but I know from my contacts that there are many church leaders who are grateful for what you uncovered and put an end to."

"I suppose you're right," Kelly said. "By the way, how's the matter we've been discussing?"

"He's going to get it. It'll be announced tomorrow."

"Can I use that?" Kelly asked.

"You won't be wrong if you do," Father Truth assured him.

That night at home Kelly enjoyed a bottle of Bodega Norton Malbec, his newest favorite from Argentina. Flipping quickly through the other three stations to see their lead stories at ten and convinced he had scooped them again, Kelly turned back to Channel 6 to watch the report he filed earlier that evening.

"A well-known St. Paul pastor will be named tomorrow to head the Archdiocese of Superior," read the perky anchor from the Tele-Prompter. "Here's Sean Kelly with the exclusive."

Kelly smiled as he sipped his wine. In the week following his groundbreaking reports, Kelly suggested to Father Truth that a mutual friend of theirs and a well-known pastor from a different parish in St. Paul might make a good replacement in Superior. Kelly leaned on Becky Lewis to get his opinion heard in the Cardinal's office in Chicago, and Fr. Truth called numerous contacts throughout the country. Both stressed the pastor's commitment to Catholic education and the parish, as well as his natural kindness and warmth—not to mention his fundraising abilities—all of which made him the perfect candidate to help an Archdiocese heal and move forward. Apparently others agreed.

Leaving the main entrance and walking down the front steps the following morning at Assumption church, Kelly felt at least a momentary sense of inner peace. As he got near his car in the parking, he noticed the lady who drove the Mercedes approaching him. They had literally seen each other hundreds of times at weekday mass, occasionally exchanged smiles and waves, but had never once spoken.

"Sean," she said, "I just wanted to commend you on your excellent reporting during this past year. It was a tragic story, but I'm glad the truth finally came out."

Kelly stood, practically paralyzed by what he heard. He recognized the lady's voice from her calls and realized he was standing face to face with his secret source.

"I'm Helen Swanson," she said, extending her hand. "I spoke with my son Leeland last night, and he echoed my thoughts on your reporting. Makes all you Domers look good. What's next? Maybe you need to look into those mysterious drownings in your hometown of Winona."

Without waiting for any reply and not appearing to want to continue the discussion, she turned around and headed to her car.

"Thanks," Kelly called after her. "I appreciate all your help. Merry Christmas"

Acknowledgements

There's a good chance you wouldn't be holding this book if it weren't for Seal and Corinne Dwyer of North Star Press. My thanks to them for taking a chance on a first-time author, providing editorial assistance and encouragement when needed, and putting up with my many eccentricities.

Megan Hahn, Mary Carey, and Jim Hannon all helped greatly with critical feedback, suggestions and proofing.

Authors Brian Freeman, William Kent Krueger, Roger Stelljes, E. Kelly Keady, and Mark Gomez all helped by answering many of my questions.

People in the world of wine who assisted with some promotional events for this book and were open to a completely "novel" approach to wine tastings/book events include Holly Evans, Scott Cass, George Rose, and Joe Mayne. Others in my so-called Wine Witness Protection Program include HT, BL, and Father Truth.

Of course, Meg, Bobby, and Patrick all helped with various insights, solicited or not, and patience.

If I've forgotten anyone, please don't shoot me. I am already working on another Sean Kelly novel and would like to finish it. I'll be sure to mention your name at the end of that book.

Thanks.

About the Author

Rob Hahn is the founder and president of Hahn Publications, which publishes *The Midwest Wine Connection* and *Minnesota Prep Sports* newspapers. He has previously worked in television and radio, including stints at WCCO-AM and WGN-AM. He is a graduate of the University of Notre Dame. *Go Irish!* This is his first novel. He lives with his family in St. Paul, Minnesota.

www.robhahnbooks.com
www.wineheads.com